This Charming Shack
By
Sharon Gartner

Angelwords Publications

Books By Sharon Gartner

This Charming Shack
This Charming Angel
This Charming Guest

Illustration and cover design - Libby Reed. ©
www.libbyreed.com

Editing Janine Ogden

IBSN -978-0-9873750-1-8

Printed in Australia

www.sharongartner.com

For all my angels here on earth.

Acknowledgements

Big Thank you to Libby and Janine for their hard work and for
possessing such amazing talent.
Could not have done it without you.

1

Thursday 3 pm

Of course I have interests.

Of course I do, everyone does, I mean you would have to be dead not to.

I'm not talking about extreme interests like skydiving or mountain climbing, just normal everyday interests. I'm sure there are people out there who enjoy the simple things in life like stamp collecting or needle craft, although I would rather poke my eye out with a coat hanger.

Let's see what I have got so far.

Lisa Collins:

Interested in: Men only (very important I point that out after a terrible misunderstanding with girl from the pharmacy).

Relationship status: Single (cannot say that I just been dumped by hippie boyfriend – everyone will think I'm a loser).

Interests: Singing in the car, scrounging around in op shops (well they interest me, and so what if it's not Tai Chi). Let's see, what else.

About me: I'm over five feet tall and have the most captivating eyes that will melt your heart (for men only, so girls don't get too excited). I'll engross you in the most engaging conversation and then steal your drinks when you're not looking, and lastly when there's a crowd I'll light up the floor with the most awesome dance moves you're ever likely to see.

But overall, a fairly well balanced person, subject to change every twenty eight days.

Perfect!

Right that's my Facebook profile done.

"Miss Collins!"

David Roth from David Roth Solicitors storms into the little side office where I'm sitting connected to my laptop.

"If you are finished with your important e-mail, then can I suggest we get this over with?" He sounds angry so I gingerly log off and follow him back into his office.

"Miss Collins, is there a problem?" The truth is my appointment with the Solicitor started an hour ago and so far I have managed to stall him.

Buying a property is a big deal and I'm feeling a bit apprehensive about the whole thing. Two days ago I was absolutely sure about my over-ambitious actions but then again, two days ago I still had Joe.

David Roth sits at his desk opposite me rubbing his brow.

"Miss Collins, as your lawyer do I need to remind you that you have already signed an unconditional contract for the purchase of Abattoir Estate?"

"*Abby'toir,*" I correct him.

"Pardon me?"

"It's pronounced *Abby'toir.*"

That was the name on the property listing over the internet.

A large old-style homestead nestled below a hillside on three and a half acres of peace and tranquility. The old house had been empty for over four years and is in dire need of repair. According to the realtor the previous occupants had left it to a distant relative who lives in a castle in Scotland. So it wasn't a huge surprise to the realtor when I made an offer so low the bank made a mistake and thought I was applying for an overdraft on my cheque account.

David Roth is now looking at me perplexed. "Well whatever," he sighs, "the point is, we need you to sign these so we can go ahead and arrange settlement".

"No problem," I smile, reassuring him. I picked up the pen and my hand hovered over the big yellow sticker with the big pointy finger that says 'SIGN HERE'.

David Roth is now tossing a stress ball into the air. I'm facing a really big dilemma as I'm not entirely sure if I want to move to the country anymore.

Let me explain why.

I bought the place in the hope that I could share it with my boyfriend Joe, my boss and owner of 'The Organic Café'.

A quaint little place decorated by local artists in the heart of Sydney's Rose Bay.

I applied for the job because I was desperate, the advert read 'Only Vegetarians and Vegans need apply'.

I was neither but going vegetarian couldn't be that hard, I mean giving up meat is nothing like giving up smoking, it's not like you crave for meat.

We started dating shortly after I landed the job but going completely vegetarian was more difficult than I thought, not to mention having very pale skin due to low iron levels.

So in my lunch break I would make excuses and run to the nearest McDonald's to devour a Big Mac (I didn't tell Joe about lunch time rendezvous with Big Mac's, didn't see the harm in just a teeny white lie). Joe had often talked about living off the land to be completely self-sufficient. I personally couldn't see the point, who wants to slave over a plough just to put food on the table when there are supermarkets out there that have done all the hard work for you. But Joe had the most gorgeous green eyes that would melt your insides whenever he looked at you and I was in love, so surely making your own compost could be rewarding. It was going to be a surprise for his birthday, I had it all planned. I would casually announce over a romantic dinner of tofu and beans about my little purchase and Joe would get all choked up with emotions that he would fall on his knees, beg me to marry him and we could live off the land and make lots of cheese and babies.

It was only after he caught me at Denney's Diner tucking into a plate of pork ribs that it all ended.

"We are not right for one another," he said as I frantically wiped BBQ sauce from my chin. And besides who cares if one type of plastic gets mixed with another type of plastic in the recycling bins. It's all going to the same place anyway, isn't it?

So now I'm stuck with a dilapidated house, three and a half acres of wasted space and no job. I glanced across at the Solicitor who is flicking casually through a mountain of paper work on his desk. I tried again to stall by asking where the bathroom was.

Saw how fast his head snapped up from the paperwork, followed by a toxic stare that would strip paint from walls and decided that it would be safer to sign the stupid papers than to be burnt at the stake at the next lawyers' convention.

"Fine!" I sighed and scribbled my signature.

Left office

Dragging my heels along the pavement, the heat from the sun was beating down on my head and I couldn't help thinking I've screwed up big time.

I'm also scared what Mum and Dad might say when I tell them but not as scared as telling Dad that I have not seen the house in person, only over the internet.

My phone beeps and I find a seat amongst the bustle of pedestrians hurrying along the cobblestone square of the open mall.

"Hello."

"Lisa, its Millie, your aunt's had a nasty accident; you have to come right away!"

"It's too late Millie," I groaned. "I've already signed."

There's an awkward silence on the other end of the phone.

"What am I going to do?" I cried in despair down the phone catching the attention of passers-by.

"Alright calm down," Millie sighed, "let's just think this through".

Millie's my best friend in the world. We worked as barmaids at an Irish Bar and Grill before I went to work at Joe's Café. I share a flat with her and her weirdo, lunatic boyfriend Sid. Millie and Sid met in high school before Sid moved away with his family. They kept in touch over the years with letters until one night, five years ago, Sid came into the bar where Millie was working a shift and they have been together ever since. Sid believes he was abducted by aliens and is the head of the cult *"The Lost Souls Movement."*

Sometimes he and his weirdo mates would sit for hours in fields with the cows 'till the small hours of the morning in the hope that the offending beings would return. Forget Star Trek, this was a lot sadder.

"You can always sell it," Millie's voice appeared on the line again.

"No one wanted to buy it in the first place," I sighed. "That's why I got it so cheap, apparently the house has some superstitious story to it."

"Well then, tear the house down and sell the land."

"I don't think I can. It's listed as an historical dwelling, it's protected."

I can hear the cogs in Millie's mind ticking over. She was the level headed one of our dynamic duo, she was the voice of reason on everything. She was also very bossy.

"It's protected!" she snapped. "Lisa did you get a building inspection done?"

"Um..."

"Oh my god!" Millie was now the panicked one, "Lisa a historic site means simply that; historical, old, falling down around your ears! Did any alarm bells go off in your head when you realised that? This is the worst thing you have done yet. You need help."

I hate it when Millie yells at me. I can feel the lump in my throat swell and I'm trying so hard to fight back the tears.

Millie's voice softens. "Look maybe there's a way out, maybe you revamp the place and sell it."

Millie words ring in my ears as I glance up at the shop window in front of me 'Property Investment'. The sign across the shop front is jumping out at me. I had a sudden thought that I could get into property investment.

I never liked Joe's alternative ways anyway.

I mean free range, organic, caged; an egg is an egg and if he wants to eat stuff that's grown in its own faeces then he's welcome to it and I'm glad he found out that I'm not a vegetarian. I couldn't eat another bit of crappy cabbage and leek stew that tastes like old slippers. I don't need him, in fact I'm over him!

I can hear Millie's faint voice on the end of the line. "Lisa are you still there? Don't do anything I'm coming to get you."

Millie's over-reacting, she's so paranoid especially after the last little incident.

"I'm fine," I reassured her, "I'm coming home; I have a great idea."

"Don't do anything until you get home," she warned.

Okay, Millie's not *exactly* paranoid. She thinks I have a problem and has been assigned to me as my supporter since she dragged me along to a support group called *I.B.G (Impulse Behaviour Group)*.

A bit like Alcoholics Anonymous but for people with impulse behavioural problems, which is a waste of time because I'm totally in control of my actions.

I thought Joe was the one and I was so sure he felt the same about me, now he's gone I need a new focus and Millie will be so proud when I tell her my brilliant idea.

I.B.G Meeting

Okay, Millie's not so hot about the property investment idea.

She did agree that fixing the house up and selling is good but buying more property now was not so good. She made me cancel my appointments with the lovely guy from the realtor office and apologise for wasting his time, as he had several investment properties all lined up for a viewing this afternoon.

All agreed that the move to the country to fix up shambled mess would be good for me - consequences and all that. I told the group that I am a big girl and can make my own decisions and announced with dignity that indeed I am moving to the country but not because they said so.

Moving day

The last of the boxes were carried to the moving truck as they shut it's doors.

"Where do you want this one luv?" asked the more robust member of the team from Budget Movers, the same guy who was dripping sweat all over my possessions.

The move itself didn't take long but cleaning the old place before putting my stuff away proved to be a mission even James Bond wouldn't accept, but it kept my mind off Millie. It was hard to leave the flat, I so didn't want to go and clung to Millie like a pre-schooler.

Millie insists that the move will be great for me and give me a new focus and promised she would come and visit over the weekend. The moving truck roared off on it's departure and all of a sudden I felt like an isolated lonely rural person. I never thought that being so far away from civilisation could make one feel like the only person in the world. I reminded myself the small village of Taromeo was situated only ten kilometres away so there must be people otherwise it wouldn't be called a village. But still, a good hour's drive into the city, an hour away from my friends and the things that are so familiar. I turned my attention to the boxes sitting at my feet, stacks of them all marked *Saucy Girl,* a range of adult products that I had after a result of a tiny business venture that never worked out. I pushed all eight boxes aside and crashed on the sofa. The place looked so different to the pictures on the internet, it's really in dire need of repair.

Some of the previous owner's possessions still remained hidden under dust covers in every room (bonus! I'm planning a garage sale already). The bookshelves that covered the four walls of the sitting room bowed under the weight of the many books littering the shelves.

The realtor had been very cagey on the details of the sale, just that the previous occupants were now deceased and all chattels including the furniture were listed in the sale. I couldn't think about renovations right now, the task at hand seemed daunting enough.

I have to admit that the country is so peaceful and I'm starting to feel connected with my inner self. My thoughts turn to Joe and what he was missing, he would have loved this place. Bastard!

My eyes are growing heavy with all this tranquility and need to drift off into blissful sleep.

Middle of dream

I'm dressed in skimpy shorts and a bikini top, my long blond hair hung loose down my exposed tanned back. Beside me was Joe, he also was stripped down to his shorts and he looked so sexy with his tool belt around his waist hammering a nail into a wall. *Bang, bang,* the noise sounded so realistic. *Bang, bang,* there it goes again.

"Hello anyone there?"

I'm sure I heard a voice. My eyes snapped open and a woman with grey hair had her rather large face pressed up against the window looking straight at me. I jumped off the sofa in a staggering daze and realised it was dark inside the house.

Making my way to the door tripping over boxes in my haste to talk to another human being, the door swung open before I could get to it.

"There you are!" the woman said crossly, "I was about to give up on you. Here take this would you it's burning my hands!" She thrusts a large casserole dish into my hands.

The dish felt lukewarm to me but I was still in a sleepy daze and wasn't going to start getting picky.

Not sure if there's formalities needed here, no one has ever brought me a casserole before.

I decided to make an introduction instead and give thanks. She cranes her neck inside the door and takes in the chaos. "I'm Barbara Crankshaw, we have the farm down the road. I see you still have a lot of unpacking to do and on your own as well I hear, not married or anything?"

Ah, so the legendary bush telegraph is alive and well.

"No." I smiled tightly. "I've just come out of a relationship."

"I thought so. Gill from the estate office told me he thought you were on your own."

The old woman has now managed to get half of her hefty body through the door. I'm not sure I want this woman here, she seems meddlesome but the angel on my shoulder insists I welcome her inside just the same.

"No thanks," she snaps when I offer her a drink, "got animals to feed".

She gives me the impression that bringing me the casserole and welcoming me to the neighbourhood was just another chore on her list of things to do today. And she was fast running out of daylight hours.

"Well I should introduce you to my nephew sometime," she said as she observed me for a moment.

"Yep he's about your age, lovely boy, he's on his own as well."

"Oh um, great." I manage to smile.

"Well I must go, anything you need sing out, we are at the farm that's first on the left."

I watched her leave and wonder why country people choose to 'sing out' haven't they heard of text messaging?

Later

Taking a deep breath I pushed the little button and jumped when sound blasted around the room. Yes! I have television! Bed was made up, all furniture in their correct positions and shambled mess looking a lot less shambled. With the noise of television blaring in the background I'm starting to feel a little more at ease.

Cannot seem to get used to the silence around me; slightly freaked out because while browsing through the bookshelves I came across a stack of Hustler magazines hidden between *Tom Sawyer* and *Wuthering Heights*. What makes it so creepy is that they weren't old Hustler magazines, they're somewhat new ones and I'm worried the spotty teenage boy, who obviously left them here for his own private party, is going to come back and demand I hand them over.

First official tour of house

It would have been so grand in its day. I wandered around stopping to take in every room, imagining myself as lady of the manor strutting around in a long flowing dress.

The house was like a maze with rooms connecting off other rooms. In total there were four bedrooms, a formal dining area, a large country kitchen complete with electric and wood-burning stove, a larder with its many shelves stocked with jars of dusty old preserves and a large living room that ran the whole length of the house. I must admit, for its age it wasn't in too bad a shape. Millie will be so impressed when she visits.

The casserole that the old lady had brought earlier was heating nicely in the oven so I plonked myself down onto the sofa and stared at the TV.

God it's so quiet even with the idiot box going, I need a distraction. I can't go and check Facebook as at present there's no internet.

I started thinking about getting a dog then remembered Millie's lecture about impulse decisions and decided not to think about a dog. Heaving a sigh I picked up the phone and punched in Millie's number.

"How's it going so far?" she asked.

"Oh fine," I sighed, picking a thread off my jumper willing myself not to start blubbing.

"I haven't unpacked everything yet but I did meet a neighbour. Nice lady, a bit snappy. She brought me a casserole. Oh and she wants to hook me up with her nephew."

"Ugh, you're kidding!" exclaimed Millie.

"Your neighbour wants to set you up with her *nephew*, very bad idea Lisa, I would soon put a stop to that."

God, Millie is such a drama queen.

"He's the same age as me and he might be good looking for all you know."

Millie chuckled. "Wouldn't count on it, I mean why else would his aunt set him up? It's because he's too inbred to find himself a girl. You're probably the first decent thing they have seen on two legs."

I shuddered. I have no experience with the country types other than watching *Deliverance.*

Millie continued, "I'm a bit concerned about you spending your first night alone so I will keep my mobile beside the bed tonight."

"Millie thanks for your concern," I sighed, "but I'll be fine, I have to get used to being on my own sooner or later."

"I'm more concerned about the hillbillies, Lisa, just make sure you lock your doors."

Now I'm peeing myself with concern but I don't want to let on to Millie. I get up, flick another light on and change the subject.

"Now Millie," I said, settling myself back on the sofa, "when you come to visit I want you to bring your colour charts. And I'm thinking about hosting a dinner party, not right away, after I clean the place up a bit which is where you come in because I want you to be my head designer."

"You want me to design a dinner party?"

"No, I want you to be my head designer. It could be a little sideline earner for you in my property empire. What do you say?"

Millie had always dreamed about being an interior decorator and it seems to be the perfect solution. I could pay her a percentage from my profits on this place and then go into business together.

"A dinner party?" she asked in her flat annoying tone.

Honestly did Millie even comprehend what I had just offered?

"Well yes!" I tutted, "that's what country folk do don't they? You know, have dinner parties."

"Don't you think," Millie started in her 'I know best' voice that caused me to roll my eyes to the heavens, "that you need to learn to cook first and anyway you weren't planning to stay there so why bother hosting a party?"

I opened my mouth to dispute such a statement when an ear splitting shrill filled the room, I got such a fright that I'm pretty certain my heart jumped out of my chest and landed on the floor. I held my hand over my ear.

"What the fuck is that?" Millie's faint voice shouted down the phone.

"It's okay, just the smoke alarm!" I shouted back.

A strange smell is coming from the kitchen.

Oh shit the casserole!

In smoky kitchen

The casserole looked like burnt dog poo which got me thinking about dogs again.

The smoke finally cleared from the kitchen but the drone that was in my inner ear from the noise of the smoke alarm was still making its presence known.

Let me tell you that pushing the button and holding it down for three seconds does not silence it.

Neither does madly waving a cloth in front 'till your arms hurt, smashing it against a tree or hitting it with a hammer. In fact the only way I could stop the ear piercing shrill was to take the battery out.

With the offending casserole dish soaking in the sink and its contents in the bin I stepped out onto the wooden verandah to fill my lungs with fresh air. It was almost a full moon out. The countryside lit up like a black and white photograph, the only sound was a gentle wind rustling through the trees. I lit the roll your own cigarette I had found next to the Hustler magazines and drew the smoke deep into my lungs.

It was a bit cool out but spring was in full swing and summer wasn't far away.

I watched the treetops sway with the breeze aware that it's just me alone out here with nature. I started thinking about dogs again.

I contemplated this over the stale cigarette.

If I get a dog then that means I would have it for it's entire life span which really doesn't fit into my plans.

I saw something flash between the trees, it looked like a man but I think my eyes must be playing tricks after a long and hard day.

Millie's concerns about being out here with hillbillies were now dominating my thoughts.

Bloody Millie.

Now I seem to be arguing with myself over seeing a man lurking in trees. My brain and body were not communicating well and my body was now visibly shaking.

Grabbing the flashlight from inside the door (Millie's text message suggested it, along with the axe) I shone it between the two gum trees where sighting of hillbilly was but it seems as if I may have been mistaken because nothing is there.

Now I'm yelling into the darkness. I'm now asking hillbilly to state his name, sounding a lot braver then I was feeling.

Satisfied there's no hillbilly lurking amongst the trees I stubbed the strange, stale tasting cigarette out and went back inside. I had to admit it was bit funny. I mean me out there armed with an axe, shouting into the trees, like a *'YouTube'* moment.

In fact the thought sent me into a fit of giggles and I could not control my laughter. But as funny as the situation was, I'll feel a lot better if I put a chair under the door knob.

5.30 am

Bloody noisy wildlife! Honestly all their chirping and squawking, obviously no respect for mankind, or womankind for that matter! Reaching for my mobile beside the bed I read the time, can't believe how early it is.

Bloody birds. I don't remember closing the threadbare curtains but really there's no point now is there? I mean I have no neighbours.

My first night went well, although I'm bit hazy on details (odd). I lay there waiting for my body to kick start into getting up. Then remembering what I had to do, excitement started to surge through me like an energy ball. I jumped out of bed and ran for the door towards the kitchen. Then ran back towards bedroom as I discovered that I am naked and cold (also odd as where are pj's?).

I make one cup of tea and two slices of toast in my new kitchen then decide to take my breakfast to bed along with my stack of decorating magazines I had picked up at the news-agents.

Opening the curtains exposed the outstanding view from my bedroom window.

A blanket of dew had settled on the ground making visible the cobwebs that were woven between the strands of wire on the fences. I am in awe of the way nature has an extraordinary ability to paint the picture perfect setting to accommodate my grand manor.

Sipping my tea under the comfort of my duvet I flicked through the pages for inspiration. I had visions of what this place will look like.

Warm colours and timber floors would complement the countryside beautifully. Maybe I could add a loft and some of those pull down stair things.

I drained my tea and looked at the time on my mobile again and realised I had been awake for only forty five minutes, checked for messages, infuriated that there is none from Millie. So decided to lay back and enjoy sunrise from the comfort of my warm bed. Should be getting up but it's Saturday and I'm in the countryside so no need to rush.

"Yoo hoo! Anyone home?"

I'm sure I heard a voice?

My eyes snapped open as I untangled myself from the clutches of flannelette sheets and duvet. I yelled urgently back to the voice. "Not to worry, I'm on my way," never been caught sleeping before well not by hillbillies anyway.

Struggled into my jeans and t-shirt and cursed the fact it's early morning. Glanced at my phone and realised it's not early but in fact mid morning. Voice is getting closer and zip on jeans is now stuck.

It was starting to dawn on me that country people are rude and have no patience.

I called back to the voice again. "I'm coming."

I'm so pre-occupied with the flaming zip that I didn't see casserole lady approaching and ran into her enormous saggy bosom.

"Lisa dear!" she exclaimed, "you really shouldn't leave your back door open like that. You may be living in the country but even we are not immune to the odd burglar you know."

I fluffed my hair and wiped under my eyes, trying not to give away the fact that I had been caught snoozing at this time of the morning. Mrs Crankshaw leaned in closer to me narrowing her eyes.

She was in my personal space, I took a step back to avoid this but now her hand came up towards me, my eyes followed her hand like it was moving in slow motion.

"What have you got in your hair?" she asked as she pulled something from my tangled hair.

It was my half eaten honey toast.

"Oh sorry about that." My face turns red as I take the offending toast from her. "Um, breakfast in bed," I muttered, running my hands through my sticky hair.

Mrs Crankshaw heaved a sigh and shook her head.

"I've got the morning off," she said turning her attention to the unpacked boxes, "so I thought I'd come and give you a hand."

Oh no!

I followed her into the kitchen willing her to leave

"Oh, how kind Mrs Crankshaw but there's no need to.."

"Nonsense," she interrupted as she picked up a box and dragged it onto the kitchen table. "You could do with a hand, girl on your own and all, now why don't you be a good lass and make us a cuppa."

I don't want her here. I'm not being ungrateful, it was nice of her to bring me dinner but I do have boundaries and she clearly is crossing them.

"Is that my casserole dish?"

I mumbled an embarrassed apology and explained that I slightly overdid the casserole and it would not happen again, I felt like I was back at school in the principal's office. The old lady tutted and seemed annoyed, change of subject in order.

Watching her as she carefully unwrapped each piece of crockery and separated them into piles on the table; I had a sudden thought that maybe having the old women here wasn't so bad, it would be nice to get to know her a little.

Besides her company was better than no company at all and being local she would know a bit of history about the old homestead, which will come in handy when I market the place, (have done draft presentation already).

"Did you know the previous owners?" I asked handing over a steaming hot cuppa in my best china mugs.

"Flora? Yes she and I were dear friends," she let out a sigh, "such a tragedy the way it all ended."

"Tragedy?" I asked, "was there an accident?"

Mrs Crankshaw shook her head and looked out the window in the direction of the big oak tree that covered the back lawn.

"Flora and Bill planted that tree, they never wanted children. Flora was never the maternal type but it suited them, they were so close. Her and Bill married young and lived in this house for forty years. Anyway a few years back Bill discovered he had bowel cancer, the poor man and in the later stages he refused any treatment. Broke her heart it did but she nursed him day and night and well I guess she couldn't face life without him." Mrs Crankshaw sighed sadly again.

"I'm so sorry," I sympathised but rather impatiently, waiting for her to actually get to the point.

"It was my nephew Jake who found them," she continued. "This was the strange thing, he found a note under his windscreen wiper of his ute one day; the note read that he needs to check things out on the property so he did, and that's when he found them," her voice broke into a whisper.

"Ah, found who?" I asked a little confused.

Mrs Crankshaw sighed, "Lisa haven't you been listening? Found *them;* Flora and Bill, under the oak tree."

"What, were they…oh!" my hand shot up to my mouth.

"Yes they died together, suicide pact," Mrs Crankshaw shrugged, "still don't know to this day who put the note on Jake's ute".

I was so horrified and didn't know what to say.

No wonder the estate agent had been so cagey about the details, people died in this house and by choice.

A sense of dread is coming over me, thinking that I may possibly be living in a haunted house amongst hillbillies.

The sound of gravel crunching alerted me to an approaching vehicle.

"That will be the rural postman," Mrs Crankshaw informed me, "why don't you go and introduce yourself and I'll carry on with these boxes."

Feeling numb inside I put my empty cup in the sink and strode towards the post van. Not at all bothered that I looked a fright and had honey through my hair as it's only the postman.

"Hey there lass," he greeted with his slightly Scottish accent.

"Rob's the name," he stuck out his hand. I muttered my name back still slightly dazed.

"Lisa you say, nice name."

Rob, with his sagging abdomen and lack of hair, rocked back on his heels taking in the surroundings.

"Well you certainly have your work cut out for you here, I see you met Barb," he said, gesturing his head towards Mrs Crankshaw's ute, "fine lass she is. So what are your plans for the old place, a bulldozer?" he chortled at his own joke.

"Not sure." I said, locating my voice, which had a slight wobble to it.

Well it wasn't entirely true but I didn't want to start telling him what I had in mind for the place, other then an exorcism.

"And on ya own too," he said, "no husband I hear."

I'm starting to believe country folk have nothing better to do then snoop.

"Well never mind," he continued, "I like a woman with a power drill and an apron." He stuck his head back inside the van and pulled out a business card and handed it to me. "Privately contracted to do these rounds," he said after noticing my puzzled look. "And another thing to watch; your power bill lass. There's been some lights left on before you moved in, mainly the outside one. Old Flora must have forgotten to turn out all her lights and the mains come to think of it, before she, you know?"

I nodded in acknowledgement as I still cannot locate my voice.

"I noticed it every time I drove past, one of the lights in the house was on. The light bulb would have blown by now... morning Barb!" he yelled to an approaching Mrs Crankshaw.

"Morning Rob" she nodded and turned her attention to me.

"Lisa dear," she asked as she held up a very large purple dildo. "What is this and where does it go?"

Rob drove away with a half amused smirk on his face.

I didn't care how it was going to happen but I just willed the ground to open up and swallow me whole.

Mrs Crankshaw now stood over the kitchen table where the

contents of the *Saucy Girl* box was now on full display.

I averted my eyes from the contents sprawled out on the table.

"So you mean woman actually buy this stuff?" she asked as she picks up a deluxe version of the studded vibrator. It took some explaining but she finally accepted that I wasn't a nymphomaniac.

"Well I'll be buggered!" Mrs Crankshaw exclaimed. "Don't know how they could take to such a thing, rather have the real one any day."

I wanted to cry.

"Must go," she suddenly announced, placing the dildo on the table, "Max will be expecting lunch." She patted me on the arm as I continued to sit there wallowing in my own humiliation.

"Say would you like to come for dinner tomorrow night? It's pot luck – you know what pot luck is don't you dear? It means everyone brings something to contribute."

"Oh of course" I said, managing a smile to let her know that there is no way I'm still mortified about the sex toys sprawled on my kitchen table.

"You can do dessert; Jake will be there so you two have a chance to meet."

Oh god, I completely forgot about the hillbilly nephew. I need to back out of this but how?

Facebook Status Update. Lisa Collins:

So embarrassed right now, snooping country folk.

2

Sitting at laptop

I now have internet and am feeling more connected with the outside world. Still humiliated over this mornings event but am going to put the incident behind me and move on.

Internet is a very useful tool and I am going to send thank you card to people at *Google* because I found out some interesting things. For a start I found out that I could apply for a special grant to help with the repairs on this place. Because it's listed as a historic building there are grants available to help with the maintenance. I finished downloading the application form and logged on to my resume.

It's all very well being a property developer but until I sell this place and make a tidy profit I still need a job. Eric had delivered the local paper this morning and I could not believe my luck.

Applications are invited for an age-carer at the local retirement home, morning shifts only which would suit me perfect and I already have an interview for tomorrow morning at ten thirty.

I picked up the phone to call Mum and Dad and let them know where I am, I've been dreading this moment.

But after Millie's threat of 'you tell them or I will', I think it would be better coming from me. Mum and Dad used to live in

Sydney where I grew up but since Dad retired they have been travelling around Australia with the other grey nomads.

The only source of contact I've had with my parents over the last few months is by a mobile phone that Dad had brought before their journey began. He's still not sure how to use it.

Dad's voice appears on the line and I can hear the roar of the Winnebago engine in the background.

"Hello!" he shouts down the phone.

"Dad, it's me."

"Lisa darling how are you? Just one moment I'll pass you over to Mum."

I smile; Dad and I don't talk much beyond the pleasantries. Me being an only child and a girl, Dad never knows what to talk to me about.

Dad's a footy freak and my boyfriends over the years have been subjected to great interaction over which team they supported. Poor Dad, he really missed out on having a son.

"Lisa sweetheart!" Mum's voice yells down the phone. "How are you luv? Dad and I are on our way to Darwin."

I hold the phone away from my ear while she tells me the places they just visited. Honestly my parents think they are talking on a two-way radio. "Mum," I interrupted, "you don't need to yell, I can hear you fine."

"What?"

"I can hear you fine."

"What?"

"I said I can hear you!" great, now I'm shouting down the phone.

"Dad's just pulling over!" Mum yells through the phone again.

I really want to hang up about now. I love my parents but god knows sometimes they want to know every last detail. Dad would want to know how many termites were in the place and Mum would want me to describe what the estate agent was wearing. Or they could just die of shock at my latest impulse purchase.

It could swing either way.

I took a deep breath.

"Mum, I've brought a property and it's in need of repair and it's an hour's drive from the outer suburbs of Sydney and not to worry because I'm not going to be living here for long, only about a year and once the renovations are done I'm going to sell it and did I mention it's in the country?"

I stopped to take a breath. I can faintly hear Mum relaying my outburst back to Dad.

"Mum?"

"Oh Lisa," she said in a tone I couldn't recognise, "you really need help."

"I'm sorry, I should have told you before but it kind of just happened."

"That's what you said last time!" she snapped.

Dad's voice now appears on the line. "Did you get a pest inspection done, what did they say about termites?" I groaned, but to be honest I was quite relieved.

Dad and Mum had never done anything reckless in their lives up until now. Dad always played it safe. I was surprised when they bought the Winnebago straight from an add in the newspaper but not before Dad had it inspected a dozen times. The seller reduced his price just to get rid of Dad's endless enquiries.

I didn't feel the need to tell them that I hadn't a pest or building inspection done, after all by the time they make it back to Sydney the place will be finished.

"Don't worry about it Dad, the place is great and it will give me a head start on the property ladder."

"Well it's a bit risky luv if you ask me but you're a big girl, I'm sure you know what you're doing."

I didn't have the heart to tell them I hadn't the faintest clue.

"I'll pass you back to Mum."

In the background I could hear Dad start the engine. Mum appeared on the line.

"So dear, tell me," she shouted down the line, "what was the estate agent like?"

First tour of surrounds

Feeling brave and not thinking of snakes whatsoever. I noticed concrete sheds located at the back of the property, possibly an old chook house and the remains of what was once a vegetable garden. Don't know anything about gardening and am unsure as to how I'm going to cope with dirt and snakes but I'm confident the solution will present itself.

The concrete shed was made up of two rooms and what looked like to be cattle yards running off the end of it. Got the courage up to step inside and notice the old table and hooks hanging from the tin roof?

It is a big building and has a very pungent smell about it. Seen enough, it has sinister vibes and the thought of hillbillies are making me shudder.

Brainwave

I am going to ask Mrs Crankshaw about getting an animal to eat the untamed grass, thinking of a goat 'cause they eat everything. Insects biting at exposed skin, need repellent.

Back at house

After pouring myself a wine and applying Stingoose to my bites I stepped onto the veranda again to survey the land and wait for another brainwave.

Wine seemed to be going straight to my head on account of very little food being consumed. I am now hungry so I turned to go inside when felt something brush against my leg. Terrified and unable to move, I'm convinced I'm about to be bitten by a snake.

Meow!

Oh thank god, it's just a cat.

The cat is friendly and I have no idea where it came from but am guessing must be from the Crankshaw's as they are the nearest neighbours. Offered it a tin of sardines while I slopped baked beans over toast, nice to have company for dinner.

Sudden realisation

I have been in the countryside for 48 hours and have not thought of doing anything impulsive. Millie will be impressed, I am making progress.

Plate of baked beans in hand I joined the cat on the sofa and flicked on the TV. Trying not to think about the interview tomorrow because I really need this job and am feeling apprehensive. The mortgage payments were cheaper than what I was paying in rent at the flat I shared with Millie but I did a budget this afternoon and was shocked at the cost of renovations. The cat is now getting familiar and wants to snuggle under the blanket with me.

Having thoughts about dogs again.

Sometime after midnight

The television was now showing infomercials and the cat is now doing unspeakable acts with my stuffed rabbit that I have had since my ninth birthday. Decided to nickname the cat Randy Puss. I switch off the telly and stumble through to my room when Randy Puss started to growl. Paranoid those hillbillies are breaking into my home, I stood still and listened for any signs of forced entry. Randy Puss is still hissing and growling and now I'm very scared.

I'm trying to locate the stupid light switch as Randy Puss puts his heckles up. Sudden realisation; cats can sense the supernatural.

I am now shouting into the darkness at ghosts to go away.

I thought back to the time I watched Bruce Willis in *The Sixth Sense*.

I know that if ghosts appear they want you for something so I asked the ghosts what they wanted.

No answer. By now bile was rising in my throat and hot tears were coming down my cheeks. I know that they are out to get me and I don't want to die. Finally located light switch and flicked it on.

Nothing!

Except for a branch from a tree outside blowing across the window.

Randy Puss had stopped growling and jumped from the sofa.

"Pff, silly," I told him. "It's only a branch, what did you think it was, ghosts?" Randy Puss ignored me and stalked past me into the bedroom. I check the bolts on the doors and made my way to bed. Told Randy Puss as I climbed between the sheets that there is no such thing as ghosts but decided that Randy Puss may settle down if I left the light on tonight.

Interview day

I piled my hair on top of my head and twisted it into a French knot. Stood in front of the mirror and surveyed myself.

Black dress pants, white fitted shirt complemented with silk scarf and black high heel boots.

It speaks volumes, it tells my potential employer that although I may be only applying for a carer's job in a small crusty retirement home, I am a smart, intelligent and graceful lady that takes pride in her appearance.

Randy Puss was still curled up on my bed and I leave him there because of the milk situation. I ran out of milk again, I swear I had enough, and I don't have time to take Randy Puss back to the Crankshaw's and make a coffee run as well.

Driving to interview

I'm going over the possible questions in my head, not feeling so confident now.

I'm just going to have to pin my hopes on the outstanding reference from my days at the geriatric ward at the hospital and I'm sure my charm will win them over.

My interview was at ten thirty. I glanced at the clock on the dashboard it read 10.25. But the clock was ten minutes fast so I'm making good time.

Turned the radio up to drown out the knocking noise coming from underneath my bonnet, so annoying.

I pulled the car over to check the directions on my lap. *Twin Oaks Retirement Village* was situated about two kilometres from the village down a tree lined road. I had jotted down the directions that the receptionist gave over the phone but I wasn't really paying attention. I'm sure she said it was down Tucker Road or did she say….no, must have been Tucker Road.

I put the car into gear and set off again. The car jolted a little, I wish it would stop doing that. I planted my foot down further and turned the radio up more.

I saw the sign up ahead that said *Twin Oaks Retirement Village,* turned right into the tree lined road, when car shuddered and came to a halt.

"No!"

I turned the engine over and thumped the wheel in frustration. Told the car how stupid it was and decided only one thing for it.

Running down road

Clutching my resume I have been running for what seems to be a lifetime. Sweat was pouring from my brow and my lungs feel like they were going to explode.

Bloody receptionist, wait until I have a piece of her! She didn't mention the bloody residence was two bloody kilometres down this bloody road! I'm so late and I can't run fast in these high boots. Without stopping I kicked them off and sprinted barefoot down the asphalt road ignoring the jabs from the loose gravel beneath my feet.

Arrive at lovely retirement home

A heavily tattooed woman with a Sinead O'Connor hair style seemed to gasp at me from behind the reception desk.

Understandable, I stood there dripping in sweat with my hands on my knees panting for air.

"Are you okay?" she asked.

"Lisa," I gasped, "here for interview."

The woman looked concerned and guided me to a chair and signaled to her colleague to get me a glass of water.

"Did you walk?" she asked.

"No car broke down," I said waving my arm in the direction of the road.

"Where are your shoes?" she asked again, glancing at my feet.

Before I could answer she handed me a glass of water.

I took one long gulp, grateful for the cool liquid running down my parched throat. I wiped my mouth with the back of my sleeve.

I smiled bravely at the woman but inside was feeling rather sorry for myself. I'm late and I've arrived at my job interview in bare feet, I may as well go, there's no point going on with the interview. I stood up and handed the glass back to the woman and thanked her for lovely water.

"Where are you going?" the woman asked.

"Home," I sighed, "I doubt your boss would want to interview me now."

The woman chuckled, great, now she thinks this is funny.

"I'm Debbie," she said as she stuck out her hand. "I'm the Resident Matron, it will be me who's conducting your interview today."

In tattoo woman's office

Ushering my mortified self into a chair while Debbie arranged a tow truck for my car.

She now sat opposite me in the tiny room looking over my resume. My experience with matrons didn't exactly fit the description of this person in front of me. Debbie had a kind face but tell-tale lines of a rough life ran deep into her pale skin. Crossing her legs revealed the tattoos didn't stop down the length of her arms either but down to the tops of her legs and stopped just above her knees. She looked up and smiled.

"All looks good Lisa, how about a tour?"

Tour round retirement home

It was home to thirty residents with all bedrooms consisting of two single beds and a commode in each corner. A rather large showering area was situated between the three well equipped bathrooms.

Debbie ran through the list of daily chores and routines with each resident, making it impossible to remember each one. She got to the last room on the tour where a rather large man was lying on top of his sheets. His eyes were glazed and had a silly grin on his face.

"This is Doug," Debbie said, as she straightened the bed sheet around him. "He needs around the clock care, he also has a manual catheter that needs changing every two hours which needs to be done in pairs."

I nod.

"You see," she continued, "his mind reverts back to his.... what we can make out to be anyway, his teenage years. Bless his dear heart." She smiled at him fondly, "he babbles a lot and thinks anything in a skirt is fair game."

I winced.

"Well that's about it," she said looking around.

"Your reference was great and I need to check up on a couple of referees but the job's yours if you want it? Three months probation period on the morning shift 7am 'till 2pm."

Oh bloody fantastic.

Just like that I had a job.

Pff, country life so simple.

Emma's car

A young girl named Emma, who was at the home on work experience, gave me a ride back to the village stopping on the way to retrieve my boots that were lying on side of the road.

I had never ventured into the village before and as we came over the brow of the hill I let out a small gasp. The village centre consisted of angle parking and a tree lined street.

Its historic buildings, that housed the many small shops, lined the only main street in town. It had all the amenities - a pub, bakery, small supermarket, hairdressers and produce stores. Emma dropped me at the garage where my car was in the workshop with the bonnet up.

In garage

A large figure of a man was bent over the engine.

He saw me approach and shook his head. "When was the last time ya checked ya oil?" he asked, wiping his greasy hands on a black rag.

I scratched my head, to be honest I don't think I ever had. Millie used to have her head underneath my bonnet every time she borrowed my car, I presume she had checked the oil thingy. "Well you were lucky this time," he said slamming the bonnet shut, "any further you would have cooked it, didn't you hear the engine knocking?"

Without answering I followed him into a small dusty office where he proceeded to charge me $200 for the tow and oil. He handed me a card with a phone number, "keep this handy," he grumbled, "next time you break down call us."

Disgruntled but not wanting to point out to the fat man how rude he was, I paid and left.

Dilemma

After parking in the main street a sense of dread fell over me.

Tonight I was expected at the Crankshaw's for dinner where Mrs Crankshaw will attempt to set me up with her nephew.

I decided to play it safe and pick up a couple of chocolate mud cakes from the bakery to take along, I'd be buggered if I could attempt to bake anything half decent as well.

I could decline and say something came up but after our humiliating meetings thus far I felt I needed to make up some respectable ground with Mrs Crankshaw.

Strolling up the street and looking around at the local residents standing around on the pavement chatting,

I can't help but think that Millie was right.

Maybe the only reason Mrs Crankshaw was setting me up is because her nephew is too backward to find a girl for himself. Oh god I need to get out of this one, I can't go along tonight and sit there while he makes moves on me. Oh god what am I going to do?

My mobile rang. It was, of course, Millie.

"Just about to call you, I've…"

"How did the interview go?"

"Interview? Oh fine, piece of cake, start tomorrow."

"Congrats."

"Thanks, but now I've got bigger problems. Meeting neighbour ladies nephew tonight and just heading to the bakery to buy desserts."

"Okay have been doing a lot of thinking about this one," said Millie. "Dress like a city girl, get the biggest heels you have and the shortest skirt you can find, that would be bound to turn him off you."

Millie is so strange.

Asked Millie why the reason for her strange idea as I stepped out onto the road to cross.

"Because," said answered, "he wouldn't see you as wife material, imagine herding cattle in leopard skin boots. Farmers, and lets presume he is one, they like plain girls with childbearing hips, so appear as if you never want to set foot on any farm and he won't look twice at you."

Think Millie's been watching too much of *Farmer Wants A Wife*.

I'm about to inform Millie of my dislike to her outrageous idea when the sound of tires screeching diverted my attention. Turned my head in direction of the noise, a ute was hurtling towards me and I was standing in the way like a petrified possum caught in headlights.

The ute came to a sudden halt just in front of me. It was so close I could see the driver's startled look underneath his wide-brim hat. There's a buzzing sound in my ear and I can't move.

My face is burning red and my body trembling from my near death experience.

Suddenly I snapped out of it. There were people yelling at me from the kerb. I could see the smudge marks on the windscreen and I was still standing in the middle of the road.

The wide brim hat ute driver is now slowly winding down window, his mouth is moving but I cannot hear what he's saying.

I have a sudden realisation he's yelling at me.

"Do you want to get yourself killed?"

I can feel eyes from onlookers watching me.

"Why don't you watch where you're fucking going!" he continued to shout.

I finally found my legs and ran to the safety of the curb.

My face is hot from the humiliation and the onlookers are still staring. I wanted to shout rude things back to scary ute driver but cannot locate my tongue.

Decided to give the bird instead.

"Bloody arrogant townies and ya bloody mobile phones!" he ranted as he drove off. The onlookers turned away leaving me standing on the footpath looking like a dumb ass.

Realising Millie was still on the line I put the phone to my ear.

"Millie you still there?"

"Well I rest my case," she triumphed, "see what did I tell you, they hate you."

Back home

Unloaded my mud cakes and library books I had borrowed from charming but small selection in the village library on the counter, before pouring myself a wine to calm down my still wobbly legs after my near death experience.

I must have left the back door unlocked again this morning but puzzled by this as I could have sworn I locked it.

I need to get my mind off this morning's events so decided to spend the day doing intense research.

I took my glass out into the warmth of the sun and flicked through the stack of country living decorating books I brought home from the library. I am in awe of the lovely pictures of quaint farm cottages complete with lavender and honeysuckle growing up the sides of cobblestone paths and stacks of terracotta pots strategically scattered around a charming cow painted door.

I compared my own garden. It consisted of a spindly frangipani, an out of control vine running up the side of the verandah, a wild blackberry bush and weeds. Lots and lots of bloody weeds.

Feeling a dire need to knock a wall out.

Frustrated but in control, I poured myself another wine and opened the very last book.

There were endless photos of gorgeous white canopies draped over equally white bedroom suites and claw-foot baths complete with terracotta pots spilling healthy green foliage.

I compared the decor of my own house, brown floral wallpaper and lime green carpet complete with bare patches and cream trim, complemented by an old faded pot with a stalk of a once thriving house-plant.

I shut the stupid books' in frustration, the urge to knock the ugly wall out is even stronger but I have willpower and I decide that it's better to wait 'till Millie's arrival over the weekend.

Very bothered by this sudden urge but it's the sensible thing to do.

God I need a distraction.

I drained the dregs from my bottle of wine (no point in leaving the last mouthful, very wasteful) and decided a nana nap would be perfect not only to suppress my urge to tear the house apart but need to keep my wits about me to fight off creepy advances from Mrs Crankshaw's nephew.

Crankshaw's farm

I drove towards a sign that read *The Meadows;* it seems every place around here had a name of some description.

I swung the car into the Crankshaw's rutted driveway and carefully negotiated the potholes.

I decided not to take Millie's advice too seriously after all these people are farmers and I didn't want to stand out that much.

My choice of clothes for this evening was:

A red mini skirt (tight but stylish).

Black knee high boots.

Black Chanel top (I picked up in op shop for $7.50).

The Crankshaw's residence was an older style modest home with a small collection of native shrubs to soften the box shape of the house. I parked my car next to Mrs Crankshaw's trademark ute.

The smell of rotting silage hit me and I felt like I wanted to puke. Made my way towards the house carefully negotiating the muck in my shiny boots. Made it to the enclosed porch, found the door and after wading through the masses of gumboots and buckets, I rang the doorbell and waited.

Baal!

What the hell was that, some sort of doorbell?

Baal!

There it goes again.

I turned in the direction of the strange noise. The most adorable looking face gazed up at me from a basket in the corner.

"Oh aren't you cute," I informed it, in my voice that can only be reserved for baby goats. I bent down to pat it placing the mud cakes carefully on the ground beside me. The goat started to nibble at my fingers.

"Yes you are adorable, yes you are, yes you are, yes you….."

I'm sensing I'm not alone. My gaze followed the long legs covered in denim, the loose checked shirt that hung loosely over the top of the jeans and then finally my eyes lock with his. He had a trace of stubble round his chin. His wide brim leather hat showed his high cheekbones. But it was his eyes, his deep blue piercing eyes that sent a shiver of delight through my insides.

He was looking down at me with an amused smirk on his face. I couldn't break away from his mesmerising eyes. I studied his face hard, for some reason he looked familiar.

I felt the colour drain from my face, it was the same guy who almost ran me over in the street earlier. He hasn't spoken yet but I'm positive it's him which is just my luck and who is he anyway? Well hopefully if I don't mention it he may not realise it was me who stepped out in front of his moving vehicle.

I tried to get up but the heel from my boot slipped on the concrete and I seemed to lose all sense of balance and fell backwards into the mud cakes. I mean I just sat in them.

The door swung open and Mrs Crankshaw appeared.

"Ah, hello Lisa thought I heard the bell, what are you doing down there?"

Well what reason can you come up with when you have your butt in the dessert?

"I see you have already met my nephew Jake," she continued clearly not waiting for an explanation.

This is Jake! Oh Millie's so going to pay for this one.

"Lisa get up of the ground you'll get piles!" Mrs Crankshaw fussed.

Jake spoke for the first time since my arrival. "Actually Aunty, we met earlier today," he stepped over to me and with one swift yank, pulled me to my feet.

"Not the first time today Lisa here has stepped into my path," he scoffed as he patted me on the shoulder and walked inside, leaving Mrs Crankshaw staring at the chocolate mess on her porch.

Mrs Crankshaw tutted as she showed me to the bathroom to clean myself up. I ran a flannel under the water and rubbed vigorously at the chocolate stain. The more I rubbed the worse it got and now it looks like I've had an accident in my pants. Defeated, I threw the cloth into the laundry hamper and sat on the edge of the bath. I cannot believe it, Jake's gorgeous and I'm stuck in these ridiculous clothes. Why couldn't I have ignored Millie's stupid advice and dressed sensible, like normal country girls do?

Mrs Crankshaw tapped gently at the door before entering the bathroom. "I brought you these," she said handing over a pair of old dungarees.

I wanted to scream at her that she was out of her mind but instead informed her that it would be a lot better if I just nip home and change clothes.

Mrs Crankshaw looked horrified, "Lisa there's no time to do that, the other guests will be arriving soon just put these on, no-one cares what you look like."

She shut the door leaving me with the most hideous pair of dungarees I've ever seen.

I feel like I'm twelve again and Mum is insisting that I wear the very undignified brown lace up shoes she brought me for school and not my cool trainers that all the other kids were wearing.

I sheepishly entered the Crankshaw's living room still in my red-mini. "They don't fit," I told Mrs Crankshaw even though I hadn't tried them on. I had to salvage any dignity I had left and figured chocolate covered miniskirt was much better than a pair of the old lady's pants.

Jake entered the living room and handed me a glass of wine. He had taken his hat off which exposed his dark curls that complemented his olive complexion.

"Don't get too attached," he grinned, twisting the cap of his beer.

"I beg your pardon," I spluttered.

"The goats," he said gesturing towards the back porch, "don't get too attached, they are cute now but even the orphan babies we hand rear end up in the same place."

"Oh and what place is that?" I asked, trying to steer the conversation away from our earlier encounter.

"Lisa dear have you tried goat before?" Mrs Crankshaw interrupted, wiping her hands on her apron before Jake got a chance to answer.

I suddenly felt sick.

Yes *okay* I know where supermarket meat comes from but to eat something you have nurtured is something else and eating goat! What kind of sick person would want to eat a goat?

Jake smiled at me when I didn't answer. "Its okay," he mused, "tastes like chicken."

Now I know he's having a go at me, if he thinks that I'm some city girl that goes squeamish at the sight of a bit of goat meat, then I'm going to prove him wrong. I'm going to show Jake that I'm all about the country.

"Actually I'm after a couple of goats myself," I said with an air of grace to my voice.

"Oh, what sort were you after?" Mrs Crankshaw asked.

"You know," I waved my hand and took a sip of wine.

"Boers make good eating," Jake smirked.

"Well you're in luck dear" Mrs Crankshaw continued, "because Pamela and Chuck will be here shortly, they often have goats that don't quite make the grade, have a word to them when they get here."

"Thanks, I will," I smirked back at Jake.

God he's so gorgeous I could almost forgive him for being so arrogant.

I heard the goat bleat again out on the porch.

"That would be Pam," said Mrs Crankshaw, "Jake could you get that?" she called over her shoulder as she made her way back to the kitchen.

Jake opened the door. The woman's face lit up.

"Jake darling," she trilled.

"Pamela, looking great as usual," Jake greeted her by planting a kiss on her cheek.

Behind her appeared two little faces, they piled into the sitting room one after the other, with their electronic toys in hand.

Both kids smiled politely at me as they took their positions on the sofas' like programmed robots.

"Lisa this is Pamela," Jake introduced us.

For having had two children this woman had the most amazing figure. Immaculately dressed in a white top, her hip-hugging skirt highlighted her flat abdomen and flowed down the length of her long legs.

Gold jewellery hung around her neck and wrists and her dark shiny hair was cut and straightened perfectly in a bob style.

She had a sophisticated aura about her, the way she carried herself and I felt a pang of envy. I thought country-women were supposed to be, well, bland. She looked at me from head to toe before shaking my hand. She turned to Jake. "Jake darling" she purred, "could you be a dear and fetch me a glass of wine please."

Jake beamed at her and ran off at her beck and call. She turned to me. "So Lisa, you must have bought the old abattoir?"

"Its pronounced *Abby'toir*, I corrected her.

She looked at me puzzled, Jake came up behind her and handed her a glass.

"And what made you move out here?" Now Jake was also waiting for my answer. If I tell them I don't plan on staying then Jake would definitely be turned off. They don't have to know that I bought the place because I was hoping to impress my vegetarian ex boyfriend that dumped me after the contract had gone through. And now I'm left with an old shack that I plan to fix and sell again to make a tidy profit and move back to the city to buy myself a stylish apartment so I don't have to endure the country much longer.

No, I definitely cannot say that.

"A change of lifestyle," I answered. "You know, get away from the rat race back to nature."

"Hmm," Pamela nodded. "We have a lot of townies come out here with their big rural dreams but it's really hard work and most of them don't last more than a couple of months, but good luck to you".

What a bitch! It's obvious she's trying to show me up in front of Jake, well I'm not letting her treat me like that. I'll show her that I will last longer than a couple of months.

Mrs Crankshaw approached us. "Where's Chuck?" she asked Pamela.

"Oh, he's down at the shed with Max."

"Right then, well dinner's nearly ready, Jake why don't you take Lisa with you and go and tell the men dinner's ready?"

Jake ushered me towards the door and I could feel Pamela's eyes watching me. So hoping she hasn't noticed the brown stain on my behind.

The cool crisp air was a huge welcome to my flustered face.

Jake passed me a pair of gumboots. "Better put these on," he said looking at my shiny, knee high boots.

I didn't argue, I didn't want to get my new shiny boots dirty and also it shows Jake that I'm not afraid of looking like a farmer. I slipped my feet into them and fell into step beside Jake as we slopped our way through the yard.

"So you're a farmer too?" I asked hoping to break the tension.

"Yep, that's my place over there," he said pointing to a light filtering through the trees in the far distance. "Got a couple of hundred acres or so, the farm used to be combined with the dairy unit here when my grandfather had it, and his father before him, but after he died the farm got split between the brothers. Uncle Max took over the dairy and Dad kept the rest. I took over when Dad died from lung cancer a few years back."

Jake spoke with ease about his mum being an amputee and living in a retirement village in Sydney and how fond he was of his aunt and uncle. His deep voice was captivating. I listened with interest, admiring the way his expression changed as he told his families history.

He was nothing like Joe, he had ruggedness about him and unlike Joe it was clear that Jake belonged on the land. Joe wouldn't have lasted out here in the elements and the stench, he was more comfortable being an inner city hippie and now I'm somewhat grateful we separated.

I can see now that I was never suitable for someone like Joe.

Now Jake on the other hand, well we have so much in common, for a start we… well, I'm sure we do, it's just a matter of time.

We stopped in front of a four wheel motorbike and Jake mounted it. "Well aren't you getting on?" he asked as I stood there dumbfounded.

I said a little prayer that skirt wouldn't tear in the process and climbed on.

I wrapped my arms tight around Jake's waist.

"Ah no need for that, there's a bar behind you, hang onto that."

Hastily retracted my arms from around his waist while Jake kicked the bike into gear and roared off.

One hellish ride later

We arrive at the shed with most of countryside splattered up the side of my legs. The smell of effluent wafted up my nose and I began to feel queasy again.

The herd of cows was in line, waiting to go back out to pasture and behind a high pressure water hose was a small man with a greying *ZZ-Top* like beard.

"Foods ready Uncle Max!" Jake called out and the man waved his hand in acknowledgement.

Jake approached the other man standing off to the side of the pens watching the slow action of the cows.

"Chuck." Jake mumbled.

"Jake." The man grumbled back, their greeting seemed a little tense.

"This is Lisa, Lisa this is Chuck, Pamela's husband."

I was astonished, I mean talk about an odd couple.

Chuck, who was dressed in a tweed jacket and *R M Williams* boots, was as about as attractive as *Basil Fawlty* from *Fawlty Towers*. I stuck out my hand "How do you do Chuck?"

"It's Charles," he sniffed, ignoring my hand.

Max came up and slapped Jake playfully on the back, "who's this pretty lass then?" he beamed in delight.

I smiled, Max had cheerfulness about him that anyone would instantly warm to, "I'm Lisa," I beamed back shaking his hand, which by the way was covered in muck.

"Yes Lisa, Barb told me you'd be coming tonight, lovely to meet you. How you settling in down at the old Abattoir?"

What is it with these people?

"Its pronounced *Abby'toir*," I corrected him.

All three men were looking at me dumbfounded until Max chuckled "Well lass, great to have you here. You'd better watch out for this one," he said digging Jake in the ribs, "she looks like she could break your heart."

I flushed and dared not look at Jake.

"I'll give you a hand to put this lot away Uncle" Jake said, "Chuck could you take Lisa back up to the house in the ute?"

Disappointed I followed Pamela's husband out to the ute and

call me paranoid but I'm sure Jake's avoiding me. Well I cannot blame him, after all I'm ridiculously dressed thanks to Millie.

Also have chocolate cake stuck to my butt, mud splattered up my legs and my hands are covered in shit.

Pamela's husband made no attempt at conversation as we drove back to the house but I wasn't bothered, I found him just as rude as his wife.

Back at the house

Seated around the table, Mrs Crankshaw had purposely sat Jake and I together. Pamela took her seat on the other side of Jake as her husband sat next to me at the head of the table. After they gave thanks for the food the conversation switched to farming as the dishes of cottage pie and lamb casserole were passed around the table.

I listened with interest waiting for my opportunity to contribute to the conversation but I knew nothing about cow's udders. I'm so bored and a bit put out by the lack of attention coming my way.

Jake had his back to me and was in deep conversation with Pamela. I watched Pamela with interest, the way she gracefully buttered her bread roll and sipped at her wine, very mannerly.

If I'm ever going to attract Jake's attention I will have to start convincing him that I'm all about the land and not some ridiculously dressed townie.

The conversation continued between Jake and Pamela, she laughed at something Jake had said then brushed her shiny hair back off her face in one swift, elegant movement.

I was starting to think Pamela had a thing for Jake. Ha! As if she had a chance, I mean Jake must be at least half her age.

Finally a break in conversation and attention was now on me. And about time too, after all I was the guest here.

"Lisa here is after a couple of goats," Mrs Crankshaw said to Pamela.

Pamela nodded and turned to her husband.

"Well we do have those two mongrels that didn't make the grade?" Charles addressed me after shooting a glare at his wife. "They are quality goats," he assured me, "but because we only accept the highest grade of meat, anything that doesn't make the grade gets sold for pet food."

"Oh," I replied, not knowing what else I could say that sounded like I knew what he was talking about.

"Fifty dollars each," Pamela piped up, "keeps the books honest and Charles can deliver them tomorrow if you're interested?"

"Oh that would be marvelous," I trilled.

"You're forgetting dear that I can't deliver them tomorrow, I'm going away on business in the morning," Charles reminded his wife.

"Well then Jake can deliver them; if you don't mind that is" she said, patting Jake on his hand, her eyes firmly fixed on her husband.

"Yeah no problem," Jake replied through a mouthful of food.

"What about Mike?" Charles hissed. "After all he is the farmhand and not completely useless, why can't he do it?"

"Because I have other things I want him to do!" Pamela snapped back. It felt like watching a tennis match with me in the middle, if Jake felt the same way he wasn't showing it, cramming food into his month.

"What sort of business?" I asked Charles, breaking the silence.

"I'm an investment banker."

"Oh so you're not a full time farmer?"

"No he prefers to leave the farm work to others," Pamela answered for her husband.

"I don't want to be too much trouble," I said, sensing that this tense exchange was somehow my fault.

"It's no trouble," said Pam, glaring at her husband.

The children didn't seem to notice their parent's exchange either, must be a common thing around the Horton dinner table.

"Lisa dear you must join the Country Women's Association," Mrs Crankshaw spoke while spooning her third helping of peas onto her plate. "Pamela here is the president and a great job she does."

"Oh why thank you Barb," Pamela smiled in a coy way.

"Yes Lisa you must, we do a great deal around the community, fund-raising, that sort of thing. It's jolly good fun and a great way to mingle with the community."

"Oh well I'll certainly think about it," I said, trying to hide the fact that I had just spilt gravy down the front of me. Jake saw this and handed me a napkin.

"So Pam," Mrs Crankshaw piped up, "have you entered any of your pickles in the fair this year?"

Great, back to Pamela, it's all about her isn't it?

I had a sudden thought that entering ones wares in a country fair could be an opportunity to show Jake that I am all about the country.

"Excuse me, sorry to interrupt, but did you say there was a fair coming up?"

"Yes, two weeks from now," Mrs Crankshaw said.

"What sort of competitions do they have?" I asked.

"In what?" Pamela asked, giving me a puzzled look.

"Oh you know, jam making, that sort of thing."

"I didn't know you were interested in home-wares Lisa?" Mrs Crankshaw said, "let me fetch you a program."

"I do all sorts of things," I said.

"Like what?" Pamela asked me once again.

"Oh you know, flower arranging, chutneys, that sort of thing."

Well I did do a sand saucer at school when I was in the third grade and if I remember, I beat Fanny Frances that year on account that sand saucers were all about clutter, not theme as Fanny Frances found out after her little stream made out of tin-foil failed to impress the judges.

Mrs Crankshaw returned to the table and passed me a program. "There you go my dear, if you are interested in entering anything let me know, I still think they would accept late entries don't you think so Pamela?"

"Yes I should think so."

I flicked through the list of entries they had. Jam seemed to be my best bet here, it can't be that hard, can it?

"Well I think I might enter my famous blueberry jam" I said.

"Blueberry jam?" Pamela asked me again.

Honestly, Pamela's hearing isn't the best.

"Alright then," said Mrs Crankshaw, "I shall put an entry in the jam section for blueberry jam."

The children asked to be excused from the table and Pamela reminded them that dessert would be served soon.

I cringed at the word dessert.

"We will be having apple pie with ice-cream," Mrs Crankshaw said to the children as they left the table. "Lisa did make a fabulous looking mud cake but there was an unfortunate accident with it, wasn't there Lisa?"

"Yes unfortunate" I mumbled, my face burning.

Jake had an amused look on his face as he poured Pamela another glass of wine before topping up my glass.

The usual banter was spoken over apple pie and ice cream. After the dishes were cleared I excused myself for the evening, one more glass of wine and I would be dancing on the dinner table or worse, start bitch slapping Pamela for stealing my thunder. Jake seemed to be suffocated by her the whole evening and I never got a chance to get him alone for one moment. Every time I glanced in his direction I felt well, it was hard to describe really... oh that's right, need to mention about Randy Puss.

"Mrs Crankshaw, your cat is at my place."

"Cat?" She looked at me puzzled.

"Yes a tabby cat, it turned up at my place, must have walked a long way."

"Lisa dear, we don't have a cat."

"Oh?"

"It must be a feral cat, there are a lot of them around."

"Oh, okay."

Looked definitely like a tabby to me?

"Well thank you for dinner," I said sincerely, "I have to work in the morning but I would like to return your invitation. I'm planning to host a dinner party one evening and would be delighted if you could all come," I announced as I made my way to the door.

Ha, that will impress Jake.

Max came over to see me off, I said my goodbyes,

Pamela merely nodded at me. A bit rude of her considering I was the guest for the evening.

"You're quite welcome dear," Mrs Crankshaw said wiping her hands on her apron, "and a dinner party sounds, um, great, Jake why don't you walk Lisa to her car?"

At car apologising for earlier incident in town

"I don't normally take calls on my mobile," I said, "I only have a mobile for emergencies you know and that call was important. I also do normally watch where I am walking, I must have had a lapse in concentration."

"Ah that's okay," Jake smiled, "I would've felt terrible if I'd hit you."

Jake started to scuff his boots into the dirt as I fiddled in my bag for my car keys. In the kitchen I could see Mrs Crankshaw's face pressed up against the window as if she was willing us to start snogging or something.

Jake started to say something, he looked embarrassed.

"Um, I'm sorry about tonight, I think I know what Auntie Barb's intentions were, you see she is good to me but she seems to think I need a wife and tries to set me up with anyone she can think of. She thinks I'm desperate or something."

Desperate! Oh the shame. Jake continued, "but you seem really nice so maybe we could be friends?"

I nodded enthusiastically, trying to cover my embarrassment.

"Friends," I said as I stuck out my hand. Jake took my hand and shook it, sending shivers through me. "We'll just see how things go shall we?" he smiled in a smooth manner.

I climbed into the car, not trusting myself not to throw myself at his mercy. I started the engine and headed for home not giving Jake another look and not feeling great about the whole evening.

Facebook Status Update.

Lisa Collins: Does anyone have a jam recipe?

Lisa likes: Farming and The Farmer Wants A Wife.

3

On phone to Millie

"She did everything to show me up in front of Jake! I mean honestly, the woman was a show pony if not a bit of a bitch."

I was, of course referring to Pamela Horton.

Millie was surprised to hear how gorgeous Jake was but Millie was only surprised that she was wrong for a change, not to mention the advice she gave me about the clothes.

So, so wrong.

"I'm sorry, why is that Pamela woman a bitch? You have lost me." Millie said.

"Because Millie, she was rude to me and she was all over Jake, trying to keep him away from me."

"Lisa you are doing it again!"

Millie's voice cut through me and I'm just going to ignore that comment. It's okay to fancy somebody and that's just what I was doing, it's just an interest, nothing more.

"Lisa, you're a man-oholic, you promised me you would stop."

"But this is different!" I wailed. "I'm not breaking any promises Millie."

Change of subject in order or I will end up getting a lecture again.

"Do you know where I can get blueberries?"

"Blueberries? Have you not tried a supermarket?"

"Well I need about a pound."

"What for?"

"I'm making blueberry jam to enter in the upcoming country fair." There was silence on the other end of the line, I thought we had been disconnected until Millie's voice appeared on the line again. "Lisa I hate to be the one to break this to you but since when have you entered anything in country fairs. Has this temporary madness got anything to do with Jake?" she said in her stern voice.

"Oh don't be ridiculous Millie. Everyone enters something in the fair, that's the country way, how hard can it be? Now do you know where I can get a pound of blueberries?"

"Blueberry jam?" Millie chuckled.

"Oh never mind!" I snapped. "I'll find them myself."

My first morning at the retirement home in my new job
Going well so far.

The residents were charming and it was amazing how comfortable I felt chatting to them. Now with morning tea over with and the residents back on their allocated armchairs, Debbie the Matron was showing me how to apply Doug's catheter.

"First you have to get the penis hard," she instructed.

I watch Debbie's movements as Doug lay back with his hands behind his head, a distant look in his eyes.

The catheter was attached to a condom type thing. "Now roll it down the penis," Debbie continued like she was demonstrating for a safe sex video. "Then fasten it with tape, there." She surveyed her work looking satisfied. "That needs to be changed every morning, normally before breakfast, but night shift had to put a new one on before they left this morning, he must have pulled it off during the night."

My job is none too glamorous but is a big novelty finishing at two in the afternoon after years of working shifts at Joe's cafe. Taking care of elderly is extremely satisfying.

Home

Missed a call from my parents, I will phone them later.

I checked over the fences and brought buckets of fresh water for the trough in preparation for my new arrivals. I had chosen to wear a pair of jeans and checked shirt, tied at the ends in a Daisy Duke style, complete with gumboots. A bit of make-up applied and I was ready to show Jake how countrified I was.

An hour later

I heard a vehicle pull up and checked my appearance in the mirror. This would be the first glimpse Jake would have of me in normal clothes so better get it right.

I stepped out to greet Jake with all the country grace I could muster, but it wasn't Jake.

It was Pamela jumping from her Range Rover. Her hair was smartly swept off her face and pulled neatly into a bun, her crease free white shirt was tucked into her jodhpurs that seemed to hug every curve of her lean figure, obviously dressed for riding. Very English.

"Hello Lisa," she trilled making her way to the door "Jake's on his way but don't bother to pay me yet, I'll invoice you, I'm actually after a favour."

I was shocked at her tone, it seemed to be far more pleasant than the night before and she even looked more relaxed. "You see, as you know the weekend after next is the country fair and the CWA runs a refreshment stall every year and I know you haven't joined us yet but I'm in a bit of a dilemma because one of our ladies cannot make her slot at the tent, due to family problems. I was wondering if I could count on you to fill in for her."

So now she's being nice to me, well I will just have to tell her I'll think about it.

"It will only need an hour of your time," she continued to persuade me, "and there will be someone with you, nothing hard, just serving tea and coffee. So can I count on you?"

To be honest, it sounded great, if I was to get into the thick of the community Jake would see that I'm committed to the country and not about to run back to the city like Pamela seems to think I am.

I hesitated answering just to see if Pamela would plead or beg. Sensing my hesitation Pamela touched my arm lightly. "Sorry to put you in this position, I'm sure I can find someone else, thank you anyway."

"No wait!" I cried as she turned to go. "I mean, I'd I love to help out," saying it with more enthusiasm than I intended.

"Oh fantastic, Barb said that would be a pushover, well love to stay but my daughter has a riding lesson. I will get back with the times. Tar la."

I didn't waste time seeing her off and raced back inside and opened my drawers, frustrated as I have no damn jodhpurs. Quickly fixed my hair into a bun and pulled the shirt tales out of knot, survey myself in mirror once again.

There that's better now I look like I'm going on a hunt.

Back in the kitchen

Poured a glass of wine while I waited on Jake's arrival, that's when I noticed a half empty bottle of beer was sitting on the kitchen top.

What the hell!

It was still slightly chilled like it was not long out of the fridge. Must been going mad because I sure as hell did not open a beer.

I had brought a carton of beer earlier for Jake's arrival so I had something to offer him besides tea.

After all, farmers drink beer after a hard day on the land. I was racking my brains trying to remember if I had drunk the beer and had forgotten that I did so, when the sound of Jake's ute arriving pulled me from my thoughts.

As he reversed the ute up to the pen I saw two of the cutest little faces peering through the bars of their cage. Jake jumped from the cab and began hurling them out by their feet. Extremely barbaric way to handle goats but I'm not one to judge.

"Are you going to give them names?" Jake asked leaning on the fence, watching me get acquainted with the new arrivals.

"Not good to name anything you're going to eat," he mused.

I glared at him, but in a flirty way.

"Well I think they deserve a name," I said as the goats crowded around me and nibbled on my hands and clothes. I have never named a goat before, I felt like a new mum bonding with its infants. I was so in awe of their sweet faces I had almost forgotten Jake was there.

I apologised for ignoring him and offered him a nice cold beer if he helps me decide on names.

"Yeah sounds fair enough," Jake agreed. "But I'd prefer a cup of tea, I don't drink during the day."

Very sensible man.

I'm in the kitchen perving out the window at Jake while he tightens the gate hinges.

I have to say he is looking very sexy, very broad across the shoulders and he has his shirt sleeves rolled up to reveal his deep tanned forearms. He was without doubt the most gorgeous looking man I had seen. Such a shame that he didn't have a wife or girlfriend, seems like such a waste of a perfectly good man.

Not that I'm complaining that he hasn't a wife or girlfriend.

Pouring boiling water over the tea bags in the mugs, horror and dread run through me. I didn't ask him how he likes his tea. Shall I call him in or take a tray of milk and sugar?

Damn, why didn't I think to make some fresh muffins.

Dilemma diverted I found Jake nestled under the oak tree, aka 'tree of death'.

"You have got to get those fences fixed," he said as I handed him his cup followed by the milk, sugar bowl and a packet of Oreos. "They won't hold them for much longer, goats are cunning things not to mention jumpers, maybe some hot wire and some netting might be the way to go."

I brushed his concerns aside as I had much more important things to talk about than fences like why wasn't he interested in finding a girlfriend. But the words failed me and I couldn't think of a single thing, besides how wonderful the weather was.

Luckily Jake broke the silence first.

"Lot's of work to be done around this place," he commented, taking in the surrounds.

Perfect opening to tell Jake all my plans I had in mind for the place like planting vegetables and making my own wine and getting a cow. Thankfully I paid attention to Joe when he talked non stop about small holdings otherwise Jake here would think I was ignorant.

I was babbling but for some strange reason I could not stop talking. I wanted to stop but my mouth just didn't stop moving, Jake looking at me with amusement.

"What?"

"Do you always talk this much?" he asked, pulling his hat further down his face with amusement.

How dare he!

"I'm sorry!" I snapped at him, "I didn't realise I was boring you!"

"No, you're not boring me, you're just running before you can walk, you've only been here for a week. Running a property takes up a lot of time even with the small holding you have, not to mention funds."

"Are you saying I'm not up to this?" I said waving my hand around the wonderful shambles that was my home.

"Keep ya hair on, I'm just saying there's a lot of work involved."

"Yeah well I'm quite aware of that Einstein!"

Anger boiled inside me, it was so clear that the comment Pamela had made to me last night had persuaded him that I could not cope with the demands of country life.

Jake regarded me for a moment, I could feel his eyes on me as I tried hard not to look at him.

He drained his cup and got to his feet. I stood up in unison with him and we nearly bumped heads. He was so close that I could feel his breath on my face. So sure he is going to kiss me. But instead he handed over the empty cup.

Bastard!

"Thanks for the cuppa," he grinned. "But better be going, haven't been round the cattle yet." He turned on his heel leaving me feeling suddenly foolish for my defensive outburst. Clearly he doesn't like strong-minded woman.

He reached his ute and turned back to me, "Bonnie and Clyde" he shouted.

"Pardon?"

"The goats, how about naming them Bonnie and Clyde?"

He's so sexy and brilliant.

Dilemma

The long weekend approached and I'm waiting anxiously for arrival of Millie and Sid like a lonely rural person.

Millie had agreed to my proposal about being head designer.

She is so excited and thinks it would be a wonderful idea getting into the business of property investment. But I'm feeling guilty because I'm not sure if I want to be a property investor now. Reason being is that I think I'm much more suited to country life, apart from isolation which takes some getting used to and the rats in the ceiling keeping me awake (Randy Puss is obviously no hunter). But I'm extremely excited about their arrival and can't wait for Millie to check out my fabulous home.

The sound of Sid's car with the ghastly hole in the exhaust pipe announces their arrival. I'm so excited I didn't give Millie a chance to open the passenger door.

"Whoa!" Millie exclaimed as I pulled her from the car and hugged her all in one swift motion.

"You act like you haven't seen a single sole for years."

Millie looked at the old place for the first time and I noticed her face dropped into a look of alarm. "Well aren't we going to be busy," she said, rubbing her forehead.

Sid climbed out of the car looking like he hadn't slept for days.

Dilemma diverted

I had a bottle of wine and three glasses chilling nicely on a table under the shade of the porch. By creating the perfect setting I was hoping to impress Millie so she will see just how lovely the countryside is.

And she will see my point when I tell her that I've made a decision and that I will not be returning to the city, as I am to become a woman of the land.

"This looks a bit fancy," Millie said as she settled herself down on the chair.

"Well Millie, we are in the country now," I said, opening the corked bottle with a real corkscrew. "We do things a lot more tastefully in the country."

Millie upset my ambience by taking herself on a tour of the house.

Back on the porch, Millie filled me in on what I'd been missing in the city and I filled her in on the charms of living in the country. Millie looking bored.

"So what colours did you have in mind for the house?" she asked, changing the subject quite abruptly and reaching for her colour chart. "Because I was thinking of a scarlet for the living area and a purple down the hallway and maybe a lime green for the kitchen."

I was starting to think that asking Millie to be project manger was not such a good idea after all.

"I was thinking more of a traditional look keeping with the era of the house," I informed her. Millie rolled her eyes at me.

"Boring, you have only got small windows; there is not a lot of light in that living room, bright colours will lighten it."

"It's not dark," I argued.

"Oh really, so why do you have the light on at three o'clock in the afternoon?"

God Millie is so bloody observant.

Sid cleared his throat. "Why don't you put a couple of French doors in the living area, that will let in more light and keeps the tradition of the house, in time you could add a deck out that way, if you want my opinion," he quickly added.

I looked at him shocked and have to admit it was very brave of him. Sid is usually hen pecked and has worthless opinions.

"We didn't ask for your opinion," Millie hissed.

"Do you know about this stuff?" I asked him, silencing Millie with my hand.

"Yeah, Dad was a builder. I used to go on the job all the time. It doesn't have to cost much. You could pick up the doors second hand at a demolition yard. You might need a permit but I could check it out with the local council, and I've got a mate who could put the doors in for you for cash. But first I would contact the historic places trust and find out how much building work you're allowed to do, that's if you want to," he shrugged.

Sid's normal and has valid opinions, who would have thought.

I'm now visualising French doors opening onto deck and Jake and I sitting out there in the evenings sipping sherries after a long and hard day farming.

Millie is now puzzled by the fact that Sid actually has a dad and Sid pointing out that everyone has a dad (another brave move by Sid).

I'm still deep in thought on the possibilities of evening sherries on the deck with Jake. Need to put a plan into place or Millie will just take over.

"Okay Millie, I will let you paint the hallway any colour you want, but you must leave the living area to Sid. Agreed?"

Millie looked defeated. "Do what ya like," she sniffed, "it's your dungeon."

Next morning

Sipping my coffee and watching Sid in the pen with the goats doing some type of meditation.

Very weird, but because it's Sid I am used to his weird ways and not phased at all.

He spotted me and got to his feet.

"How long have you been doing that?" I asked.

"Since sunrise," he said, "feet are starting to go numb."

Both of us glanced at the goats with mutual uncomfortable silence. I'm not sure how to talk to Sid, he's often away on another planet, well, his soul is, so he believes.

"Don't you think it's cruel to have goats locked up behind fences?" He asked.

I'm not sure if his question is a hypothetical one or if he's serious, but I'm not in the mood for a debate either way so I casually shrug at his comment.

Millie joined us at the pen, clearly still irritated from being banished to the hallway duty.

"I'm going into town to buy paint." She announced with her hands on her hips. "And by the way you have a major rat problem, the banging kept me awake half the night *and* I almost lost my balance on the huge great hole you have in the floor in that spare room."

Too early in morning to argue with her so I shrugged my shoulders, Millie's in a pre-menstrual mood anyway so best to say little.

"Sid, I'm ready to go, hurry and change into some normal clothes would you."

Sid must sense PMT mood as well as he hurried back to house without saying a word.

"So do you need me to get some timber to patch that hole in the floor?" Millie asked.

"It's not a big hole," I argued, "and besides it goes with the character of the house."

'It's a dump!' Millie exclaimed. "I dropped my roll of deodorant on the floor this morning and had to chase it as it rolled down the sloping floor, Lisa your foundations are shot, forget paint, you need to get some structural work done."

"Oh I will," I said, waving her concerns away, "but not until I spruce the place up a bit. Breathe some life into it." Millie looked annoyed.

She rolled her eyes then joined a miserable looking Sid and left for town.

Hope she comes back in a better mood.

I now have blueberries for the jam, frozen, but blueberries all the same. So my task today is make jam for the fair next week.

I'm loving the sun but am starting to get quite smelly in flannelette pajamas.

Making my way back to the house to get dressed and create tasty jam, a figure off in the distance caught my eye.

I tried to shield my eyes from the morning sun to get a better look. It appears to be a man staring back at me, but then again how could I be sure, he was some distance away.

I walked towards the fence that separated the property boundary from the forest to see if there is any sign of a car or any sort of transport that might explain that there was a man on the top of the ridge, as it is a long way to walk.

Okay, maybe there is an innocent explanation for his presence as he could be hunting, but very concerned as hillbilly hunter with big scary gun watching me from top of ridge does not seem normal.

I glanced up at the ridge again but lost sight of him. I'm thinking I could have possibly imagined it, but seems a good excuse to phone Jake and ask if any hunters use the area.

Phoned Jake (got number from directory, charge for service but so worth it)

Feck, bugger, damn! Jake's not home. I left a message anyway but now cannot stop thinking of him. Very bad to be thinking of Jake, as all of a sudden I feel very turned on. Not surprising, as it's been six weeks since I broke up with Joe which almost makes me a born again nun, according to Millie.

Hormones now raging over more thoughts about Jake and feel intense need to strip wallpaper. Jam making can wait, it's unimportant, so is personal hygiene at this point. Taking one corner of the hideous wallpaper and ripped, now I cannot stop. Feels good to divert frustration, but not in a perverted way.

Millie and Sid back

Millie's so impressed with my morning's work of hideous wallpaper removal. It's very therapeutic stripping wallpaper, I have even forgotten about scary hillbilly hunter.

Millie must be still in her PMT mood because Sid excused himself from wallpaper duty by hiding. I'm still in my pj's, the radio blaring in the background and I still cannot get Jake out my mind. Millie's talking non-stop and I'm not really listening to her, she's probably telling me what a dickhead her boyfriend is anyway.

Millie stopped mid sentence and I thought that was my cue to put in my involuntary "uh hah," when I turned to see Millie gawking at what seems to be a door under the half stripped wallpaper.

I gawked at the sight of the door as well.

Millie stripped the rest of the wallpaper away from around the frame and the two of us stood in mutual astonished silence.

Sid came up behind us. "It's a door," he observed.

"Nice observation Sid!" Millie snapped.

Curiosity swept through me like a wave, a hidden door, how cool is that! I suggested opening it.

"Sid, go and get something to break the door." Millie instructed, sharing my enthusiasm.

"Oh I don't know man, I got a bad feeling about this" Sid said.

Sid always has been a wet blanket.

"Oh for goodness sake!" snapped Millie, "just go and get something before you receive a bad feeling."

Sid sulked away and came back with a hammer and raised it over his shoulder ready to attack.

"Wait!" I cried. "You will break it, I think we should we just push at it."

"All right, stand back," Sid sighed.

He backs up enough to take a running thrust at the door. Smashing his shoulder against the wood he bounced off the solid door and landed on the floor.

"You moron," Millie muttered as Sid rolled on the floor clutching his shoulder.

Millie felt above the door frame, "ah ha!" she said triumphantly, pulling down a key from on top of the frame, "oldest trick in the book."

"Millie that's extraordinary!" I exclaimed.

"Yes I know," she said smugly "guess those old mystery novels paid off eh?"

"No, the key!" I exclaimed. "It's extraordinary, must be an antique."

Millie rolled her eyes at me. She has had a habit of doing that since she arrived and if she doesn't change her attitude soon I will be forced to strike her off this project. The key fit perfectly and after a bit of fiddling, the door unlocks.

The smell of mildew filtered from the room. The light from the hallway revealed another passage behind the hidden door. It was dark so I fetched a torch and shined the light into the room. The passage seemed to stretch beyond the torch light. I strained my eyes into the darkness, there appeared to be a room at the end.

Millie pushed me forward. "Go on," she urged.

"Why do I have to be first?"

"Because it's your spooky house," Millie replied nervously.

"Yeah I agree," Sid spoke up.

I pointed out to Sid that he is the man so he should go first.

"I'm scared of the dark," he snapped back.

"Oh give that to me!" Millie exclaimed.

She grabbed the torch and started her way down the darkened passage.

"Watch your footing," Millie warned, "there might be holes in the floor."

Millie sarcasm is wearing thin, PMT or not, there's no excuse for it.

"Does anyone else think it's weird there's no cobwebs?" Sid asked, looking up at the high ceiling.

Millie came to a standstill. The room itself was no bigger than my storeroom. We stood in silence, bewildered at our discovery. The room was empty apart from what appeared to be an old piece of furniture hidden underneath a cloth against the wall.

Gathering the courage to take a step further into the dark room, I pulled at the dusty sheet to reveal an old oak wardrobe.

"See if it leads to Narnia," Sid joked.

"Wow!" Millie exclaimed. "That must be worth a mint."

"It's in good condition too," I added. Moving the torch light around the room I was already thinking of the possibilities for the use of this room, a library perhaps, or it could be my drawing room, although I have no idea what a drawing room's function is.

"I wonder what they used this room for?" Millie asked.

"It used to be part of a bigger room," Sid added, pointing to the remains of an old fire place.

"At some stage they put this wall up and closed this room off altogether."

"Yes but why wallpaper over the door?" Millie picked something up off the dusty timber floor, an old newspaper. She brought it closer into the torch light.

"It's dated 1947. How long did you say the previous people were here for?" Millie asked me.

"Forty years."

Sid started counting on his fingers.

"Then it wasn't them who built this room!" I snapped at Sid, getting extremely frustrated with his dim-witted ways.

"Help me move the wardrobe," I instructed.

"What for?" asked Millie.

"I want to get it into my dining room. It would make a great addition to the renovations." For once Millie agreed with me, I was starting to think this old house may be a bit of a goldmine, another reason to stay in the country.

Sid held up his hands nervously, "don't go messing with stuff, it might be haunted."

"A haunted wardrobe?"

"Oh stop being a big baby and help!" Millie snapped at him.

"We'll tip it on its side, I'll push it, and Sid you take the weight."

Millie and I grabbed the bottom of the wardrobe and put our shoulders into it. "Ready, one, two..."

Sid let out a high pitched scream.

Millie and I dropped the wardrobe and clung to each other in fright at Sid's reaction.

"What! What is it?" Millie screeched. "Is it a snake?"

"A rat!" Sid exclaimed. "It shot out from underneath the wardrobe."

A shiver ran down my spine. "Where is it now?" I asked.

"I don't know, I didn't see where it went!"

Sid's voice had suddenly changed, it now sounded like he had gone back to that stage at puberty where things hadn't quite dropped.

"Oh god you've got to help me," he pleaded "I'm scared."

Randy Puss made an appearance and lunged at something near Sid's feet.

"There it is!" shouted Millie when she found the torch and shone it near Sid to reveal two yellow eyes looking back at her. "It's down by your feet Sid."

Sid screamed again, this time it was more like a scream from the movie 'Jaws'. He ran towards the door, the rat following Sid and in turn, Randy Puss chasing the rat. Millie and I burst into fits of nervous laughter, we were trying to hide our disgust for the unhygienic creature and also trying to hide our discovery that we think Sid may be a bit of a namby pamby.

4

Needed afternoon nap

The excitement was too much. Must have slept for some time because it's late afternoon when I rise. Millie had finished the wallpaper and I can hear the shower running. I stumbled to the kitchen to make a drink when I notice Sid's car gone as well. Millie had been very busy, I noticed the kitchen table littered with papers and colour charts as well as post-it notes to remind her about enquiring to Historic Trust about building work. I need to tell Millie about my change of plan and don't want to be a city girl any more.

The sound of a car approaching seems to be the perfect diversion, I looked out to see who (wasn't Sid's car, not noisy enough) and Jake's familiar ute came into view, I'm so excited I nearly pee my pants.

While running to the mirror to check my appearance, I realised I'm still in pj's and a tad smelly. I doused myself in spray deodorant and hastily discarded pj's for skimpy, sexy shorts.

Satisfied with my look I went out to greet Jake.

"Didn't I tell you to get that fence done?" He grumbled, keeping his back to me as I approached him. "Found these two sauntering down the road."

I realised Bonnie and Clyde were on the back of Jake's ute.

"How did you two get out?" I asked them in my voice that was only reserved for escaped goats.

"Probably through the open gate," Jake pointed to the gate.

"Bloody Sid must have left it open," I scorned, before quickly adding, "Sid is my friend's stupid boyfriend."

He unhitched the goats that were tied to the tray with ropes and carried them back to their pen, I thought it was only good manners to invite him in since he did bring my strays back. Jake accepted, sounding a lot less put out now.

In secret room with Jake

I couldn't help myself; wasted no time showing Jake our find this morning.

After all, he grew up here, he may provide me with some information.

Not that I'm showing off or anything but I can't imagine Pamela having hidden rooms in her house. Jake seemed amazed at the hidden room and suggested that I get the wardrobe appraised.

We are having a lovely chat about history and stuff but I'm not really paying attention, his eyes are distracting me again.

Thinking about jumping him but may come off a tad too keen.

We were about to leave the secret room when Millie appeared.

Oh no!

"Well he-llo," she greeted Jake with an evil twinkle in her eye,

"I'm Millie, you must be Jake, I've heard a lot about you."

"Um could I talk to you for a moment?" I beamed grabbing at her arm. Millie was not shy in coming forward, I also hadn't yet filled Millie in on my new plan which included Jake.

"In a moment," she said brushing my hand away.

"Nice to meet you," Jake greeted back.

"Jake just brought back the goats," I said, "Sid must've left the gate open, Jake found them wandering down the road."

"Oh well," Millie shrugged, "no biggie. Jake why don't you join us for dinner? Lisa was just about to make dinner, weren't you Lisa?"

She didn't just say that did she? Millie gave the thumbs up to me behind Jake's back, I shot her another warning glance.

"Well you wanted a dinner party," she shrugged.

Millie is such a bitch.

"I got a better idea," he said, "why don't I take you ladies out for dinner, my shout."

"Well since you're buying," Millie grinned.

Bloody Millie, she needs to learn some manners. I'm so embarrassed by her rudeness.

"What about Sid?" I reminded her.

"What about him?" She shrugged, "I'll leave him a note letting him know, he'll be right." She turned to Jake, "us girls will go and get changed, you make yourself at home," Millie said as she pulled me by the arm.

In bedroom deciding what to wear on my first date with Jake (and Millie)

"Now Millie, you have to promise me you won't embarrass me, okay?" I said running the brush through my hair, trying to decide what would be suitable to wear to a restaurant.

"He's gorgeous!" exclaimed Millie. "And don't worry, I won't embarrass you."

"Well you already have with your lack of grace, honestly Millie you will need learn some manners."

"Someone's got a crush," she sang.

"Just promise me you won't embarrass me, okay? And another thing, don't tell him that I plan to sell the property as soon as it's finished."

"Why?" she asked, puzzled, if not a little alarmed.

"I'll explain later, now I wonder where Jake's taking us to, do you think it would be a classy restaurant?"

"Who cares where he's taking us," she shrugged, "he's buying remember and *what* are you wearing?"

I had chosen a cream full-length skirt that hugged my waist and flowed out, along with a matching top. I pointed out to Millie that going out for dinner one needs to balance ones dress sense.

Millie huffed and walked over to my pile of clothes sitting on the bed and pulled out a pair of jeans and a black crop top and threw them at me, before leaving the room.

Jake and Millie were conversing over who was driving. It was a lengthy discussion, but soon it was decided we take Jake's ute. I checked that I had locked my back door and then I, thanks to Millie, was wedged between the two of them and well aware that my thigh was touching Jake's leg as we headed off towards town.

Ranor Hotel

Jake must have decided to stop off for a drink before dinner.

It was buzzing with people and Jake got a greeting of whistles and banter from the locals as we approached the bar. The barman approached us and Jake introduced him as Rodney.

"It's karaoke night," Jake informed us, "and it looks like a full house too. Have a seat and I'll bring the drinks over."

Millie and I settled ourselves at a table. The bar interior was dull but the place had a certain buzz about it, like the feeling of apprehension you get before a big night out.

The Eagles Greatest Hits belted from the jukebox and in the far corner two men with goatee beards and long hair were immersed in a game of pool.

"Jake's gorgeous," Millie exclaimed when we were safely out of his earshot. "Why haven't you jumped his bones yet?"

"Millie I've only just met him and besides that was the old me, if he wants me he will have to court me proper."

"Have to what? And what do you mean, the old you?"

I had a tiny thought earlier today that Jake may be an old-fashioned values man and is playing very hard to get so I'm thinking that maybe it's about time I did too.

I also need reassurance from Millie.

"I don't think he's very keen on me," I said in a sorry voice.

"How could he not be," she sympathized, "you're a nice looking girl, better than the feral looking mob I've seen here so far."

That's what I wanted to hear, Millie's fantastic in reading thoughts.

"Maybe he's shy," she continued. "Why don't you make the first move? Got nothing to lose."

"Except my dignity," I added. "By the way, where is Sid?"

"How the hell do I know, he's sulking because he didn't like me calling him a baby."

Jake arrived back at the table with the drinks. A triple vodka for Millie and a glass of dry white for me.

"Drink up," he suggested. "The courtesy van is running tonight so no one has to worry about getting home. If you need a lift just go and see Chubbs." Jake pointed to a rather robust gentleman sitting at the bar nursing a rather large beer.

"But he's drinking," said Millie.

"Yeah?"

"So how can he be the sober driver?"

"Oh don't worry 'bout that, he's allowed a pint an hour,

he will see you home safely. What do you want to eat?"

"We're eating here?" I asked.

Jake looked puzzled. "Yeah, unless you have somewhere else in mind?"

"No, no, here's good."

There wasn't much of a choice on the one sided bar menu but I settled for a steak sandwich and a knife and fork to eat it with, I was hoping to go somewhere quieter.

To be honest I felt appalled that Jake suggested we dine here surrounded by drunken on-lookers; clearly it must be a country thing. The steak was tough and watery underneath the layers of soggy bread, I had trouble chewing through it. Jake devoured his buffalo sized steak as if it was his last. He picked up my glass to get another, I had gone through two glasses of wine so far and I was starting to feel a bit tipsy despite the fact I had just eaten half a piece of watery steak complemented by lashings of mayonnaise.

Millie asked me who the woman was that Jake's talking to. I turned towards the crowd to see Jake in deep conversation with Pamela. She was dressed in jeans that ran all the way up her lean legs, that I might add, seemed to go on forever, tight shirt and cowboy boots.

To finish off the effect, her dark hair hung loosely down to her shoulders. I was so pleased I didn't wear my skirt tonight.

I explained who she was to Millie.

"She looks good for her age. How old did you say she was, in her forties?"

"Oh shut up!" I snapped.

The music started and Billy Ray Cyrus's *Achy Breaky Heart* started booming from the speakers.

"Great, here comes a night of hillbilly music," Millie groaned.

Everyone one got up and started to line-dance led by (of course) Pamela. I watched as she kicked her legs and swayed her hips in perfect sync to the music. She was quite the picture and I noticed Jake watching her.

Next week I'll book myself in for line-dancing classes.

Millie, not to be outdone, chugged down her drink.

"I'll show this lot how dancing's done."

"Oh no Millie don't," I pleaded, "you promised me you wouldn't embarrass me."

"Well if the new you, whomever that may be, is going to sit here all night and be anal then that's fine, but I am going to enjoy myself."

She headed towards the line of dancers. I watch for a while cringing at Millie's every dance move until Jake came back to the table with my drink.

I feel like a fish out of water amongst all these people. Jake must also be a mind reader because he grabbed my hand.

"Come on," he said downing his drink, "I will introduce you to some of the locals."

We pushed our way through the gathering crowd. I have to say the contact of his flesh sent shivers tingling through my body. He introduced me to Chubbs, the designated driver nominated for the evening, who looked to me like he was intoxicated, but then again it could just be the state I was on route for.

"Another drink?" Jake asked as he took my empty glass and made his way to Rodney.

I turned my attention to Chubbs and kick-started a conversation by asking what he did for living.

"As little as possible," said a voice belonging to a skinny, middle aged man beside him, who was introduced to me as his sidekick Stubbs, who was apparently the local slashing contractor. The name Stubbs was because he only had three fingers on each hand. I was praying that it was accident related.

"So you brought the old abattoir?" asked Chubbs.

"It's pronounced *Abby'toir*," I corrected.

"The old Simpson property," Stubbs piped up, "shit is that still standing?"

"Got a bit of work to do then," said Chubbs.

"Yes, well I do intend to restore it to its' former glory," I said as Jake came back and handed me my wine.

"Forget that. You should get in with this prick," Chubbs said pointing at Jake. "He's loaded, if not a bit of a tight-ass though." Jake didn't seem to notice me blushing, and responded with some uncouth banter.

So Jake's loaded, well I'm just going to have to show him that I'm not all about money.

A few of the store owners came and introduced themselves, including Tim who owns the bakery, "oh, it's the mud cake girl," he realized.

 "Mud cake girl?" Jake asked. "Why do you call her that?"

"Oh she came and brought one of my mud cakes the other day. That was after you attempted to run her down."

Jake nodded, "oh that's right, that wouldn't be the same mud cake that you slaved over all day and then sat on was it?" Jake smiled at me and moved off to talk to some old guy with a rather large purple nose.

I'm so embarrassed.

But over it, I'm so enjoying myself. I chatted to Stubbs about the logistics of slashing paddocks and joked with Chubbs about who could drink more.

Mingling with country folk is so cool.

Later

Jake seems to have disappeared as I could no longer see him, I could see Millie however, on the stage where she had taken over not only the dance floor but the karaoke machine as well, and was trying to talk Tim the baker into performing *Stir It Up* by Bob Marley.

Later still

I've had sudden thought that I need to give Pamela a piece of my mind. I mean how dare she talk to *me* like I wasn't good enough. Somebody needs to tell her that all this show pony stuff doesn't impress anybody.

Later still

Pamela's lucky I can't find her.

Much later

Having the time of my life, I laughed, I danced with most of the locals, even beating them in a game of pool.
I had always sucked at pool.

Much, much later

All this popularity with the locals is proving to be wearisome and I cannot find Jake anywhere. How rude it is to abandon someone on a dinner date.
Millie signaled to me to join her on the tabletop for a dance but I declined.
I stood back away from the crowd to give myself a break from all this mingling. Fishing my mobile from my pocket I scrolled down to my address book and started punching numbers. I was in the mood for talking not dancing. Majority of my calls went to voice mail, which I also found rude. I mean why bother having mobile phones if no one is going to answer them.

I came across my old friend Neroli's number.

I almost forgot I had it. She and I had a falling out a year ago, couldn't remember why, but who cares, one does not hold grudges. I will just call her to say hi, I mean I know Neroli, she will be so pleased to hear from me.

I pushed the call button on my mobile, tipped the rest of my drink down my throat and signaled for Rodney to get me another.

Facebook Status Update.
Lisa Collins: I'm so drunk.

5

Following morning (I think)

I'm not too sure, but the sun streaming through curtains burning my eyeballs confirms this.

My head was thumping and my mouth felt like it was glued shut. I opened one eye and breathed a sigh of relief that I made it to my own bed. I smiled to myself at the thought of Jake, he must have brought me home last night, I hope I didn't make spectacle of myself. Tried hard to remember back to the events of last night but it's hopeless. I sure hope Millie made it home, I'd better go and have a look. Attempt to lift my head, too much effort.

Millie's a big girl I'm sure she would have got home.

I heard a rip coming from under the sheets. I think someone farted and I'm sure it wasn't me!

There it was again! Oh, and I appeared to be naked.

I rolled over to see a strange man sleeping next to me, ARRGGH!!

I jumped out of bed and grabbed the sheet to cover my naked body. Hangover forgotten.

He opened his eyes. "Hey," he said, grinning at me.

"Who the hell are you?" I asked him.

"My name's Matt, I told you like a million times man."

"What are you doing in my bed?" I screamed at him.

He sat bolt upright, exposing his naked torso, he held his hands up in defence.

"Whoa man!" he sounded alarmed, "you called me remember and then you invited me back here."

"I most certainly did not!"

He reached for a packet of cigarettes from the bedside table. "Well if you didn't invite me then why did you willingly get into my car? I mean you were in no fit state to drive."

I took a moment to digest this predicament, I had to give him the benefit of the doubt, after all I couldn't remember a damn thing.

"You didn't take advantage of my... you know, did we?" I asked.

"Yeah man, you were gagging for it, practically begged me to take advantage," he chuckled.

Mortified, but again I had to give him the benefit of the doubt.

He lit his cigarette. "Yep, you rang me and told me you were at the pub, and the celebrations were on because you caught a mouse or something, thought that was a little strange at first, but I wasn't doing much so I thought why not."

"I called you? Well, who are you and why would I have your number?"

"I dunno," he shrugged, flicking his ash into an empty can. "You called the bosses work phone actually. We normally get after hours calls but boss was at a barbecue so I was on-call, pretty rude for a Saturday night."

Now I was confused.

"Why would I have your bosses work number?" I asked. "What sort of business would I have with your boss?"

"It's the only garage around these parts, I'm the apprentice mechanic," he explained. "So I'm guessing you have a car. Actually I know you, you're the chick from the other day, yeah now I remember," he nodded.

I tried to digest this new information but got distracted when the strange man climbed out of my bed, even more distracted by his nakedness.

He walked passed me pinching my bum as it stuck out from the gap in the sheet. "Since you were a good host last night, I'll make the coffee," he said with a grin that spread across his face. He climbed into a pair of boxers that had skulls imprinted on them.

"I think I remember where the kitchen is," he said as he departed leaving me with my shame.

I collapsed on the bed, still trying to piece together the events of the night before. I could hear him rattling around in the kitchen. I only hope that Millie wasn't up and she wouldn't see the nearly naked man in the kitchen. Thinking about Jake and trying to remember when I last saw him in the tavern. I'm hoping he wasn't there long enough to see me in that state, but then again he may have been and if he was, then that's his problem, after all he did abandon me. I just hope I didn't make a fool of myself.

Grabbing my mobile phone that lay on the floor beside the bed I checked the outgoing calls.

So shocked at the discovery that I had called everyone last night. Oh my god, including Neroli.

I swore I would never speak to her again, not after what she did. I couldn't have spoken to her for long though as I can't imagine we would have much to say to each other.

Oh god, forty minutes!

I think I also better check the last call made just to be sure that strange man hadn't been lying to me, let's see, last called made was Monty Auto's.

I have a sudden realisation that I may have made a tiny fool of myself last night.

Sitting in bed with strange man called Matt sipping coffee like a married couple

Finished explaining to Matt that I'm not normally the kind of girl who picks up just anyone for a shag.

"Oh, god no!" he exclaimed with a look of horror on his face.

"I don't think you're a slapper or anything."

I felt myself go numb.

"You were just really pissed," he continued. "Oh man it was so funny how you were trying to get that fat guy to belly dance. Well better go," he said draining his cup, "didn't let the old lady know I wasn't coming home last night, she will be going nuts right now, my bad."

Horror and dread came over me.

"Old lady! Please don't tell me you're married?"

"What? Married?" He asked me, a little puzzled by the question. "Na man, my mum."

"Your mother, you still live at home?"

"Yeah for now," he said reaching for his pants, "saving up to get me own place, get away from the old lady, she's always nagging me and stuff."

Suddenly my hangover haze started to lift and the coffee kicked in.

I took in Matt's appearance as though I was looking at him for the very first time. The fluff round his chin that was trying to be passed off as facial hair, his long tousled hair, the fresh scars on his face resulting from acne.

The fact that he was an apprentice.

Cringing, and dreading the answer, I asked him how old he was.

"Just turned nineteen last week," he said looking awfully proud of this.

I couldn't move, even though I prepared myself for the shock, I still could not move.

"Pardon?" I screeched, trying to locate my voice.

"Party was da bomb," he continued not noticing my bubble of self-loathing.

"My mates and I got this keg of beer and oh my god, far out, we were so wasted. Can't wait 'till my twentieth. That party's going to rock!"

He stood up and pulled his jeans on so they rested on his hips so least half of his boxers were proudly on display. Throwing his feet into his boots without lacing them, he turned to me, "um, do you want me to call you, or something?"

"There is no way I shall be pursuing this relationship." I told him so in such a hoity voice.

"Yeah, that's cool, totally hear what you're saying," he shrugged, grabbing packet of cigarettes from the bed-side table. He opened his month to speak and then quickly shut it again. He may be a spotty teenager, but he can recognise a mature woman in the process of a meltdown.

"Um, later," he mumbled as he closed the door behind him.

I grabbed my pillow and put it over my mouth to muffle my screams of humiliation.

Later in the kitchen

Millie was in fits of laughter.

"It's not funny!" I snapped.

"No, you're right, it's not funny," she said wiping a tear from her cheek, "it's bloody hilarious." Millie started roaring again. "How could you not recognise he was young enough to be your son?"

"Oh shut up! This's serious, now half the village must think the new girl is a bit of a slag and I know he lives round here. I mean what if I ran into his *mum,* and what is that god awful smell?"

I was so wound up I couldn't stop thinking about it. Jake and I were getting on so well and things were staring to heat up between us. Now I've gone and blown my chances. I mean what if he found out, what will he think of me then?

"Calm down," Millie suggested, wiping the tears from her cheek.

"Why didn't you stop me Millie?"

"I did try," she pleaded, "when you were dragging the poor guy out of the bar by his shirt you told me to, and I quote, 'fuck off'."

I buried my head in my hands. "Oh my lord and in front of the patrons, I'll never set foot in the town again."

"Half of them were just as intoxicated as you," said Millie.

"Besides you're a single lady you can sleep with whomever you please, no one noticed, no one cared. Or," she shrugged, "you could just deny everything."

We sat in silence for a while, each lost in our own thoughts. Deny everything I thought, what a great idea, it's his word against mine and let's face it who would believe a spotty youth over a mature women in her thirties.

"I wonder if he's the type to kiss and tell," Millie said, then went into fits of giggles again.

A sudden thought occurred that Millie's not lecturing me like she normally does, in fact she seems amused. Realised that Millie's cure for hangovers has always been more alcohol, so that may have a lot to do with it.

"Are you still drunk?" I crinkled my nose in disgust. "Oh my god Millie how could you drink first thing in the morning?"

"It's not first thing in the morning, it's two in the afternoon."

"What! Oh no, what about my babies, Bonnie and Clyde. I haven't topped up their water trough."

"Don't worry, Jake did it this morning."

I felt myself go cold.

"Jake was here?"

"Yep, he brought some fence wire for the goat's pen, he also said to say sorry for running off last night but something came up. He's coming back later to put the fence up."

"Well he could have said something last night, how rude running out on a date and what *is* that smell?"

"Maybe when he saw you getting on so well with the locals he thought you'd be okay."

"Well I wasn't and how did you get home last night, not from that guy Chubbs?"

"No he was too drunk to find his own feet, he fell off his bar stool and the bar manger had to drag him out by his feet. Oh, Sid, he turned up at the bar last night after he got my message, he went to see someone about smudging your house.

That's where he went when he took off yesterday and that's what that smell is that you are complaining about. He's smudging your house getting rid of the negative energy and evil sprits."

Just as the day couldn't get any weirder, Sid appeared in the kitchen chanting to himself. The smell of white sage trailed off his smouldering stick. He waved the stick around the kitchen before exiting the room.

"Isn't he great?" Millie said dreamily as she watched him go. I felt sick and my head started to pound.

"I'm going back to bed," I announced to Millie, "please wake me up when Jake gets here and don't say anything to him."

"'No worries, cougar," she started to giggle to herself again.

Still in bed

After the third failed attempt to drag myself up. My stomach is turning and I've missed a call from my parents. I'm never drinking again.

Millie poked her head around the door.

"I'm going out to get more food," she said in her 'I'm feeling great' voice. "You need to get up and get yourself out there, cowboy has arrived to fix your fence."

"More food? I brought heaps the other day," I told her.

"Well someone's eating it. Now get out there!" Millie hissed.

Outside

I made Jake a cup of tea. The nausea is gone and the pain killers are finally kicking in. Jake had his shirt off exposing his tanned torso that sent me into a spin. I watched him as he swung the hammer on top of the posts, drinking in the sight of him.

He looked up and caught me staring.

"Afternoon," he grinned at me.

I felt myself blush and handed over his mug.

"They won't get out of that," he announced proudly.

After surveying the new fence I'm thinking mice wouldn't be able to escape that, but I didn't say so. I thanked Jake by fluttering my eyes at him. I think he likes the damsel in distress types.

"No worries," he said, taking a sip of his tea and wincing.

"Sorry about last night," he continued, "something came up. You looked right at home so that's why I just slipped out. Did you get home alright?"

"Oh yes," I said. "The local mechanic dropped me off and then he went straight to his house, in fact he never came to the door, just dropped me off and left, never said goodbye just…you know."

Jake was now looking at me as if I was mad.

He turned to lean on the fence. "I hear you're helping out at the fair next weekend. How's the jam making going anyway?"

Oh shit, I had completely forgotten about the jam.

"It's fine," I assured him, "just the ribbon to put around the jar and all will be ready."

Well it wasn't a complete white lie. I have yet to find a suitable jar or a pan to cook it in, not to mention instructions on how to make jam. But I do have a ribbon.

We fell into easy conversation. I think that's because I still have enough alcohol in my system from last night to relax me. We chatted mainly about the land and animals and about his mum, whose health was suffering.

"I'm sorry to hear that," I say, showing my sensitive side, "do you have any brothers or sisters?"

"One brother, but he's not around these days."

"Oh no, is he dead too?"

Jake chuckled. "Na, he ran off after Dad died, Rick had always been a bit out of control. He didn't even come to his funeral, Mum was sick with worry. We get the odd letter now and then but he doesn't want anything to do with us."

I sympathised in my sympathetic way.

"Yeah well, that's Rick for ya," Jake shrugs.

We were still deep in conversation when Millie arrives back. Jake and I are so comfortable in each other's company it's like we are soul mates. Millie insisted she make everyone omelets for dinner as the sausages that I had defrosting in the fridge since yesterday had disappeared.

Jake accepted the invitation for dinner and after a meal of omelets and chips we all sat outside on the porch enjoying the warm balmy night and just for a fleeting moment it felt like Jake and I were a couple entertaining friends.

Well it would feel more like it if I wasn't so on edge with worry every time Millie opened her mouth to speak, and the fact that Sid was embarrassing me by chatting to Jake for most of the evening about his extra terrestrial encounter and his quest to find ET life.

Okay, Jake seemed to be intrigued by Sid's story, but I was sure he was only trying to be polite.

But then again as long as Sid's talking about his sorry life then Millie's not filling Jake in on the sordid details over the little misunderstanding concerning the youth in my bed.

I excused myself and went to the kitchen, willing Millie to not open her month and talk to Jake about last night.

I'm feeling better but now I had an incredible craving for some Coca-Cola. I searched the kitchen for the bottle I swear I had brought just yesterday. Slamming the cupboard door in frustration, I looked in the fridge and remembered that the sausages that were resting on the plate were gone and no one bothered to take the empty plate out. It had to be Sid, but I don't remember him being so hungry and…. Sid doesn't drink Coke. And he cannot eat sausages, he's allergic to preservatives.

Well someone did. Slamming the fridge door I returned to the porch.

"Sid, how did you get in the house last night, you didn't have a key?" I asked.

"Didn't need to, back door was wide open."

"Well I locked it last night," I shot back.

"Well you can't have," Sid argued. "Otherwise how would I have gotten in and read your note that you were down at the pub?"

I slumped down on the chair trying to think back to the events before we went out.

I was so sure I locked the doors, like I was so sure that I didn't take the bottle of beer from the fridge the other day.

Come to think of it there have been an awful lot of strange things going on around this place since I moved in.

My blood ran cold. The thought of ghosts entered my head again. But then since when has ghosts liked sausages and Coca-Cola?

"I think someone's been breaking into my house," I announced.

Millie gasped. "What makes you think that?"

"Because the sausages are gone and the bottle of Coke I bought, but that's not all, food has gone missing and the other day something strange happened and I cannot explain it."

"You sure you didn't offer any to your guest last night?" Asked Millie with a sly grin on her face.

I glared at her, willing her to shut up.

"I'm sure I would remember doing that Millie," I said through gritted teeth.

"I'm surprised, you didn't remember getting home," Millie jokingly shot back.

"You don't remember getting home?" Jake asked, puzzled.

"Of course I do," I smiled, kicking Millie under the table.

Millie opened her mouth to speak when Jake suddenly jumped from the table checking his watch. "Well I'm calling it a night, good to meet you Sid. Thanks for dinner," he said.

I watched him stride across the gravel, my jaw dropping at such a hasty exit. Had Sid said anything to offend him?

I exchange curious glances with Millie and Sid, as Jake wasted no time in turning over the engine and driving off through the iron gates.

"Well that was weird," Sid mumbled.

I was going to point out that old saying of the pot calling the kettle black, but let it go.

Security check

"Maybe it's him."

"Who, Jake?"

I pondered this as Millie checked that all the door locks were working. "Well he did disappear last night at the pub, he knew you wouldn't be here, maybe he's trying to scare you?"

I thought about it then dismissed it "Na, Jake's not creepy like that."

"How do you know what he's like? I mean he bends over backwards to help you, but doesn't want to get into your pants, now that's creepy."

"No Millie," I sighed, "that's being a gentleman."

I slumped down on the floor, my head was swimming in all directions.

"I think I'm overreacting, I mean there could be a perfect explanation for all of this, it could be Randy Puss?"

"Have you ever been to Jake's house?" Millie asked as she jiggled the door. "How do you know he hasn't got naked pictures of you and a bottle of hand cream in his lair?"

"Well I've never been invited, you can't just invite yourself to someone's place Millie, it's not good manners."

"Who cares about manners, it certainly sounds like his aunty hasn't any. Take a cake or something to his house, a little thank you for all he's done, you're not being forward doing that."

Jake never struck me as being the creepy type. He was too gorgeous for that. But Millie's right, I don't know Jake well enough and after his hasty exit tonight not to mention the fact he offered no real explanation for leaving me at the tavern. Maybe it wouldn't hurt to drop in on him. So first thing tomorrow I shall go and call in on Jake and take him a little home-made something to say thanks.

Painting time

Millie took the lid off the paint tin and waited for my reaction. She chose a sort of lime green for the hall and I flinched.

It was ghastly and I told Millie that it would never grow on me and she needs a re-think on her chosen colour scheme. She told me that it was fine and that it was about time I pulled my head out from my behind and I told her.......

Never mind.

The point is, now I'm sitting on the porch alone and Millie and I haven't uttered a word to each other for the last few hours, and now she has finished the first coat in the hall and is packing to return to the city.

We haven't stopped arguing since Millie arrived and I'm feeling guilty because I haven't told her yet that I plan to stay in the country, but she's been working so hard and she has even got on my laptop this morning and made a budget spreadsheet for the renovations and found out from the Heritage Trust that we can go ahead and add the doors in the living room. Sid has been great too. He and Mrs Crankshaw have spent all afternoon weeding the vegetable garden. Mrs Crankshaw arrived to collect my jam for the country fair that I haven't even made yet. She saw Sid in the garden and went over to give him some advice and now they are down in the garden weeding and chatting like old friends.

Millie tapped me on the shoulder. "Hey I better get going soon," she said gingerly. "Got to be at work tomorrow."

I so want to tell her that I'm staying and I'm not interested in being a property developer any more but when I looked at her with her shirt splattered in paint and smelling of turpentine and the worn-out look on her face I couldn't possibly tell her just yet.

I mean that wouldn't be fair, so I'll wait 'till tomorrow when she has had a good rest and then I will phone her and tell her not to worry because there is no hurry because I'm to become a woman of the land.

The country fair was only days away and Mrs Crankshaw was getting impatient so I promised her that my wares would be ready for collection the next day.

Millie threw her bag into the car as Sid waved off Mrs Crankshaw.

"I'll be back the weekend after next," she said gathering me into her arms and giving me a tense hug. Millie and I had smoothed out our earlier rift but then I made a comment about her choice of fabric for the drapes and now she not only looks tired, she looks bewildered. I watch them drive away and the place feels lonely again.

In kitchen

I pulled the frozen berries from the freezer.

I borrowed a jam making pan from Debbie at the Old Peoples Home. I was surprised however the pan had horrible black marks on it and smelt a little strange.

My recipe I had got from an old cookbook of Mum's said for every pound of fruit, add a pound of sugar.

There seemed to be no recipe for blueberry jam so I followed the recipe for apricot jam which incredibly only consisted of water, sugar and fruit.

Throw ingredients together and cook slowly. It couldn't have been easier.

The recipe said to prepare the fruit first, but blueberries don't need preparing so I throw the fruit into the pan with the water.

I fished around for sugar, I must have some here, I never take sugar in my tea so I only keep a minimum of sugar in the house. I found the unlabelled jar containing sugar, measured a pound and added it to my pan. Twenty minutes later and my jam was bubbling away on the stove, I needed a jar to present it in. I found a coffee jar and after emptying its contents and peeling the original label off, my jar was ready to house the very jam that would win over the town folk and more importantly, Jake.

I planned to bake a cake to take over to Jake's tomorrow, as I wasn't due at work until tomorrow afternoon.

Debbie likes her staff to work at least one of the three shifts just to get to know the whole routine of the residents. So it gave me the opportunity to drop into Jake's for morning tea.

Jam done

It's cooling nicely, so I started on the chocolate cake I intended to take to Jake.

My oven must be playing up as the cake was cooked on the outside and uncooked in the middle.

Alas, the cake ended up being a weapon to throw at the magpie's that were threatening the newly dug vegetable patch, but all is not lost, I could pick up a mud cake from the bakery before heading to Jake's house

Unveiling

The moment I was waiting for, I had brought a sheet of fancy labels and a charming checked cover to go on the lid of my jar. The conserve itself was the colour of vibrant purple, if anything it added to the charm of the red checked cover and the tartan ribbon.

I wrote with my best pen on the label and stood back to admire my creation, wondering if Pamela Horton's wares were half as good.

I put the pan in the sink and ran my finger around the pan for the taste test. I waited for the sweet and fruity texture to burst on my taste buds but it didn't taste sweet. My taste buds are going hysterical.
I spat the contents into the sink and chugged down a glass of water, it tasted salty.

In state of utter panic
I re-read through my recipe trying to figure out where I went wrong. Mrs Crankshaw would be here any moment to collect it. Lets see, water, yes, fruit, yes, sugar… then it hit me with a bolt, I pulled the jar containing the sugar out of the pantry and dipped my finger in it.
I have used salt instead of sugar.
On phone to Mrs Crankshaw
I managed to put her off 'till the morning telling her that I had

been so busy baking I hadn't had time to finish my jam. All entries had to be in at midday tomorrow so I came up with a plan. First thing in the morning I would go to the store and buy a jar of blueberry jam and switch the contents in my decorative jar, no one would know the difference.

Okay, yes I'm aware that's cheating but really first impressions count and when they ask for a recipe I could say it's a family one, top secret.

I hadn't time to listen to my conscience right now.

At bakery

Tim served me, he remembered me from the pub.

"Hey there Lisa how's your friend?"

"Don't know who you're talking about."

Well Millie did say to deny everything.

"You know" he went on, "your friend. The one from the karaoke."

Oh *that* friend!

"Millie, she's good thanks."

"Bit of a fiery one that one."

"An understatement."

"She certainly wouldn't take no for an answer."

"Yes I heard you singing, you're very good at it."

"Thanks," he said modestly.

"You're welcome."

"But that's not what I'm talking about," he added.

"Oh."

I paid for my cake and left. I wonder what he meant when he said Millie wouldn't take no for an answer.

In small but very cute supermarket

I checked the store first, firing stuff into my basket hoping no one I recognised is there. When the coast was clear I made my way to the jars of jam on the shelves, no blueberry. Closest thing to that was blackberry.

Oh well I could just say that blueberries were currently out of season and I had to use blackberries instead. I mean blueberries/blackberries, what's the difference. I fired the jar into my basket and scurried to the checkout before anyone can spot me.

Arrived at Jakes house

The ute was in the drive so I knew he was home.

Nerve's started to kick in. It was like going through ground hog day. The house was an exact replica of the Crankshaw's house. I suspect they had a bulk discount on that particular design of house. Except it was just as run down as my own property, there were chooks running free around the place, cobwebs around the windows and it looked like Jake never cut his grass.

That job was obvious deployed to a very large goat that greeted me as I knocked at the back door.

Jake answered and seemed pleasantly surprised to see me so I relaxed a little. He invited me into the kitchen and filled the kettle for a cuppa. The house was in the same state inside as it was out, no sign of a women ever living here or any naked pictures or jars of hand cream.

On the wall there was a photo of Jake and his brother when they were about four, dressed up in bow ties holding hands with a women who I can only presume was his mum. There was certainly no weirdness going on here.

I produced the cake. "For everything you've done for me, you know, fencing and stuff."

"Thanks," he said, taking it from me. "Straight from your oven I see," he chuckled.

"Oh, ha-ha well I didn't have time to bake. I've been so busy making jam."

"It doesn't look right, something's missing." He examined the cake carefully before snapping his fingers. "I've got it, it hasn't got your lovely butt stuck to it".

I started giggling.

There was something about the way he said butt. No, there was something about the way he said lovely butt, *my* lovely butt in fact.

I don't know what came over me I was still giggling like a

schoolgirl. Then it happened, without warning, he grabbed me, pulled me close to him and started kissing me.

It was unreal the way his tongue was now playing in my mouth. Now I shall spare you the details but I could feel myself throbbing for him as he pushed me against the wall.

His mouth and his hands were everywhere, it was going so fast I couldn't be sure whether my bra was on or off. I could feel the hardness in his pants; well basically I turned to jelly. Every bone in my body was screaming and before I could throw my underpants at him and scream for him to take me, he hastily withdrew from my grasp, leaving me panting for breath.

"Anyone home?" The familiar voice of Mrs Crankshaw snapped me out of the spell. Jake turned his attention back to the tea making.

Damn and blast that women.

"Ah Lisa dear, thought that was your car outside." Mrs Crankshaw smiled as she made her way to the kitchen.

Jake automatically got another cup down from the cupboard without acknowledging her.

I checked my appearance for any tell-tale signs but really I wanted to scream at the woman to just to go away.

"Now dear, has Pamela spoken to you yet about the roster for Saturday? No, I don't think she's had time, her husband just got back last night from his business trip."

Jake dropped the mug he was holding, shattering it into small pieces. "Sorry," he grumbled, bending down to pick up the broken pieces.

Mrs Crankshaw continued as if time was money. "Anyway, I'll drop a roster and map to you later and I put your entry in too by the way."

"What entry?" I asked.

Mrs Crankshaw tutted. "Your jam, I hope you don't mind but you did leave your door open, it was sitting on the kitchen bench."

Oh shit

"Mrs Crankshaw, it's the wrong one, you see..."

"Wrong one? Rubbish, it had blueberry jam on the label, you did say you were doing blueberry."

"Yes but I wasn't satisfied with it, you see it could do with a little more um…"

"Well it's too late now dear I've delivered it to the judges' tent, I'm sure it will be fine."

She turned her attention to Jake and helped him clean up the shattered pieces of crockery.

Now what am I going to do?

My salty blueberry jam is up for judging tomorrow. I have to get that jar back or suffer the humiliation.

Or I could just sneak in there tomorrow before the judging starts and pull it off the table, yes! No one would ever know.

Perfect

"Lisa would you like a piece?" Mrs Crankshaw asked.

"Ha? Oh cake, yes please."

She talks to Jake about the cattle and drenching and blah blah. I wished the old lady would leave. I was desperately trying to catch Jake's eye but he avoided it. We sat and ate the cake and drank tea while Mrs Crankshaw did all the talking.

I was still in a state of shock, with the jam and the passionate encounter I just had with Jake, who by the way was looking very agitated.

So when Jake got up and declared he had work to do, giving the cue that morning tea and morning delight for that matter was over, I crept away like a mouse feeling a little dejected as I said my goodbyes to both Jake and Mrs Crankshaw.

I was even more put out that I spent the rest of my time, before I was due in at work, sitting on a chair by the front gate with my phone on my lap waiting for Jake to appear or even call.

He didn't bother to do either.

Damn that Crankshaw woman. She doesn't know the first thing about matchmaking. I mean if she saw my car out front when she arrived at Jake's then you would think that she would just presume that a passionate liaison was happening and turn the car around and leave.

Honestly her timing is impossible.

Facebook Status Update.

Lisa Collins: OMG, OMG, OMG, OMG.

Lisa changed from 'Single' to 'In a relationship'.

Lisa is attending Taromeo Annual Country Fair.

6

Evening before county fair

Pamela had called in to see me at work and of course I had to be right in the middle of emptying a bedpan.

She filled me in with the information about the stall. I have to hand it to her she seems so in control and so poised.

I could see why Jake was fond of her, not that she was Jake's type of course but he seemed to look up to her. So maybe I should put my reservations about Pamela to one side and take a leaf out of her book. So a couple of hours in her company may be a good thing.

Still no word from Jake.

Home

Had missed a call from my parent's, will call them later.

I was attending to Bonnie and Clyde's pen when I discovered the window high up under the eve of the house.

I'm puzzled as I hadn't noticed it before, but then again, from this angle it was hard to tell that it was there. Walking to the side of the house for a better look it appeared to have been painted over at some stage and now the white paint was starting to chip away.

Walking back into the house I couldn't help but be curious. I mean how cool is this house. First a hidden room and now a secret attic. But best wait until Millie arrives for another decorating visit, not that I'm scared or anything, but it's best this sort of thing is done in pairs. And if there were anything up there of any value then I would want to share it with Millie. Oh bugger it, I'm going up there.

I figured that if there was an attic then there must be a manhole somewhere inside the house.

There certainly wasn't any evidence there had been a staircase, and after searching the rooms, except of course the wardrobe room, I came up with no sign of a manhole.

There's only one thing for it, I'm going to have to go up the ladder.

It's awfully high but I couldn't wait, I *had* to find out.

I grabbed the ladder from the shed and positioned it under the window.

"Safety first," I said to Randy Puss who had appeared at my feet. I had the basic safety precautions covered. My mobile phone in my pocket and a pillow tied to my back with a belt. Well ninety eight percent of accidents end up with spinal injuries.

Cautiously making my way up the ladder I positioned myself and leaned towards the window.

Top of ladder

Cupped hands together against the pane to see through the gap in the paint and then tried to scrape more off with my fingernails, but was met with darkness.

The torchlight only seemed to catch my reflection, damn! There was only one solution, I had to sacrifice the window by breaking it.

I slowly started to make my way down the ladder to grab something heavy for the task. The ladder wobbled a bit, but it was okay. I continued down, carefully minding my footing on the rickety ladder.

Then it happened.

My mobile started to vibrate in my pocket causing my unsteady nerves to jump in fright, which in turn unbalanced the ladder, which started to slide sideways down the eve of the house.

This was the exact moment when my life flashed before my eyes, it's true, it just happens in slow motion. This is it, Lisa Collins, sophisticated property developer, ended life in such an undignified manner by falling off a damn ladder.

The ladder stopped moving. I breathed a deep sigh of relief.

I'm not out of woods yet, the ladder is resting on the downpipe where the corners of the house meet, the bottom of the ladder was balancing on one leg.

Oh shit! Now how am I going to get out of this?

There was nowhere to go. One move from here would cause the ladder to crash to the ground taking me with it. I carefully fished my mobile out of my pocket. There was a text message from Millie,

'r u busy'.

I text back. *'up a ladder help'.*

Message reply. *'lol at work so bored'.*

 I was going to text her back and tell her that this wasn't a joke but Millie was an hour away and I could be dead by the time she got here. I snapped my phone shut in frustration. God what was I thinking.

Still up ladder

Well there was Jake, I could call him.

No, absolutely out of the question, even stuck up a ladder in a life or death situation I will not be chasing him asking for his help. He didn't even have the common decency to contact me after he kissed me!

Still up fricken ladder

Someone else came to mind, and I was running out of options.

So what choice did I have? I couldn't stay up here forever.

I flipped open the phone and scrolled down my contact list.

Finally down fricken ladder

It's great to be alive and have my feet firmly on the ground.

I thanked Matt for coming to my rescue.

"Yeah sweet as, all part of the service. But why didn't you holler out to the dude in the field there?" Matt said pointing to towards the forest.

 "What dude?"

"The hunter dude or something, he's gone now but I saw him when I pulled up, well he looked like a hunter, he had a pack on his back."

I went over to the fence to see if I could see the stranger, probably was the same guy I saw the other day.

"He's not there *now*," Matt said. "He started walking back up the hill when I pulled up."

I invited him in for a cold beverage, it was the least I could do, after all I called and told him I had a flat battery and of course he arrived with his jumper leads only to find out that I was stuck up a ladder clinging to life. A cold beverage seemed to be the polite thing to do.

In secret room

I showed Matt the mystery room with the wardrobe, not showing off, but how cool is it.

"Freaky man," his eyes were like saucers as he took in the dark room.

"Imagine the parties you could have here, like get everyone stoned and take them for a tour of the house, it would be like the haunted mansion and 'who done it' and that stuff."

Well bless him; his brain obviously hadn't caught up with his growing body.

Back outside

Matt examined the window.

"We could smash it," he suggested.

"Well that's what I was intending on doing, 'till the ladder slipped."

"Then shall we?" he suggested with an evil grin.

Matt up ladder

"You sure about this?"

"Yes do it," I shouted back holding the ladder steady. Matt held the towel up to protect his face.

I sure hope Millie budgeted for broken windows.

I turned my face away and listened to the sound of glass breaking. After the last of the fragments fell away I waited for confirmation of what was up there.

"Is it an attic? ... Matt!"

I could hear him mumbling with his head through the space, he sounded distressed.

"Matt, what is it?" I cried. I'm starting to panic now; I mean what if it's like a dead body.

"Matt, are you crying?" *Shit.* "Matt get down here!"

He made his way down the ladder.

"You *are* crying, what is it?"

"Oh man you need to have a look."

Back up fricken ladder

OH!

I was so taken back I almost fell off the ladder again.

It was a room all right; a room full of marijuana hung upside down on the rafters to dry.

It looked dusty and had obviously been up there for some time.

But still, it was dope and it was in my ceiling. I made my way down the ladder to a very misty eyed Matt.

"Isn't it beautiful," he choked.

Matt back up the fricken ladder

He pulled one of the offending plants out the window using a long handled crook before nailing a board over the broken window. I couldn't stop pacing as Matt examined the plant.

"It's been here for a while," he said. "Yep, I'd say someone's long forgotten about this baby."

Or dead I thought, thinking about the previous owners.

He tutted. "Disgusting what people do."

"Matt you have to promise me that you don't tell anyone about this," I warned.

"Oh *god* no, of course I won't."

"Not a soul, okay?"

"Agreed, but you should think about getting a lodger in," Matt continued, "girl on your own way out here. If you were my sister and that, I wouldn't like her out here on her own."

I was touched by his concern but assured him that I was a big girl and could look after myself.

"So what about this?" Matt asked, pleading with his eyes.

"Oh okay, have it if you want."

"Man you're such a cool chick," he grinned.

Matt's phone started to ring to the tone of 'Smack My Bitch Up'.

"Aww suck, it's the old lady. Better go, she was expecting me home for dinner like an hour ago," he snapped his phone shut. "If she's carries on like this, I'll get my washing done elsewhere."

I didn't need to thank him again. I felt like he was paid his due as he carefully put his plant in the back of his truck and covered it like a newborn baby.

In the distance the sound of a shotgun rang through the air.

"Think hunter dude got something," Matt said getting into his truck looking like the cat amongst the pigeons.

Morning of country fair

A good night's sleep was owed to a few nightcaps to calm my nerves. I did give a thought to Matt's advice about getting a lodger in, especially with the strange goings on around the place lately, it might not be a bad idea.

But now I had to get up because I was due at the CWA refreshment tent and before then I had to retrieve my jam from the judge's tent.

Randy Puss meowed at the door to let me know it was breakfast time. Goodness knows where he is putting it. For a stray cat he seemed to get fatter every day.

Realising the time, I downed my toast and coffee and started making my way into town.

Arrived at fair

Festivities were everywhere, kids with candy floss, rides, vintage machinery displays and craft stalls selling knitted tea cosies.

I found a map from information and made my way to the home-wares section. I was greeted by Pamela who once again looked like she had just stepped out of an episode of extreme makeover, the host, not the victim.

Just my luck.

"Lisa good morning," she greeted in a shrill tone of voice "are you lost? The refreshment tent is that way."

"Yes, I know but I was just wondering if I had time to view the wares, you know check out the competition."

"Sorry Lisa but the tent is closed now.

Judging begins soon then it's open to the public."

"Oh but I just want to… you know?"

It appeared that Pamela didn't, judging by the look on her face.

"Well the thing is," I leaned closer to her and lowered my voice, "I may have mis-spelt blueberry on my label."

"Oh Lisa, no one cares about the label it's the taste and texture that they judge on, you should know that," she was eyeing me suspiciously now.

"Of course," I smiled, "it's just I'm a perfectionist and it …"

"We haven't got time," she interrupted looking at her watch. "Now come!"

I trailed behind her, *shit, shit,* now what? I could make a run for the tent while her back was turned. The tent was getting further away and Pamela continued to walk like she was on a mission. This was my chance, I turned on my heal and ran back towards the home-wares tent.

Home-wares tent

I banged on the closed canvas. "Excuse me."

"We're closed," a voice called back.

"I know," I said with urgency, looking behind to see if Pamela had noticed my absence. "I need to withdraw my entry."

The voice was closer now. "Judging has already begun," said the voice behind the canvas.

"Yes but I need to withdraw my entry," I pleaded.

"I'm sorry but it's too late," the irritable voice said.

"Look, if you just let me in."

"Please leave!" the voice snapped back. "If you need to withdraw you need to see the official at the committee tent."

"But this is urgent," I pleaded. "I think there's been some err... some tampering."

"Tampering?" The faceless voice sounded alarmed so I ran with it.

"Yes tampering," I said, "I had heard that the jam entries, especially the blueberry variety, have been tampered with."

There was a silent pause.

"Hold on," came the voice.

"Lisa!" I turned around to see Pamela marching towards me. There was nothing I could do now. If Pamela found out that I'm trying to withdraw my entry then she's bound to mention it to Jake and I'll never live it down. I turned and made my way back to her. "Sorry," I said when I caught up, "I thought I dropped um ... something."

Arrived at refreshment tent

Pamela introduced me to Maggie.

"She's another one of the CWA girls," Pamela trilled. "She will show you what to do. Barb Crankshaw will be here at ten thirty to relieve you." Pamela turned to Maggie. "You'll be right here? I'm going to watch Alice at her show jumping."

Maggie was a small lady, I'm guessing around her mid forties. Her strawberry blond hair was pulled back at the base of her neck. She was a very ordinary looking women but she had a kind face.

She muttered something as she watched Pamela walk off into the crowd swinging her perfect hips. Maggie started on my instructions.

"Well there's not much to do, it's a self help thing so all we need to do is keep the tea and coffee containers topped up, butter some scones and keep the urn's hot."

I learned that Maggie and her lawyer husband, complete with six children, have a small holding of forty acres and had lived in the area for the past fifteen years.

Her voice was soft when she spoke but there seemed to be resentment behind her brown eyes, like she would explode if you pushed her buttons. Didn't want to find out, so I busied myself with the first task of buttering scones.

First customer

"Well look who it is, it's our new youngin." It was Chubbs the drunken designated driver I met at the tavern the other night.

"They rope you into their little club did they?" he bellowed, "you just watch these ladies, they will lead you astray."

Maggie giggled. "Oh get away with you," she joked.

"But they do make a mean scone," he said swiping one from

underneath the fly net.

"Oi you," Maggie blushed and smacked his hand away.

Chubbs turned to me. "So Lisa, Jake tells me you could do with some chooks at that place of yours. Well I've got just the thing, got some Rhode Island Reds if you're interested?"

My insides were fluttering, Jake said that! That means he *does* think that I'm worthy of country life. Although I have no idea what Rhode Island Reds are, maybe they are ones that lay eggs?

"Yes well I have been meaning to get some."

"Great then I'll sort a box out." He said swiping another scone.

Next hour

Locals kept coming with their friendly banter, I joked and laughed with them as I buttered scones and served the tea. I had to admit I was having a great time mingling with folk and I was so pleased that Jake had noticed my countrified ways.

I was so busy I hadn't noticed the time until Mrs Crankshaw turned up.

"Phew," she puffed coming into the tent. "Warm one out there today. Did you hear? They cancelled the home-wares judging."

I froze.

"Cancelled?" Maggie asked looking puzzled.

"Yeah I heard that," Chubbs said emerging for his forth scone that morning.

"Apparently there's something about tampering, they had to shut down to investigate. You know with health warnings and all that crap."

Mrs Crankshaw tutted, "who would want to tamper with conserves? Honestly these shows are not what they used to be."

"It's not just that," said Maggie sounding outraged, "do you know what effort I put into my entries? Just to be cancelled over one persons' selfish attempt at cheating."

"Yes," Mrs Crankshaw agreed. "Even Lisa put an entry in this year, you must be terribly disappointed my dear."

"Oh, err yes," I said, feeling my face burning.

Later

Maggie was now checking her watch and mumbling under her breath that Pamela hadn't came back.

"Well she's not the only one with kid's events," she said to Mrs Crankshaw.

I started to think that maybe Pamela and Maggie didn't get on.

My heart started to pound; there in the crowd was Jake. I hadn't had time to rehearse what I was going to say to him. But it was too late he was walking towards the tent. I quickly busied myself. God he looked good.

"Morning ladies," he greeted as he approached. Maggie giggled like a schoolgirl again.

I tried not to look at him but was forced to when he asked me how my morning was going.

"Fine," I replied, with as much frostiness as it would take to freeze hell.

Pamela swanned into the tent. "So sorry," she trilled. "Alice got first in her grade, naturally." I could hear Maggie almost sneering under her breath.

"Yes well I've got to check that Jamie's ready for her dance," Maggie snapped at Pamela before saying goodbye to me and leaving the tent.

"You know it was probably her that tampered with the conserves, her jam's haven't won anything in the past."

"Now, now Pamela," tutted Mrs Crankshaw.

Pamela ignored her and turned her attention to Jake. "What can I get you?" she asked, fluttering her eyes at him. For a fleeting moment I swore there was a look between them, was I jealous? Or did Pamela know about Jake and mines little snogging encounter yesterday. No she couldn't have, Jake wouldn't kiss and tell.

"I just came to ask if Lisa wanted to walk round with me." I could feel his eyes on me. "I'm just heading over to the wood-chopping competition."

"She would love to," Mrs Crankshaw answered before I had a chance to speak.

I looked over to Pamela who was looking a little pale.

"Oh, I was just going to ask Lisa if she could stay here a little longer because I ...."

"Nonsense," Mrs Crankshaw scoffed. "I can handle this on my own. Lisa can go, she hasn't had a chance to look around yet."

"Sure I'll come with you Jake," I said, reminding everybody that I was still there. "It will be great to have a look around." I removed my apron and joined Jake as he led the way. I could feel Pamela's eyes stabbing into my back as we walked into the crowd. You know, I'm starting to wonder if Pamela thinks that I'm not good enough for Jake.

We walked in silence, at first looking at the different displays before making awkward small talk. The sexual tension between us was electrifying.

We approached the home-wares tent where there seemed to be a gathering of officials hovering and a string of yellow tape around the tent.

I quicken my pace.

"Hold up!' Jake called out, amused at my accelerated stride. "Wood-chopping is this way."

We arrived at a roped off arena where men with axes were now fiercely thrusting at their logs. Jake finally spoke.

"I'm, ah, sorry about yesterday at the house, I don't know what came over me." He took off his hat and scratched his head.

"But, um, well I was hoping that we could forget that it happened. We're still friends right?"

What? I could barely understand what he was saying. What had I done to put him off me? I mean the other day he was all over me like a rash. He threw himself at me and now he's *apologising* for his behaviour. No, someone has got to him and I'll bet all the home-made conserves under the sun it was that Pamela. Well I'll show her that Jake and I are meant to be together. I will just play along with his little game for now.

"Lisa you okay?" Jake was looking at me a little concerned.

"Oh yes," I said with a bit more enthusiasm than I intended. "I mean, I had forgotten about that already," I waved my hand in gesture that I had forgotten the fact he had snogged me with every part of his body.

What the hell I was saying? I just implied that I have casual snogs all the time, well apart from Matt and that was alcohol inflicted, I mean I never really did that sort of …

Oh my god he knows about Matt!

Jake looked appreciative and planted a kiss on my forehead. "Thanks," he said, "I knew you would understand, I promise it won't happen again."

We left the wood chopping and walked around some more.

Jake explained to me that the fair happened every year to celebrate spring and usually the celebrations last right to the end of the month. "Then they end the Spring Fair with a barn dance, it's a great night, I could take you if you want."

Oh phew! He doesn't know about Matt.

I could see what Jake was up to now, maybe he was a little embarrassed about what happened between us and now he's trying to do the right thing by me and take things slow.

Yes that must be it, I mean lets face it I can hardly blame him for making a dive for me the other day, he hasn't had a girlfriend for a long time, he must get lonely. I'm so pleased that he wants to take it slow.

Well I'm not *that* happy about it.

I turned to Jake.

"Yes, that will be great, it's a date," I said.

"No, it's two friend's going out," Jake corrected me.

"Yeah, that's what I meant," I quickly added.

"Hey Lisa!" I turned round to see Chubbs making his way towards us with a box.

"Your chicken's madam."

Back home

Four brown hens looked right at home in the old chicken coop.

Jake's been wonderful, he fixed up the netting and installed a new latch on the door.

He even went to the store and got some straw for their nesting boxes.

Fresh eggs daily, how organic is that!

If only Joe could see me now he would be so jealous. Maybe I should email a picture to the girls at the café, you know just to show how well I'm doing.

I watched them scratching and clucking as I gave them a feed of grain, also supplied by Jake, chickens are funny things, I wonder who invented the egg?

Well not *invent,* but lets face it, it must have been some sort of whacko genius who said 'I'm going to eat the next thing to come out of that chickens bum'.

Jake has still got me in a state of confusion. I've only been here for three weeks and it feels like a lifetime. Well let's face it, in the past three weeks I've managed to: Fall in love with the most eligible bachelor (Jake). Make an enemy (Pamela, although not my fault). Discover a secret room. Have a sexual encounter with a local nineteen-year-old youth. Discover my attic is full of illegal substances. Sabotage the annual fairs' produce tasting. And that's not mentioning the strange goings on with my food items.

Arrival of rural mail man Rob

Great, I had so far managed to avoid him since the dildo incident and I can't pretend I'm not home again because he's seen me.

Oh well I'm sure he's forgotten about it.

"Hi Rob," I greeted him.

"Hi there lassie," he beamed. "Settling in okay? Just a couple of the old bank statements for you."

I took them from him.

"So," he continued, "I hear you had a good time the other night down at the tavern, met a few of the local louts."

"What are you taking about?" I asked, scanning my mail.

"I'm just saying, good for you to get out amongst it all, great way to know who's who round here." I smiled, I was starting to like Rob, and he's so friendly.

He raised his eyebrows while the knowing grin on his face told me he knows something.

"I hear that you were exceptionally friendly to our young Matt Horton," he chuckled.

I take that back, I don't like Rob.

"Don't know what you're talking about," I shot back.

Deny, deny.

"Okay," he laughed as he slapped a hand on my shoulder. "But thought you should know that rumour has it that you two were all over each other the night in the tavern."

I hid my face behind the open bank statements.

"Ah don't be embarrassed luv, nothing wrong with playing the field. Well must be off," as he climbed in his van.

Then something hit me like a bowl of jelly with a lead brink inside. "Wait!" I ran over to the van "Did you say his name was Matt *Horton?*"

"Yes, didn't you ask his name first?" Rob laughs as he put the van into gear and roared off.

On phone to Millie

"Well that's it I'm screwed! I may as well pack up and go. *Horton,* his last name's Horton as in *Pamela Horton* and now god forbid everyone knows!"

No wonder Jake went off me, he kissed me, then he must have heard about Matt and now he's gone off me and everyone thinks I shag teenage boys!

"Alright calm down," Millie reasoned. "Did I hear you right, you kissed Jake?"

"Yes, but that doesn't matter now 'cos he thinks I'm a slag."

Millie squealed with delight. "Oh what was he like?"

"Millie can't you see I'm in a crisis here, he was fantastic!"

"That's my girl, but I think your overreacting. Even if you and Jake hit it off, it's not going to last, you're not cut out for the country, remember."

"I am so cut out for the country; I have chickens now you know."

Millie sighed, "Look I'm not saying that you and Jake are not completely compatible, but Lisa your plan is to finish the house and move on so I don't understand why you're so worried about all this. Go ahead and have a fling with Jake and whomever else you pull out of daycare but as for the others, fuck 'em. You're not there for long, or are you?"

There is an airy silence between us and I know that now would be a good time to tell Millie the project's off.

But I still can't work myself up to tell her. Millie and Sid have been saving like forever for a deposit for their own home and the commission she would get from the sale of the house would be more than enough for a deposit. I cannot do this to her.

I've convinced myself that a solution will present itself sooner or later, preferably sooner.

"Lisa?" Her accusing voice shoots down the telephone like an arrow.

"No, no, you're right, I'm not here for long, but Millie I really like him."

Millie sighed again. "Okay well here is what you should do. Go and see him, as friends, and then happen to drop in the conversation that there is a nasty rumour going around about you."

I just love Millie.

"But Lisa," she warned, "don't give up your plans for this guy. You have done that before with Joe and look where that got you."

What? How does she..?

"Promise," she warned.

"Yes okay I promise!" I shot back.

I hung up the phone and now I really don't know what to do, and to be honest, I'm a bit put out about Millie's comment. Yes, okay I made a mistake with Joe and went off and bought a house but Jake's *different*. With Joe I had to pretend I was someone I wasn't but with Jake I can be myself, well almost. And I love the country, I don't want to go.

I glanced around the charming shack that I had become so fond of and felt a stab of guilt towards Millie. But then again if I marry Jake I won't need this place, then I can sell it and Millie can have her share, everyone will be happy.

First things first, I shall go to Jake and clear the air about Matt, and then he will take me to the dance and realise what a wonderful wife I could be.

Perfect, knew solution would present itself.

Retirement home

"Yeah I heard about you and Matt," Debbie grinned at me as we were enjoying a coffee after the usual morning duties of showers, cleaning false teeth and clearing away the breakfast dishes.

Now all the residents were sitting on their allocated armchairs while the occupational therapist was taking them through their morning exercises, which looked more like the sitting down version of the chicken dance.

"Yes, well I was slightly intoxicated," I said with as much dignity as I could muster.

"No need to explain to me," said Debbie, "happens to the best of us."

"So how long has he been in the town?"

I asked casually fishing for information.

"All his life, his parents breed the Boar goats. He's got a younger brother and sister."

Every blood vessel in my body stopped working.

"Um, he's not Pamela's son is he?"

"Yep, I think he's her son from a first marriage or something, she had him young. Actually I used to babysit him," she laughed.

"Oh don't," I snapped, "I'm well aware of his age."

"I didn't say anything. Don't go defensive Lisa, I was just going to add that I used to babysit him when he was a nipper. He gets all embarrassed when I see him and remind him that I used to change his nappies."

"Yeah well … " I mumbled.

Debbie stood up and rinsed her cup out. The residents were now doing the sitting down version of knees up mother brown.

"Oh by the way, after you left yesterday a woman came by looking for you, said she was an old friend. I didn't give out your home address, it's policy, but I did say I'd pass a message on. Her name and number are in the day book."

Curious, I opened the day book.

Oh my god, I flip open my phone and quickly text Millie.

'Neroli in town!'

Message reply,

'omg lisa what have u done?'

Facebook Status Update.

You have one new friend request from Neroli Bishop

Confirm / Ignore.

Lisa Collins: Damnnnn!!!!!

Lisa changed her 'In a relationship' to 'Single'.

Lisa likes: Brides Australia and Australian Country Life.

7

Neroli

Neroli shifted her car into gear and drove out from the motel car park. She had left her mobile number with the woman at the nursing home, but it's been over twenty-four hours now. Neroli was convinced that Lisa might not have got her message.

The couple from the motel were so nice to her when she fell short of paying them for the night's accommodation and she had then enquired around town for Lisa's address. Neroli was pleased when Lisa had called her; it had been over a year since their fall out. But the night she called and offered for Neroli to come and stay with her had been the answer to Neroli's problems, even though Lisa sounded a bit drunk on the phone.

"When are we going to the farm Mummy?"

Tom was Neroli's four year old son. Unlike Neroli, Tom didn't have his mother's dark hair and Polynesian descent. He was fair-skinned with bright red hair.

The gene trait of his father, whom after the one night stand that resulted in Tom being conceived, was never to be seen again.

"Almost there my darling," Neroli told her son.

He had endured more in his short life then a lot of children twice his age.

They had been on the road for over a year now, stopping at place to place. Home was in Perth and Neroli had not seen her parents for three years but she tried to keep regular contact for Tom's sake.

Neroli came from a middle working class family; her childhood had been a dream. But now her parents have washed her hands of her and Neroli could not understand why.

She checked the directions sitting on her lap and remembered the description she was told. This must be the place. Neroli swung her car into Lisa's driveway and turned the motor off. No vehicle in sight, Lisa's obviously not home from work yet.

"Look Mum, chickens."

Tom was out of the car as fast as his legs could carry him and started poking his fingers through the wire.

"Be careful darling they could bite." Neroli warned, as she looked around the property.

Wow Lisa has done well for herself, she thought. The house could do with some work but I could live with it.

"Mummy, Mummy can we live here? It's so cool."

"Yes darling of course we can, but listen don't tell Aunty Lisa we came to live with her, not yet anyway.

Let mummy talk to her first okay, you promise not to tell?"

Tom, too excited to acknowledge her, nodded and ran towards Bonnie and Clyde's pen.

"Mummy look at the sheep," Tom called behind him.

Neroli knew Tom wouldn't talk, he knew the drill all to well. Her feet swollen from the heat, Neroli settled herself under the oak tree to wait. She watched Tom dart around the pen with the goats.

A child's paradise out here.

She just hoped Lisa would understand.

Lisa

Back home

This was the moment I was dreading since I learned that Neroli was in town. I couldn't remember the phone conversation I had with her that dreaded drunken night at the pub.

I thought I would never forgive Neroli for what she had done but now I just felt uncomfortable seeing her again. Neroli lies constantly, you never know if she telling the truth and it was her lies that ended in us falling out. I met Neroli when I worked at the Irish pub as a bar maid. Tom was a baby then, and Millie and I took her under our wing, we felt for her, single mother whose parents were both dead and her only brother lived in Canada.

Millie got her a job as a bar maid and we took turns looking after Tom, lending her money that sort of thing. It wasn't 'till she accidentally left her mobile phone at Millie's one day and Millie answered it.

It was her brother asking if we could pass on a message to Neroli that the parents had gone on a trip to Hawaii, and of course there was more confusion when Millie asked him how Canada was. After some explaining (not to mention Millie feeling like an ass) the truth came out. Her parents were alive and well and her brother didn't live in Canada, he lived in the flat attached to her parent's home in Perth.

We were conned!

She was sitting under the oak tree. Neroli came over to greet me as I got out of the car.

"Surprise!" Neroli exclaimed as she hugged me.

"Ha, ha, yes it is, isn't it."

"I'm so glad I'm here," she went on. "Thanks very much for the invite."

I hugged her back not quite sure what to make of the weird moment. "Oh, ah well, glad you could make it," I broke away.

"Is that wee Tom chasing the goat's, my how he's grown."

"I know, it goes so fast, Tom come and say hi to Aunty Lisa."

I cringed, for a start I hated being called Aunty especially coming from Tom.

Tom is not a child I would call cute and adorable, Tom was an antichrist child.

"Na, don't want to," Tom called back.

Not much had changed.

I took a moment to take in Neroli while she marched off to the pen to disarm the stick that Tom was now waving at the goats as if it was a light sabre.

She had put on a bit of weight but she looked better for it. She had also swapped her tight clothes for baggy T-shirts and long skirts.

Millie had nicknamed Neroli 'Fish Eyes' on account of her big eyes. They reminded her of a goldfish; Millie was not very fond of Neroli any more.

5 hours since dreaded house guest's arrival

"So how long are you staying for?"

It had been a long afternoon but I was pretty sure Tom was worn out after his afternoon of destruction, and I could at least have some time where my nerves could settle down. Neroli, as per usual, was in her own world where she seemed to spend most of her time.

"Well maybe a couple of days," she answered in her dream world state.

I said that was fine with as much enthusiasm as I could muster.

I didn't have a spare bed for Tom so I managed that afternoon to phone Jake (as friend's do) and asked if he had a spare mattress.

He (ha ha) asked if my house had fallen down and said that I was welcome to his spare bed if that was the case.

Neroli was a bit flirty with Jake when he dropped the spare mattress off, so I think it's better if Neroli did only stay a couple of days.

Text Millie

In code to let her know of my house guests and was waiting for her reply when the phone rang.

"What the hell is '*N styen yac sn*'?" Millie asked.

"Neroli staying yak soon, jeez Millie, I didn't want you to call while she was here."

"And where is she now?"

"Gone to bed."

"So has she changed?" Millie asked.

"No still as dreamy as ever, she still won't tell me what she's doing here or where she's been."

"And the antichrist?"

"Tom, much the same."

"So what has she been doing?"

"She didn't say."

"So how long is she staying for?"

"Couple of days I hope,

she has already embarrassed me by flirting with Jake."

"Has she got a boyfriend?"

"God Millie I don't know why don't you ask her yourself?"

"No thanks, I rather not, I'd prefer to talk to a jellyfish, makes more sense."

This from the woman who goes out with Sid.

"Did you get a chance to square things with Jake?"

"No," I sighed. "Neroli was drooling over him and I spent most of my time trying to distract her attention away from Jake, but I will, and oh the shame Millie, the whole town knows about it, it won't be long before Pamela finds out I had sexual relations with her teenage son."

"Ah they're just jealous, and so what if Pamela finds out. Its not like he's under-age. It will give you two something to talk about at the old farts club," Millie said.

"Its called the CWA and I want to change the subject now."

Millie chuckled, she knew she'd got the last say.

"What's Sid up to?" I asked (as if I didn't know).

"With the ET squad, but he does have the doors for your living room and the permit papers from the council for you to sign."

"He does!" I shot up in surprise.

Didn't want to point out that Sid's motivation is normally on par with overweight snail.

"Yeah he's been acting a bit strange, he's even registered at the employment office today."

"But he's still waiting for his soul? Ha, get it Millie, soul–dole."

"Yeah hilarious, he's only with LSM three nights a week now."

"Wow!"

"I know!" Millie said in excitement.

Bang, Bang, Bang, Bang!

Tom had found the pot lids.

I started my morning routine of getting ready for work with the four year old at my heels. I politely asked him over the clang of pot lids where his lovely mother was.

"Sleeping and I'm hungry."

As I marched into the kitchen and rustled round for some cereal Tom broke into song.

"I want fruit loops," he sang in tune to his clanging.

"I don't have fruit loops, I have cornflakes."

"Cornflakes are yuckkyyy!"

My head and ears were ringing and my patience was running out, I snatched the pot lid off him.

"Then what do you want to eat?" I hissed.

"I only eat fruit loops."

"Well you're going to have to ask Mummy to buy some because I don't have any." I didn't have time for games, I was going to be late for work.

"Go and wake Mummy," I said ushering him to the bedroom.

"I have to go to work," I sprinted out the door.

I could hear Tom start up again with the banging.
Confident that Neroli surely couldn't sleep through that racket
I drove off towards work.

At work

I can't concentrate, thinking about horrors going on at home.

Phone home

No answer. Explained to Debbie, she said as there was only one
hour until my shift ended and it was all quiet, I can go home.
Love Debbie, best boss ever.

Back home

AARRGGH!!!!

Tom had opened the sack of chicken grain and the whole of my
neatly organized, clean chook house was covered in grain and
cornflakes!

"I didn't do it," Tom informed me as he lay in front of the TV.

The kitchen was a complete mess. I stormed back through to
the living room calling for Neroli.

"She's sleeping," Tom said.

"She's what!" I went through to her bedroom and opened her
curtains, Neroli stirred.

"Oh you off to work?" she asked.

"No!" I snapped before changing my tone; remember she's only here for couple of days. "No," *smiling,* "I've been to work and I just got home."

"Oh I must have slept in," she said, stating the obvious. She flung the bedding back to reveal the baggiest flannelette pajamas.

"Has Tom been good?"

I could feel my face go hot.

"I've been at work Neroli," I said through my clenched teeth.

"I haven't been watching him."

"Oh, okay I'm getting up now anyway," she said in a matter of fact voice.

I let Neroli know that I was upset by slamming the door on my departure. I went into the kitchen to clean up and felt a pang of compassion for Tom, after all he may be the antichrist but obviously he's often left unsupervised.

Neroli came through into the kitchen, she must have sensed my annoyance as she apologised for sleeping in and explained she'd been so tired lately.

I decided to not mention the chicken coop because I reminded myself once again that they're only here for a couple of days, then I could go back to my life without the inconvenience of having my ambience upset.

Chicken coop

Tom is at my heels once again, so to get him out from underneath my feet I allocated him the task of egg collecting.

"No eggs and the bloody chicken won't move," Tom said.

I'm very shocked at the four year olds' language.

"I'll zap it with my light sabre."

"No!" I said snatching the stick from his grasp. "Chickens need time to adjust to their new home," I explained to him. "Just like you need time to get used to your new, well, your um, new um, never mind, just leave them okay?"

Dilemma

I'm trying not to get involved in too many conversations with Neroli, as they were a bit confusing.

Neroli was not an easy person to figure out. I need to know where she had been and where was she going. She hadn't gone home to her parents as they tried to avoid her visits, like everyone else did. And to be honest, I wasn't quite sure that she had any other friends.

Time I just came out and asked her.

"So where to after this?"

"Well I might stay here, its nice here, people are friendly."

My heart stopped.

"What here with me?"

"Well for now, 'till I find my own place.

Tom has to go into kindergarten soon, I think he's getting bored."

"But Neroli," I pleaded. "There's not really anything here for you, wouldn't you be better off moving closer to your parents?"

"No they think it's best if I was here."

Oh shit.

Dilemma diverted

As I drove into work the next morning I was feeling confident about Neroli's intentions to stay. Neroli doesn't stay in one place for long and I'm pinning my hopes on that she will get bored and well, leave. Feeling very optimistic.

Was also hoping for fresh eggs for breakfast, but no show, I'm also staying optimistic about that as well.

At work

I couldn't stop thinking about Jake and the upcoming barn dance that he was taking me to. In fact Mrs Crankshaw has invited me to the monthly CWA meeting tonight where the barn dance was the main agenda.

I decided to go to learn a thing or to from Pamela about being president of such an organisation. Pamela seemed to ease into the role like a hand into a glove, and as my mother used to say 'don't knock it until you try it'.

It will also give me a chance to show my face and stamp out any rumours about my romp with a teenage boy if the subject happens to come up.

Finish work

I had no desire to go home with Neroli being there, decided to visit an antique shop.

Antique shop

A rather robust gentleman looked over rim of his glasses at me and asked if I needed help, I declined. I looked at all the wonderful crockery and ceramics on display, nice but couldn't see what fuss was about. It's just old dull crockery.

I then spotted the grandest piece of periodic furniture I had ever seen. Made from oak it had the most stunning brass handles and the carving was just exquisite. I took a moment to reflect on the craftsmanship of such a piece. It would look great in my kitchen, I simply had to have it.

I asked the gentleman how much.

"This piece?" he said pulling on his glasses. "This is a 1910 Victorian sideboard hand-crafted in oak. It was often found in very wealthy Victorian times…"

"Yes, yes," I interrupted him. I wasn't interested in what it was, just thought it would look great in kitchen.

I asked him again how much.

"That would be $2,500."

Well maybe it wouldn't look *that* great in my kitchen.

"What about this?" I asked him pointing to a rather tall Grandfather clock.

"$850"

"And this?"

"The umbrella stand is $250."

"What about this?"

"The Royal Dalton set, $550."

"And this?"

"The cup and saucers," he sighed, "they are $8.50 each."

"I'll take two of those please."

As he carefully wrapped each piece up in tissue paper, I spotted a copy of the Centenary book that was printed for the towns one hundred year celebrations. I flicked through the wonderful early photographs of the towns' main street and the stores. My heart skipped a beat as over the next page is a black and white photograph of my house in all its glory.

I'm a bit disappointed as the house still looked the same and there seems to be no other pictures and no story attached just a caption that read '*Old slaughter-yards and homestead 1932*'.

Slaughter-yards? Must have been a misprint.

Bakery

"Hi ya Lisa."

"Hi Tim."

"How's your friend?"

I think we've had this conversation before.

"Fine thanks."

"Um, do you think she might be coming back for a visit anytime soon?"

"Yeah, soon why?" I asked him.

"Oh," he looked embarrassed, "no reason."

"Okay then, bye."

"Bye."

I think our Tim has a crush on Millie.

Back home

I stepped inside and braced myself for the damage that may have been inflicted by Tom.

Also missed a call from my parents', must phone them.

Neroli and Tom were sitting in front of the television, Thomas the Tank Engine was blaring away.

"Hi." Neroli greeted me as I walked into the living room. No damage, in fact the room looked great. Neroli must have had a tidy up and was being nice by offering to make coffee.

Tom looked mesmerised by his show and didn't even acknowledge me which suited me fine. I walked back into the kitchen, got the dreaded feeling that Neroli was making nice for a reason.

Neroli handed me my coffee.

"Good day?" she asked.

"Not bad," I said nonchalantly.

"Ask me about mine," Neroli said in juvenile voice.

Fine I'll play along.

"How was your day?"

"Great, I got a job."

Yes, dreaded feeling confirmed and I feel there's more to come.

"At the motels in the village, cleaning rooms," she continued.

I tried to look pleased but I'm sure I looked more like a goldfish on land.

"I've enrolled Tom into kindergarten and I start tomorrow morning, so can I stay here?"

I'm about to blow but calm myself down and remind her that she was looking for her own place.

"Oh I will, but I need to get some money behind me first and I need to buy some furniture. I'll pay you lodgings."

In toilet

I used the excuse that I really needed to go before answering Neroli.

Why do people put me in this position?

Okay, positives, the money would be good. It doesn't have to be long, some company is better than no company especially with hillbillies lurking.

Negatives, its Neroli and Tom.

Not feeling confident but I've made my decision.

Back in kitchen

"Okay Neroli you can stay, but only for a month."

"I'll only charge you for food and phone calls, and I'll help you find a place of your own."

"Thanks Lisa." Neroli squealed, "you won't even know we're here I promise."

Should have got that in writing.

Oh god now she's hugging me.

CWA meeting

I'm trying to avoid Pamela before the meeting, so far so good. Pamela hasn't given any clue that she knew of my tiny fling with her teenage son. She acknowledged me by greeting me in a polite tone, that's a good sign, but couldn't read the tone of her greeting not sure if it was, '*you cradle snatching tart how dare you deflower my little boy*' greeting; or '*go home urbanite, you're not cut out to be woman of land*' greeting.

I'm not risking it.

The meeting of the CWA was underway in the back room of the community hall.

Introductions made. Present members under the age of sixty were; me (obviously), Pamela (pushing it), Maggie, and Gloria (who I presume from her vigorous note-taking was the secretary).

Those members over sixty, wearing hearing aids and sitting with knitting needles clacking away knitting peggy squares are; Mrs Crankshaw, Fran, Betty, and Mary.

First item on the agenda was the catering for the up and coming barn dance.

Pamela led the meeting.

"Now, as per usual, we are going to need people on the night to heat the savouries and clear the supper tables, but I cannot stress enough that this year it needs to be a bit more organised, last year was a disaster."

"I thought last year worked well," Maggie said.

"No it didn't" said Pamela. "So I propose that this year, we look to hire caterers."

Maggie rolled her eyes.

"But it's bring a plate Pamela," Mrs Crankshaw reminded her "and the tickets are already out."

Murmurs of agreement all round.

"Yes well last year I noticed it was the usual select few that actually pulled their weight."

"And one of them wasn't you," I heard Maggie mutter to herself. Pamela, who didn't seem to hear her, went on.

"So I think we should propose to the local kindergarten committee that the CWA will make a donation towards their new playground if they do supper duties this year."

"Excuse me Pamela." Gloria looked up from her note taking, she looked to be in her late forties, I picked her for the arty type, I think the paint stains on her hands gave it away, white tuffs of hair were poking out of her blue bandanna and her long flowing skirt hung beautifully on her lean frame. She cleared her throat. "I think you will find the kindergarten committee are on decoration duty on the night."

"And the lions club are doing the bar and the brass band club are in charge of hiring the music," said Maggie.

"Okay," said Pamela breathing out through her nose. "Any suggestions?"

"Leave it the way it is," Maggie spoke again.

Pamela sneered at her. "It didn't work last year."

I'm so bored.

"I think," Mrs Crankshaw intervened, "that we might be too late to make changes, the dance is less than two weeks away."

More murmurs of agreement.

"Okay, we'll do a roster then. Mary could you.....?"

"We don't need a roster, its fine the way it is!" Maggie snapped at Pamela.

Uncomfortable silence around the table.

I raised my hand as if I was back at school. "Um, what exactly do we do for supper duty?"

Gloria answered me as Pamela and Maggie are preoccupied by shooting evil stares at each other. "Everyone who attends the dance brings a plate of food for supper, and it's our job to lay the supper out, provide tea and coffee and clear the dishes afterwards."

"That's it?"

"That's it."

CWA's not rocket science, I thought sarcastically to myself.

"The problem is Lisa," Pamela sneered at me, "that some of our members didn't pull their weight last year and some of the food, mainly the savouries, hadn't been heated properly."

Pamela's a mind reader.

"That's because," Maggie said, clearly directing the comment at Pamela, "somebody had turned the oven to grill instead of bake."

"What did you want me to do with a rooster dear?" Mary piped up, adjusting her hearing aid.

Pamela, ignoring Mary, got up off her seat and leaned towards Maggie.

"My point is," she sneered, "that if more of our members had pulled their weight, things like that wouldn't have happened."

"How would you know? You were too busy on the dance floor!"

More uncomfortable silence followed.

I feel the urge to giggle at the intense silence.

Pamela sat back down continuing to glare at Maggie.

Gloria broke the silence by suggesting a vote.

So the motion was carried that we will serve the supper the same way as the previous year without the help of caterers and only one person (Maggie voted not Pamela) mind the ovens.

"All for…"

"Opposed…"

"Motion carried."

"Right then, item two, campaign against cock fighting events."

I couldn't contain myself and burst into a fit of giggles.

"Oh grow up Lisa!" snapped Pamela.

Next morning

Armed with a frying pan I went out to the chook pen to collect eggs for healthy breakfast. So tired, didn't have good sleep last night, heard strange noises all night. Tiny bit glad Neroli is here.

Have eggs but cannot get to them because the brown hen is sitting on them and not happy.

Tried gently to persuade her to move, couldn't, poke stick at her to move, she didn't, continued to poke and prod at her.

The hen squawked a warning and pecked my finger.

Defeated I turned to go and was greeted by the rooster, yes

rooster. I had been conned by Chubbs, he said he only had egg laying hens and not noisy roosters. I don't like the way it's looking at me, I tried not to look it in the eye but now the rooster is flapping its wings and heading straight for me.

"Arrgh!"

Shielding my face, I tried to navigate my way to the pen door. Think there's only one way of escaping rooster's violent attacks, I raised my arm and smack it on the head with my frying pan and bolted to the door.

"Ha!" I told the slightly dazed rooster. "That's the last time you'll ever do that won't you? Who's the boss now aye! Who's the boss?"

"Who the hell are you talking to?" a familiar voice said.

"Jake! Oh hi!" My face reddened as I realised I was still in my dressing robe and must have looked a fright. I smoothed down my hair and tried to make myself look presentable.

"Um what brings you here this hour of the morning," I asked him as casually as I could.

"Checking on my stock," he said gesturing towards the hills behind the property. "I lease part of this land for grazing."

"Oh."

"I heard you scream?"

"Oh yes, the rooster, he attacked me."

Jake looked amused.

"Yeah they do that, nasty bastards. So what's with the fry pan?"

"Oh, you know, I was kinda hoping for breakfast."

Jake jumped the fence in one swift movement, god it was sexy, and undid the latch and walked into the coop.

(Brave I thought.)

"Thought so," he said, appearing a molecule of a second later. The rooster didn't even blink an eye at Jake… the bastard.

"She's sitting on eggs, nesting, it won't be long 'till you have little ones."

He closed the latch and jumped the fence again in that sexy swift movement. I watched him straddle his quad bike and I suddenly remembered I had to put right the rumours about Matt, which yes, as true as they may be it was just a silly drunken mistake. Quite out of character for me.

"Um Jake."

"Yeah?"

"Um, well, err, it's just that, um."

The words weren't coming out, I'm not sure how to begin a confession.

"Are you okay?" he asked, half amused.

"Fine, it's just that..."

"Yes?"

"Well, do you have problems with hunters in the area?"

It just spilled from my mouth, I needed to save face.

"Hunter's?"

"Yeah, I've seen a hunter around this area."

"This is privately owned land," said Jake, "any hunting needs a permit and I'm not aware anyone round here has one."

"Oh."

"Get a description of him if you see him again and any car licence."

"You got it," I shot a finger at him. Very dumb, feel like an idiot.

He kicked his bike into gear and waved his sexy wave as he rode off in a sexy manner.

Shit, I'm going to be late for work!

At bakery, after work.

"Hi Tim."

"Hi there Lisa, heard from your friend?"

This guy's got it bad.

"No," I answered. I studied him as he rung my chocolate creams up on the till, he wasn't really the type of guy that turns heads. I'm guessing by his receding hairline that he was around fortyish but he had a slightly reddish tinge to his hair and pale skin. He certainly wouldn't be Millie's type, I mean after all he seems normal and Millie doesn't go out with normal guys.

He handed over my change and I made my way to the door.

"Hey Lisa," he called to me.

"Yeah?"

He looked over his shoulder, came out from behind the counter and lowered his voice.

"Do you think your friend is coming to the barn dance?"

"I haven't asked her, I mean she's not a local."

"She doesn't have to be." Tim said a little too quickly, "she just has to buy a ticket."

"Oh well I'll ask her, or did you want to ask her yourself?"

"Oh! No, no, no," he backed away, "just wondering, that's all."

"Well, bye Tim."

"Bye."

That man certainly does a lot of wondering.

Back Home

Missed a call from Mum and Dad. God why don't they just ring my mobile.

I never thought of asking Millie to the dance, it would be fun and I can't wait to tell her who's got a crush on her. She'll be soooo appalled!

Neroli and Tom are not home and I'm planning a quiet afternoon in the sun while indulging in chocolate creams.

An hour later

Very full from chocolate creams, feeling disgusting and fat.

BOOM! I jumped at the sound of a shotgun.

I had a sudden thought that it must be the hunter. I jumped off the chair and started towards the fence.

I saw him in the distance emerging from the trees.

It was the same man that was perving at me the other morning.

I tried to yell at him to get his attention, he doesn't seem to be hearing me, so I jumped the fence and yelled again.

I started running up the side of the hill towards him and wondered briefly what the hell I was doing running towards a mad hillbilly with a shotgun. He bent down to pick up something off the ground; it looked like a dead rabbit. I yelled at him again as I got closer. He finally saw me coming, but instead of looking pleased to see a mad woman running towards him, he turned and bolted up the hill. I yelled again but he ran even faster. I tried to give the chase but my lungs wouldn't allow it.

I stopped to catch my breath, as I'm running a dangerous risk of passing out. Strange hillbilly pervy hunter is now out of sight. So obviously he hasn't got a permit. Now I'm having sudden thoughts of the old phrase 'the hunter becoming the hunted' and realise that I'm at a disadvantage with no shotgun. I'm suddenly very nervous and I'm thinking I need to make a hasty retreat to home.

Safety of house
"Hi ya," Neroli appeared at my bedroom door.

I was lying flat on my bed still recovering from the chase.

"What ya doing?" she asked in her singsong voice.

"Building a tree house," I replied, well what did she think I was doing?

"Okay then," she retreated.

God Neroli, not the sharpest tool in the shed.

Tom appeared.

"Aunty Lisa," he said as he climbed on the bed waving a piece of paper in my face, "I made you a drawing at Kindergarten."

"Oh really, show me." I said, feeling wanted and loved. I looked at the drawing, there was a stick figure with, which looked liked, a noose around its neck and another smaller stick figure with some type of sword, and I'm only presuming the red crayon is blood.

"Now who is this?" I asked Tom, who was now jumping on my bed, he stopped jumping.

"That's me killing you with my laser sword," he said.

"Oh charming."

"He drew that especially for you," said Neroli coming into the room.

"*Rah, rah, rah!*" Tom ranted as he continued with his bouncing.

"Oh, err lovely."

"Isn't he," agreed Neroli, "anyway phone for you."

I knew it was Millie, I waited 'till Neroli left the room and hissed at Tom to get of my bed and go watch TV, that didn't work so I told him if he left there is an ice cream in it for him. He flew out the door and I put the phone to my ear.

"Hi, I'm sooo pleased you called," I started, "guess who's got like the biggest crush on you?"

"Um err..."

"Sid is that you?" *Oh shit.*

"Um, yeah hang on I'll get Millie."

"Hi ya."

"Millie what did Sid want?"

"Oh nothing, I got him to call for me just in case Neroli answered. I'm not ready to talk to her yet, so is she still there then?"

"Um, yep, well actually she's um, sort of staying for a month." I held the phone away from my ear and braced myself.

"WHAT! Are you out of your mind, haven't you learnt anything, she's already burnt you once."

"Well what was I suppose to do," I said defensively. "She's got a child, I couldn't exactly throw her out after a couple of days, and she has a job now."

"What! Where?"

"At the local motel, cleaning. She's going to look for a place to rent in the village."

"Oh god, you mean she's going to *live* there."

"Looks like it but you know Neroli Millie, she'll move on soon enough."

"Don't you be gullible," Millie warned, "she'll take advantage of you."

"I'll be careful, now guess who's got a crush on you?"

"Oh god, who?"

"Tim the baker." I was waiting for the eww and oh my god or getouttahere, anything appalling, but there was silence coming from the end of the phone.

"Millie, are you there?" She cleared her throat.

"What did he say?" she asked in a whisper.

"Millie you don't actually like this guy, do you?"

"I didn't say that I liked him," she snapped at me, "I just asked you, what did he say?"

I'm not liking her tone of voice. Wished now I didn't say anything and she's kind of killing the mood.

"He just asked after you and wanted to know if you would be going to the barn dance, which I haven't asked you if you wanted to go yet, so Millie?"

"Yes?"

"Do you want to go to the barn dance at the end of the month?"

"Well we will be coming down at the end of the month anyway, so why not."

"We, as in you and Sid?"

"Yeah, anyway I have to go, talk to you tomorrow."

God Millie's a ball of fun tonight.

I don't mean to be sarcastic but I may have to suggest she has a dose of evening primrose tablets.

Kitchen

Neroli had stuck Tom's picture up on the fridge with a magnet, great, now I have to find some way for that picture to disappear.

I had forgotten to ask her how her first day went, I can be so self-centered sometimes.

I found her in front of the television with Tom. "How was your first day?" I asked her.

"Oh fine," she replied.

That's enough caring for one day. Okay, bitchy of me. But the truth is I'm not used to sharing and now that Neroli and Tom have been here a couple of days I have realised I like the house to myself. Don't get me wrong, I enjoyed living with Sid and Millie. But I mean when you're sharing you can't walk around naked or watch re-runs of Friends without asking, 'do you want to watch this?' And if you want peanut butter on toast for dinner then that's what you have. So when Neroli finds her own place I will not be taking in any more lodgers, it will just be me.

And maybe Jake, but he has his own place. So if we ever end up moving in together whose house will we live in?

Well obviously it would have to be his because then I can sell this and give Millie her share.

But then again, my house is bigger.

I open the fridge door for inspiration for dinner still thinking about Jake and the barn dance, even though I have no clue about what you wear to a country dance, dressy, casual?

Hmm, I will have to ask Mrs Crankshaw about that, okay, maybe not Mrs Crankshaw. Frustrated I slammed the fridge door shut. "Neroli," I called to her, "how does peanut butter on toast sound for dinner?"

Two weeks later

I hadn't seen much of Jake, only a couple of times in the village, during which I told him about the hunter. I was starting to think that maybe he was seeing someone on the side but then he wouldn't have asked me to the dance, he would have taken her and I presume he's still taking me, the dance was in four days and I'm so confused.

Jakes house

I decided to do the sneaky 'oh I was just passing and thought I would pop in' thing, I arrived and was deflated to see he was just leaving.

"Sorry Lisa," he said "can't stop, on my way out." But the thing is he was looking really smart and I could smell his aftershave a mile away. He had a nice clean white shirt on, the cleanest pair of jeans and his hair was groomed not its unusual unruly look.

"Oh, are you still keen on going to the dance?" I asked him.

"Yep, sure am, that's of course if you didn't want to go with someone else?"

"What me? No, I rather go with.... I mean no I haven't got anybody else."

"Great," he says, "pick you up about eight on Saturday. Got to go Lis I'm late."

He called me Lis, but the thing is he didn't even offer me an explanation of where he was going. You would think he would say something like 'sorry Lisa got to go, I have a diving course' (it's possible) or 'sorry Lisa, I have to go, I'm off to buy you a present since I'm so in love with you' (well you never know) so the only explanation is that he is seeing someone, and yes it *is* my business what he does, after all we are friends and friends should know these things.

Back home

"Just going to the loo." Neroli announced as we sat watching the re-runs of Friends.

God I didn't have to know her every move.

Her and Tom were driving me up the wall, not that it's Tom's fault he's just doing what any normal four year old does, stuffing food in the DVD player, throwing his cheerios on the floor cause they weren't the right colour, that sort of thing. Neroli hasn't done anything about finding a place to rent so I decided to give her another week and if progress isn't made, I'll find her a house myself.

The rooster continued his war against me and if he didn't settle down soon I would have to evict him too.

"The police are here," Neroli announced, coming back into the living room.

"Oh cool," said Tom and ran towards the door.

I sat frozen to the spot.

Oh my god, Matt must have got caught with his plant and blabbed. That bastard, wait until I get a hold of him.

I could see the horror of myself standing in court and the judge asking me 'now Lisa, you claim that after you slept with the youth, you then supplied him with a class c drug that you claimed you found in the attic of your home'. I cannot go out there, I'll pretend I'm not home.

"Um, aren't you going out?" asked Neroli.

"Oh yep," I reluctantly moved from the sofa to the door. Plan B: I'll just deny everything.

"Evening," the copper greeted, removing his hat, "are you the owner of this property?"

Deny, deny. "Um no," I cannot keep my eyes off the attic.

"Oh well, we're looking for Lisa Collins?"

"Yes that's me." I said trying to advert my eyes from the attic.

Shit, I was supposed to deny everything.

"Oh, okay well, we had some reports of illegal hunting in this area; we believe you witnessed somebody hunting on the neighbour's property?"

"Oh phew, of course, thank god!"

The officer looked at me puzzled.

"I mean, thank *god* you're here, yes I did see someone."

Tom stood by my side listening intently.

"Can you give me a description?" he asked flipping open his notebook.

I described him as best I could, I explained to the officer that after all I was running at the time.

"Have you had any livestock missing or shot?" he asked me.

"No I think he was just shooting rabbits."

"We have had reports of sheep being slaughtered," the officer said. "We need to follow this up."

"Are you going to take Lisa to jail?" Tom piped up.

The officer laughed. "No I'm not."

"'Cos Lisa said she was going to kill me," Tom informed him. The little shite.

"Did she really?" the officer raised an eyebrow at me.

"Well if I see him again, I'll give you a call," I said trying to shuffle Tom inside.

"Have you got a gun?" Tom asked him.

"Tom darling," I said through gritted teeth.

"No need to bother this nice man."

"It's okay," the officer bent down to Tom's level, "no I don't carry a gun," he said patting Tom on the head.

"Well, Lisa said she was going to shoot the rooster."

"Right, time for bed." I ushered him inside, if he said any more I will be going to jail for child abuse.

"Do you own a rifle Miss Collins?" he asked.

"No, god no," I laughed, "you know, kids," I scoffed.

"Okay, well if you see anything please give me a call," he handed his card and left.

Phew that was a close one. I vowed to get rid of the illegal substances in the attic.

Eve of barn dance

I sat on the porch chewing my nails, waiting for Millie and Sid to arrive.

Neroli sat opposite me painting her nails, cool and calm, and totally oblivious to the fact that she and Millie are about to be under the same roof and Neroli is at great risk of Millie tearing her to shreds.

"What are you wearing to the dance?" Neroli asked as she blew on her nails.

"Not sure, I'll find something." I said anxiously glancing over my shoulder for Millie and Sid. I felt a pang of guilt all of a sudden, I mean here I was looking forward to tomorrow night and didn't even think to ask Neroli if she wanted to go. We would have to get a babysitter, but still it's do-able. I've been too wrapped up in myself to even think about her.

I asked her if she wanted to go.

She declined saying she's really tired.

Guilt gone.

Millie and Sid arrive

Neroli ran towards the approaching car. Tried to stop her but she's outta control. Millie was barely out of the car when Neroli inflicted a hug on her. I cringed, any time now Millie is really going to spit the dummy.

Sid emptied the boot of the car of air beds and pillows I had asked them to bring because of the bed shortage. We had a very tense dinner of cold chicken and salad. Millie not saying a lot, I suspect she's holding her tongue between her teeth. Tom entertained Sid with a game of Star Wars, Millie is now on her fourth glass of wine (not counting or anything). Neroli's not drinking but may as well have been as she spent most of her time twiddling her hair and staring into space.

I had a thought of how lucky I am to have all this around me, big house, animals and most of all, good friends.

Even though friends are not talking to one another.

8

Next morning

Not off to a good start.

Sid met the bad side of the rooster when he attempted to meditate in the chicken coop and forgot to latch the door as he ran for cover. Tom, who seemed to be Sid's constant companion since Sid told him all about the alien abduction, thought his time had come when the rooster attacked him from behind as he was playing with his Tonka toy in the garden. He ran into Neroli (who was still in bed sleeping) and screamed that the aliens were coming to get him, it took us an hour to calm him down.

Millie's now angry at Sid for telling a four year old the story.

Neroli was upset because she didn't get her usual six hour sleep-in and now the rooster was roaming around free, last seen over the fence heading up the hills behind the house.

Afternoon

Much more pleasant.

I jumped out of the shower. It was a lovely spring night and prospects of a second chance snog with Jake put me in good mood.

I'm now trying to squeeze myself into pair of trendy jeans that I picked up at the local op shop, two sizes to small, but jeans are gorgeous.

Millie knocked on my door and asks if I'm decent.

I was a bit shocked at the question as I have always been decent, maybe meant as joke. Millie came in anyway.

"Have you noticed Neroli's been acting a bit stranger?" she asked me as I lay flat on my bed trying to do the zipper up with a coat hanger.

"What do you mean stranger?"

"Well for one she refused a wine at dinner last night, she sleeps a lot and she's looking, well, tired and as you said she didn't want to come out tonight."

"So what is strange about that?" I said in between holding my breath and exhaling.

"You don't think she's ill or anything?"

My stomach popped out of my jeans as I sat up.

"I don't think so, she eats a lot."

"Keep an eye on her," Millie said. "I don't know, I just get the feeling something's not right."

"You had a change of heart about her," I said lying back down giving my zipper another go.

"She may not be my favorite person but that still doesn't mean I don't look out for my fellow women and for fuck sake Lisa," Millie stormed over to my wardrobe and pulled out a lovely flowing white dress, "will you put this on, you look like a beached whale in those."

I put on the dress she picked out and let my hair fall naturally round my shoulders, I had some highlights and my nails done earlier in the week. I have to say, I look hot.

Millie is so brilliant.

Millie poured me a glass of wine as I made my grand entrance.

"Wow you do scrub up nice," she said.

"You don't look so bad yourself," I said.

Not that Millie needed a complement, she was the type of person who could throw anything together and still carry it off. Not fair really, as I need to plan my wardrobe carefully so it doesn't look like I had thrown up all over myself.

I asked her where Sid was.

"Out on the porch talking to Jake."

Sound of Jake's name made my heart leap into mouth.

I noticed Neroli walking past me holding a beer in hand.

"I think you had better get out there before that one gets her hooks into him, that's the third beer she's fetched for him."

Couldn't get out there fast enough but stopped at the door and gently made my grand entrance onto the porch. "Hi Jake."

"Wow you look nice," he greeted.

"I know, I mean, thank you." I pulled up a chair between Neroli and Jake. Sid had Jake engrossed in another tale about his alien encounter, tried to give Sid a discreet evil 'shut the hell up' stare but I haven't caught his eye and then dear god Neroli spoke.

"So Jake, have you had many girlfriends?"

I'm mortified at my friend's mission to embarrass the bejezzes out of me.

Jake smiled, he seemed amused by the question.

Must admit was on the edge of my seat in anticipation of the answer.

"Yeah I reckon I've had my fair share, why do you ask?"

"Oh I think Lisa wanted to know."

Well at this point I wish Sid's friends alien ship would come down and whisk me away. They could do any type of experiments on me, I wouldn't care as long as I didn't have to endure this moment.

Arrived at dance

Music was coming from the hall which was decorated with fairy lights.

Jake and I waited for Millie and Sid to arrive in their car before going in. Jake seemed relaxed.

I'm not so relaxed, I let Jake do the talking but I had better do something soon so he doesn't think I'm a sack of spuds. Where's Millie with the god damn wine?

"You okay?" Jake asked.

I told him that I was fine, as I'm craning my neck in the carpark looking for Millie and wine.

His eyebrows knitted together. "Are you sure, you seem a little on edge?"

"Oh yes! It's just that, well I hope you didn't take Neroli seriously when she asked you if you had many girlfriends. I mean I didn't really want to know, I was just curious you know, good looking guy and all...."

Great, now I have found my tongue I can't shut myself up.

Finally Millie and Sid were making their way towards us.

"But you know, it's like none of my business if you have had loads of girlfriends," I continued.

"Lisa!" Jake interrupted laughing. "It's okay, if you want to know anything, just ask me, we are friends after all."

"Right, will do."

The lights were low and the music boomed from the speakers. There were groups of men standing around with their pints bellowing out the laughs.

The women were sitting in pairs chatting amongst themselves.

The music was a cross between country music and rock but pleased as it also belted out the old classics.

I grabbed the first table I had seen, desperate for first sip of wine to wash away any awkwardness I had.

Later

It seemed to work as Jake and I are in deep conversation. Found out that he played league when he was a kid, knew a few cords on the guitar, didn't like fishing and had never heard of Celine Dion.

Sid was leaning on the bar with Stubbs the local contractor and seemed to be getting on very well. I didn't know where Millie was, I was too busy hanging on Jake's every word, not to mention dancing with Jake, being introduced to Jake's friends and was even about to indulge him in my favorite joke when I felt a tap on my shoulder, it was Pamela.

"Lisa, we are about to lay supper soon could you join us in the kitchen." She gave Jake a look I didn't recognise before walking off.

"Oh well," I said swigging back my glass. "Boss lady has spoken." I cracked up at my own joke and looked at Jake. He was watching Pamela as she went round gathering up all the women from the CWA.

Mrs Crankshaw sat down beside us, "Lisa dear, having a good time?"

I think Mrs Crankshaw may be a bit tipsy. I told her that indeed I was having great time.

Mrs Crankshaw grabbed Jake for whiz around the dance floor as I made my way to the kitchen as ordered by Pamela.

Sid still leaning on the bar with Stubbs sucking cigarettes and laughing about something. Seemed like the odd couple, Stubbs the fingerless hillbilly and Sid the spaced out geek.

Observed couples on dance floor, Pamela and Basil Faulty husband locked in strange waltz, both looked like they wanted it to end.

I detoured towards the main door where all the smokers were gathered.

"Hi Lisa."

"Oh Tim, hi."

"Having a good night?"

"Great thanks."

I did a quick scan of the faces outside.

"Are you looking for your friend?" Tim asked me.

"Yes have you seen her?"

"She's just gone to the loo."

"Thanks, bye."

"Bye."

I caught up with Millie.

"How are things going with you and Jake?" she asked.

"Fantastic, he hasn't left my side all night except for now of course and I think he's really getting into me. What about you?"

"What about me?" Millie shot back defensively.

Repeated question...

"Oh, yeah great."

"Sid's at the bar."

"Who? Oh! Yeah I know, apparently he went to school with that guy."

"Stubbs, really? Small world, anyway, I've got kitchen duty with boss lady and her old cronies so I better get on, wish me luck."

Millie's in such a strange mood.

In kitchen

Maggie was bustling taking cling film off the plates and arranging sausage rolls onto oven trays. Gloria, Mary, Betty and Fran were filling sugar bowls and putting tea cups out. Pamela was nowhere to be seen.

Made my presence known, Maggie cooed over my dress and set a task for me.

I noticed on the dance floor through the serving window that Pamela was dancing with Max Crankshaw.

Mrs Crankshaw came into the kitchen red faced and fanning herself with her hands. "Phew I'm on fire tonight," she said now pulling her silk shirt away from her body and fanning her bosom.

Music stopped and Pamela made her bossy entrance.

I noticed Maggie's body language screamed out loathing for Pamela, understandable as I'm finding Pamela more of a pain every time I'm around her.

"Now who's watching the savouries?" she asked as Maggie popped them in the oven.

"I am!" said Maggie.

 "Okay, what about the tea and coffee?"

"It's done."

"Creamed whipped?"

"All done!"

"Well I'll get the tables set up shall I?" Pamela snapped.

I found out the reason for all the tension. Maggie was the president of the CWA last year and Pamela had taken it over this year. Clash of personality, Maggie politely put it.

I glanced over the dance floor (no, not keeping an eye on Jake or anything) and noticed Millie dancing with Tim. I looked towards the bar, Sid didn't seem to notice that Millie was now engaged in slow dance with Tim.

Music stopped and supper was announced over the loud speaker. I tried to find Jake but could not see him anywhere.

I loaded my paper plate with sandwiches and took my place next to Mrs Crankshaw. As I ate I listened to a drunken Mrs Crankshaw tell me about a fabulous idea she had for a get together. Not sure what this good idea was on account of Mrs Crankshaw's slurred words.

Still no sign of Jake.

Millie was engaged in conversation with Tim, well more like flirting with Tim.

I decided to look for Jake. Quick detour to ladies room, eyes peeled all the time. Big queue outside the ladies. I stood in line and jiggled like a schoolgirl, the wine going through me like water, great fear that I couldn't hold on much longer. Desperate and almost peeing my pants, decided to just nip round side of building. I found a dark spot on the other side of the hall, I pulled a couple of Kleenex out of my bag and looked around for perverts. Hesitating, but as I was getting really desperate, I just decided to do it. I whipped my underpants down, hitched my skirt up and squatted.

sssssss

Trying so hard to concentrate on not splashing my shoes also very concerned about getting caught.

sssss.

Pee going on forever.

I heard voices approaching.

ssssss

Voices seemed to be coming from the back of the hall.

I strained to listen while I continued to pee out the entire contents of my bladder. It sounded like a woman crying and a man's voice consoling her. Feels like watching big brother with no picture, long silence in between muttered words and a lot of heavy breathing.

Thank god pee finally stopped!

Pulled knickers up and quietly tiptoed to the side of the building and peeped round the corner, I'm not spying I'm just... Okay, spying.

I can't believe it.

It was Jake in an embrace with another woman.

It felt like someone had just punched me in the stomach.

He had his back to me and I couldn't make out who the woman was, her face was hidden in the shadows but she was crying and Jake was soothing her.

I so wanted to fly round the corner and shout 'so what's going on here then!' I could now understand the horror of those TV wives (or husbands) who arrive home early from work to find their husbands (or wives) shagging the insurance salesman. But had to remind myself that Jake and I weren't married and we certainly were not dating and that certainly wasn't the salesman he was embracing.

Back in hall

I'm so upset I need to find Millie.

She would know what to do.

I marched back into the hall through the murmurs of conversation and spotted Millie on the other side of the supper tables.

I made a beeline for Millie and heard a voice call out my name.

"Lisa dear," Mrs Crankshaw was waving frantically at me.

Ignoring the drunken old woman I kept focus on Millie and continued walking.

"Lisa, Lisa!" she was now coming towards me almost tripping over herself to get my attention. She's making a total fool of herself.

I ignored her again, I didn't want to talk to her, she's probably just remembered the good idea she had earlier.

Millie was engaged in a conversation with Tim when I approached.

"Can I talk to you alone?" I asked her.

"Lisa!" Mrs Crankshaw called from behind me.

God what does she want!

"Lisa dear," she puffed.

"Your skirt is hitched into the back of your knickers."

In restrooms

"Did you see who it was?" Millie asked.

Queue from restrooms had gone and skirt had been returned to its normal position but that didn't stop the comments like 'nice knickers Lisa' or 'show us ya growler' as we made our way through the crowd. So embarrassing.

"No I didn't see who it was, what am I going to do Millie?"

"You really like this guy don't you."

I nodded like a lovesick teenager.

"Well then, you are a big mature girl now so why don't you just be honest and tell him how you feel, that you don't want to be just friends."

"But what about the other woman?"

"Well you didn't catch them shagging, you said she sounded like she had been crying, he's probably comforting an old friend or a cousin, after all they're a tight fisted bunch round here."

I was starting to feel better already. Jake's a very sensitive guy probably no stranger to Aunt Agony sessions.

Yes I feel much better.

Millie's so brilliant.

I asked Millie what Tim was like.

Millie shrugged. "He's alright."

I've known Millie for a long time, I know when to ask questions and I also know when to drop the subject, this is one of those times when I should drop it.

The restroom door open and the noise of the music filtered through. A red and puffy eyed Pamela appeared; she looked a bit taken back when she saw us.

"Oh! Lisa could you please spare some time and help with clearing the supper dishes?" she barked at me then left.

"Oh that reminds me," Millie said, "you should have heard her and her husband before in the car park. They had a huge fight yelling and swearing at each other."

"That would explain why she looked like she was crying," I said as we made our way back out to the party.

"Yeah well, he left telling her she can make her own way home, she threw her wine bottle at the car. Huge drama Lis, can't believe you missed it."

Fighting our way back through crowd a dreaded thought flashed through mind. I grabbed Millie's arm for support.

"What?" she turned back to me.

"Pamela. Jake must have been out there with *Pamela.*"

Millie laughed. "What, good looking guy like him and a middle aged retired show queen, I doubt it."

But even the look on Millie's face said it could be possible.

"Look," she said taking me by the arm, "he's probably being a gentleman about it. She was upset and he was just in the wrong place at the wrong time so he just tried to comfort her, after all they are friends of the family aren't they?"

"Yeah, yeah you're probably right," I nodded.

Jeez this relationship has barely began and I'm already accusing him of cheating.

"Why don't you ask him, he coming this way," said Millie throwing me into the path of Jake.

"There you are," Jake said, "I was looking for you."

Rest of the night was awesome. My worries about Jake quickly dissolved as he twirled me around the dance floor.

Maggie excused me from CWA duties, Chubbs tried to cut in and Jake told him to piss off.

Jake's a very sexy dancer.

Mrs Crankshaw was now hitching her skirt up revealing her chubby knee caps as she attempts to kick her leg in the air.

Max sat there with a glazed look and sly grin on his face at Mrs Crankshaw's attempt to kick her legs in the air. Pamela was standing on the side looking miserable. I couldn't help but feel sorry for her but only for brief tiny moment.

Millie was snogging Tim and...

Wait a second, Millie was snogging Tim!

I'm forced to tear myself away from Jake to find out what the hell is going on. Did quick scan of room to see if Sid's witnessing girlfriend snogging baker boy, but no sign of Sid.

"What do you think you are doing Millie?"

Tim quickly mumbled something about more drinks and quickly departed.

Sid's not my favorite person but doesn't deserve to be betrayed.

Millie sighed. "Lisa its okay, there's something you should know and I've been meaning to tell you but now is not the right time."

"Where is Sid?"

"He's gone home and trust me he will be okay with this."

What does she mean, is Sid into swinging?

Tim came back with drinks. I gave them both a disapproving look before returning to Jake.

I sat back down beside Jake. He asked me if I was alright.

God Millie's so selfish; I'm not in party mood anymore.

"You wanna go?" Jake asked me. Didn't want to ruin his night as well but he is very keen to leave as well and suggested I come back to his place.

Now I can't get stupid coat on fast enough. Should tell Millie that I'm going, but no time. I need to get out of there fast before he changes his mind.

Jake's place

Well, let me confirm some rumours.

It is possible to have sex a thousand times in one night, *okay* slight exaggeration, and let me tell you that it wasn't half bad either. I tried to text Millie to let her know what I was doing, not at the time you understand, afterwards, well in between times.

Jake lit a cigarette as we lay there in the darkness.

"I didn't know you smoked," I commented.

"Only after sex," he said taking a long drag and blowing smoke rings into the air.

"And how often is that," I teased.

"About a packet a day."

He's so funny.

The mood relaxed and now I feel it's time to pop question.

"Jake?"

"Yeah."

"Be honest!"

"Yes, your acrobatic move did do it for me."

I slapped his arm (although I was pleased, not quite sure if he liked that or not). I put my serious voice on "Are you seeing anyone at the moment?"

There was a long silent pause before he answered.

"No."

"I just wondered because I saw you with someone behind the hall, I didn't know who it was."

(Well I did know who it was but didn't want to say.)

He rolled over to face me and open his mouth to speak then closed it and gave a long sigh.

"Don't you worry about that," he said in a flat tone as he got up, stubbed his cigarette out and left the room.

I feel like I'm the nosiest person on earth. Of course Jake is not seeing anyone else otherwise he wouldn't be here with me. I wished I hadn't said anything, it's Millie's fault, she was the one who said to be honest. And besides if he was seeing someone else he wouldn't just come right out and admit it would he?

God I'm so confused.

Jake jumped back into bed and pressed against me. "I'm good to go again," he joked.

"So you are," I grinned.

Convinced Jake is not seeing anyone else.

Facebook Status Update.

Lisa Collins :D

Lisa is now 'In a relationship with Jake Crankshaw'.

9

Next morning

"Wonder how Aunt is today?"

I'm so happy. Jake made me breakfast before driving me home.

Not one to brag, but did have sex again this morning.

He swung his ute into my drive and stopped the engine. I could see Tom running round the yard hitting everything with his offending stick.

"Hi Aunt Lisa," he called.

I wish that kid would stop calling me Aunt.

"Lis, you know I like you right?"

My head shot around at the sound of Jake's voice, my stomach lurched into my knees.

I stared intensely at him willing this not to happen, but have that dreaded feeling I know what he's about to say.

"I don't think I can get into a relationship right now."

He puffed out his cheeks and started to rub his face with his hands.

"I guess what I'm trying to say is can we still be friends? See what happens, you know take it slow."

I breathed a sigh of relief, for a moment there I thought he was going to completely throw me away. Jake is not only a sexy love machine, he's also a very sensitive man with traditional values.

I can understand the taking slow thing, can't rush a good thing my mother used to say.

Although he wasn't taking things slow last night.

But if I accept the idea of taking it slow then it could go on for bloody ever. I think I need to pretend to be a tiny bit cross.

But then he may dump me altogether.

God I am so confused.

Need to let him know I'm not really okay with it in a nice way.

"Jake," I began as I climbed out of the ute "I'm not the type of girl who usually, you know, does that, soooo ..." I trailed off, Jake smiled, "I know what you're saying and I know you're not."

Good, glad he got the message.

The roar of a car engine came hurtling up the drive. I didn't recognise the red Ford ute until it came to a screaming halt besides Jake's ute.

Oh no no no!

Matt climbed out from behind the wheel.

"What are you doing here?" I hissed.

"My bloody mother," he said as he slammed the door and pulled his swag from the back of the ute. "She kicked me out. I told her to stop interfering with my business and she told me to start being responsible and I said - oh hey Jake."

"Hey Matt."

"Yeah so anyway, I thought I could crash here for a couple of days?"

I turned to see Jake's expression. Not good, cross between mock amusement and pissed off.

Jake muttered something that sounded like catch ya later but can't be sure because blood is rushing in my ears so I'm hard of hearing. Slamming the ute into gear he reversed out at the same speed Matt came in when he arrived.

Oh bloody, bloody hell!

"Haven't you got a mate or something you could crash with?" I hissed at Matt.

"Nah, they all live with their mums'. I do have a mate whose place I can stay at, but he's away for a couple of days so I thought I could crash here 'till he gets back."

"I haven't got any room," I pleaded with him "I've got a friend and her little boy staying and a couple of friends for the weekend."

"I'll take the sofa, I sleep anywhere."

I stomped over to the porch and sat down with my face in my hands. Jake's angry and spotted youth wanting to take up residence on my sofa.

Worse still, as it was Pamela's spotty offspring and if I let him stay, Pamela's going to find out about the little tiny affair I had with her son and Jake's going to think that Matt and I are sleeping together.

But then again having Matt here might drive Jake to absolute jealousy and then Jake may decide taking things slow is a dumb idea and decide on hasty engagement.

And what Pamela doesn't find out won't hurt her.

I told Matt he can have sofa for couple of days but if asked by Pamela about his temporary place of residency then we've never met.

He seems pleased with the offer.

Neroli came out onto the porch and I made the introductions.

"He's cute," Neroli commented after Matt went inside.

"Cute as in little boy cute?" I said, she checked him out again and shrugged her shoulders before taking a seat beside me. "So where did everyone get to last night?"

" Sid and Millie are here aren't they?"

"No they didn't come home last night, so where did you get to?"

"I was at... Neroli what are you wearing?"

It looked like she was wearing a tent, only four sizes too big.

"It's comfortable," she shrugged.

I could only guess that Millie was with Tim. But what of Sid?

Maybe Sid caught Millie with Tim and wasn't okay with it like Millie said and has killed them both and dumped the bodies in the scrub.

Nah, Sid couldn't kill an ant with ant bait.

Matt came onto the porch sipping a beer, my beer I may add.

"Hey Lisa, I didn't hoe in on anything with you and Jake Crankshaw before did I?"

"What?"

"Well you seem keen on him, Jake and I are mates, if you want me to put in a good word, you know tell him what a great shag you are."

"No! I mean no, it's fine Matt thanks."

Neroli looked from Matt to me.

"Have you guys slept together?"

I was about to lose it.

In bed

Only mid-morning but need to catch up on some sleep. Text Millie and got a reply that she's on her way back and not lying dead in the scrub. She didn't say *where* she was but still, I'm relieved that she's not in a ditch after jealous boyfriend attack.

I feel sick at the image of Jake's face this morning when Matt turned up. I started thinking about past relationships and why I always end up alone.

Let's see, there was Samuel. We met at a party for mutual friend, he told me he was personal trainer and we started dating, soon after I started triathlon training. Two months into the relationship he rang me at work and asked to meet me as it was very important.

I spent all of that day rehearsing my 'yes I will marry you' speech and phoning friends to tell them of up and coming news. Arrived at the cafe only to be told that he joined a missionary tour of Africa and was leaving tomorrow.

Jason the jockey left for the USA shortly after I started taking sodden riding lessons.

Andrew called it off after he discovered that I was not Jewish after all.

There was Joe of course and Darren, well he turned out to be gay.

Knock at door

Millie came in.

"Hi, I brought you a cuppa and I met your friend Matt," Millie sat down on my bed.

"So how did things go with Jake?"

I remembered that I was meant to be mad at Millie so was a little frosty with answers.

"Fine, 'till Matt showed up." Relayed the whole story (in frosty tone). I asked where she ended up last night; she completely did a back flip and said that we are not talking about her we are talking about me. I was not going to be fooled so I asked her if she had been with Tim, spat the word Tim I might add.

Millie's not in attack mode, she's very calm and poised. Now I'm scared because Millie's *never* calm and poised. She ran her fingers through her hair.

"Look I didn't want to tell you but Sid and I have split up."

I couldn't believe what I was hearing, split up?

"Since when?" I asked dazed and confused.

"A couple of months."

"A couple of months!"

"Lisa you don't need to repeat everything I say."

I sat there in shock. How could two people who are your friends, be separated right under your nose and I never suspected?

"Why didn't you tell me?"

"We didn't want anyone to know, especially our families, not at the moment anyway; Sid's going through a tough time. I still love him enough to want to be there for him."

"So you still love him, then why did you break up?"

"Lisa I don't want to get into it now, can we talk about this another time please."

I could feel tears welling up.

"It's not a big deal; Sid and I are still living together."

"What about Tim?" I asked.

"I didn't sleep with him you know," Millie shot back in defense. "We ended up talking all night."

I was confused, it had been a confusing day so far.

"Don't worry about it," Millie smiled, "I will tell you everything in good time. Now get your arse out of bed and come and entertain your guests, honestly your host skills are piss poor." She shut the door behind her.

Well at least she's snapped out of her strange mood.

Two days later

Matt's still here.

I am a selfish person. I like my space, I like my house clean, Matt happens to be the biggest slob and I can see why his mum threw him out. Pamela still not aware that I'm harbouring her teenage son. Well at least I don't think so; passed her in street today and she didn't throw acid in my face.

Neroli hadn't made any attempt to find her own place so I gave her two weeks, no excuses. Matt's response was that he had to give his mum some more time, she obviously hadn't realised yet what a mistake she made kicking him out.

Neroli did start to cry so I gave her another week (well I'm not totally selfish). I was in a depressed state of mind and the fact that I hadn't seen Jake didn't help. The rain that had been falling for two days also didn't help to lift my mood.

I was a bit annoyed with Millie for keeping me in the dark about her and Sid, annoyed that my hen still hasn't got off her bloody eggs and the rooster had made its way back home and was now roaming around the property in attack mode.

So now when you go outside you have to take the whacking stick (there is one posted at every door to the house).

Matt asked if I had my period.

Jake's house

I decided to do the 'oh I was just passing' visit with Jake.

I drove the rutty road towards Jake's in the lashing rain.

Pamela in her show-off SUV was coming the other way. I waved to her as our vehicles passed each other. Pamela waved back to me and I can't help but notice the sheepish look on her face. But then again if I had public screaming match with Basil Fawlty husband I would look sheepish too.

Jake's ute is out front when I pulled up which is a good sign. Quickly ran from the car to the shelter of his porch, dodging the goat in my path. There was a cigarette burning in the ash tray by the back door which was wide open, but I knocked anyway, polite thing to do.

Everything was quiet and I started to think Jake was hiding from me when he appeared wearing only his jean's.

So sexy.

He looks startled. "What you doing here?" he asked.

I told him I just came to see him in a sexy voice but didn't quite come out right, sounded more like a strangled cat.

"Lisa I was just about to do my rounds,"

he said pushing past me towards the kitchen. "I've still got cattle out there calving."

I offered to help, after all two hands make light work, great way to prove that I will make fantastic farmer's wife but he declined saying it's far too wet and fencing and blah, blah.

I feel a bit deflated by this so I decided on the direct approach. I moved in closer to him and slipped my arms around him; he pulled himself from my grasp and moved around me to the pile of clothes on the floor.

Seems a bit frosty towards me and I feel like I want to cry.

"Is it because of Matt?" I asked him.

"Matt Horton?" he chuckled. "No Lisa, it's got nothing to do with Matt Horton."

Detected a slight bitterness to his voice. I wanted to explain that there is nothing going on with the spotty youth but Jake slid his arms around my waist after locating his shirt and promised to come round later after he finished with his cattle.

But something's not quite right. It's like Jake's got premenstrual man syndrome.

Arrived back home

Tom was on the roof of the chicken pen.

"Get down from there!" I growled.

"Can't!" yelled Tom. He pointed to the rooster that seemed to be pacing around the pen looking for a way back in, stupid thing finally comes home to roost.

Told him to stay there while I grabbed the whacking stick.

My plan was to open the door and with a bit of luck the stupid thing will go back into the pen. I pushed the door open and stood back. Bloody thing didn't move so now I'm waving and flapping my arms around like a dramatic dancer.

"Don't worry Aunt Lisa," Tom yelled, "I'll get it." He threw his light saber at the rooster, hitting it on the bum; it squawked and ran into the pen.

"Ha! Good job Tom." I lifted him down from the roof and retrieved his light saber. "We make a great team eh."

"We should kill it," he said, "I could stab it with my light saber."

"Yes, well maybe not today."

Inside

Neroli was down on her hands and knees cleaning the skirting boards. Strange woman, but have to admit the place looks clean and smells like a hospital. I left her to it, seems happy enough.

Matt arrived back soon after and asked what happened to the house as it looks clean. How he can see anything from behind that mop of hair is beyond me. Neroli served a three course dinner she had prepared by hand, Tom was also tucking into the lemon muffins Neroli had baked earlier.

Jake phoned, said he wasn't coming over, too tired.

After dinner

I forced Matt to help me clear away the dishes.

Tom was standing at the sink playing with the bubbles.

Everywhere Matt went Tom was right behind him.

"Can I sleep with you tonight?" Matt asked.

I spluttered at the prospect of having sex with the youth a second time.

"The sofa's killing my back," Matt continued, "don't worry, I won't attempt to shag you again unless you're up for it?"

Did consider it for a tiny moment.

Then I said that he could, but no shagging.

Mrs Crankshaw arrived (uninvited)

"Ah Lisa dear," she shrugged off her waterproof parker and sat down at the kitchen table.

"I thought of a great idea the other night."

"Is it the same idea you had at the dance?" I asked her while filling the kettle.

"Yes but it's taken me a couple of days to recover, not as young as I used to be."

A two day hangover, that has to be in the Guinness Book of Records.

"Anyway," she went on. "You know the sad news about Betty?"

"No."

"Ah well the poor dear has been diagnosed with breast cancer."

"Oh that's awful."

"Yes sad isn't it. I asked her if there was anything the CWA could do to help her and her family, and she suggested a fundraiser and the proceeds go to breast cancer research. So I thought, you've got some of that merchandise..."

"What merchandise?" I asked.

"Your sex toys."

"Oh, that merchandise."

"Yes and I thought if we hold a party and the proceeds go towards that, then women might buy it if they knew it was going towards a good cause."

"Why don't we just do a nude calendar, like those women did in England?"

"Lisa don't be ridiculous!" Mrs Crankshaw snapped.

Matt entered the kitchen.

Bloody hell, told him to stay in living room out of sight, does he not listen.

Tom is at his heels and are both headed towards the cake tin.

Mrs Crankshaw is now looking confused and her eyes are darting between Matt and me.

"His mum kicked him out," I said quickly, "he's only staying 'till the end of the week."

Great! Now Mrs. Crankshaw is bound to tell Pamela that I am

harbouring her teenage son, then she would want to know why I'm harbouring her teenage son and then she would find out that I shagged her teenage son and that will only give her more reason to bad-mouth me to Jake.

I mean what *is* her problem.

"He's sleeping in Lisa's bed." Tom piped up through a mouthful of banana cake.

"No Tom," I gave him my warning smile, "he is sleeping on the couch."

"Nah you said..."

"Tom! Go and brush your teeth."

"Does your mother know where you are?" Mrs Crankshaw asked Matt in a stern voice.

"Nah, but when she does I'm sure she will come crawling back."

Mrs Crankshaw rolled her eyes. Matt grabbed his cake and went back to the living room.

"Lisa, a word of advice," Mrs Crankshaw started when Matt had gone. "I know you have the best intentions dear but it doesn't look good, an aged woman like you letting young men stay over. Matt's only nineteen you know, far too young for you."

My face burned red. I explained to Mrs Crankshaw that nothing was going on, Matt just turned up and I didn't have the heart to turn him away.

Then Mrs Crankshaw, confused, asked why he would turn up here in the first place.

Change subject.

"Fundraiser sounds good." I quickly said but then added that it may be a good idea if Mrs Crankshaw informs the CWA that it was her idea for the Kinky'n'Nice party.

"Oh don't be embarrassed Lisa everyone does it, including senior members of CWA."

One mental image I could do without.

Next night

Matt arrived home with some DVD's and insisted we have a movie night since it's been raining now for three days. I have a tiny problem with a leaky roof so I phoned Millie to tell her. She said it's not her problem and I informed her that indeed it was as she is the project manager. Millie told me to shove the project manager up my backside so I hung up.

She phoned back and apologized for being an ass and told me that Sid will come out and deal with it this weekend. Strange, wonder why the sudden change of heart.

Matt's choices for movie evening were 'The Fast and the Furious' and 'Jackass', a movie where a bunch of morons do stupid stunts all in the name of entertainment.

Matt argued that the movie was not stupid but indeed a classic. Neroli announced she wasn't feeling well and was going to bed. I wasn't surprised with all the cleaning she had done the previous day.

I hadn't heard from Jake and was very alarmed, but kept telling myself that I'm sure he has a good reason. I sat through Jackass, listening to Matt's "awwwhhh man" and "wicked," thinking about nothing but Jake.

Stupid, stupid movie.

Time for bed

Matt was already in bed and giving his best stage performance of 'snore' the musical. Crawled into bed beside him and checked that he wasn't naked.

I didn't have to go into work in the morning, Debbie had asked me to work her weekend shift so she could go to a wedding, her wedding as it turned out and not in a church wearing white.

In fact the ceremony was to be held in the medium security prison chapel with her longtime boyfriend who is currently serving two years for aggravated assault. I'm so tired and need sleep. Smothered Matt with pillow to shut him up, didn't work but kicking him did.

Neroli

Neroli tiptoed into Lisa's bedroom. She knew the time had come as she was feeling uncomfortable all day and now was the moment of truth. Her secret. She had known for months and certainly didn't tell anybody about it. But then Neroli wasn't convinced that it was happening herself, denial was a strength she could muster but now she couldn't hide it any longer.

She stood over Lisa and watched her sleep for a moment, her thoughts dark.

Maybe she could grab Tom and be gone by morning. An option, and possibly a safe one, the very thought of disappearing into the night made her even more anxious, where would she go?

She couldn't possibly go back to her parents they gave up on her a long time ago and Neroli could never understand why her parents didn't pay any attention to her troubles.

Neroli never meant to hurt anyone. People always found her more interesting if she told them lies, if she was just herself people wouldn't bother to speak to her.

Running away now was tempting, then she won't have to worry about telling anyone, but somehow Neroli knew this wasn't an option, she couldn't do it to Tom anymore. She was scared and needed Lisa's help.

Lisa

Still in bed

Got the strangest feeling that I'm being watched.

I felt Matt beside me, he had managed to creep onto my side of bed, his ever present erection stabbing me in the back. I opened one eye and looked at the time on Matt's digital alarm clock, 12.43pm.

Bloody hell I have only been asleep for twenty minutes.

"Lisa, are you awake?"

God it's Neroli, what did she want?

"Um Lisa…"

"What is it Neroli?"

"Um, well…"

"Neroli just spit it out, what do you want?"

She took a deep breath. "My waters just broke!"

Facebook Status Update.

Lisa Collins: WTF!!!

      5 minutes ago

Lisa Collins: Anyone know the number for the ambulance?

      4 minutes ago

Lisa Collins: Anyone know how to deliver a baby?

      2 minutes ago

Lisa Collins: Buggerrr!!!

      Just now

10

Driving frantically down the M1, 1.05am

I glanced at Neroli who apart from moaning through her contractions had not said much.

I phoned the hospital to let them know of our impending arrival.

Waited for Neroli to pass through another contraction before asking questions.

Can't believe she did this to me. Neroli's so selfish.

"Is it early or late?" I started.

"Well it is 1.00am so I suppose it's early," replied Neroli.

The thought of Matt at home nursing his swollen head after banging it on the sideboard following Neroli's shock announcement worsened my temper, together with lack of sleep I started to fray.

I wasn't quite sure if she was avoiding the question or was simply that daft. But Neroli owes me answers.

"The baby," I said through gritted teeth, "is it premature?"

"Oh I don't know," replied Neroli.

"Well," I persisted, "when did you have your last ultrasound?"

"I didn't."

I took a deep breath. "You haven't had an ultrasound, what about a doctor?"

Neroli shrugged.

"Tell me you saw a doctor Neroli."

She stared blankly at me.

The rain started to get heavy as we drove through the darkness.

I was about to swear when she shifted in her seat and started her breathing, her contraction seemed to go on forever.

"You okay?" I asked her as she started to ease.

"Yeah its fine," she said.

"Good!" my anger returned, "'cos when we get to the hospital, I will have the first go at the fucking gas in the hope that it might mush my brain enough to develop a sixth sense and then I might start to understand what fucking planet you're on!"

The silence cut through the air as we approached the bright lights of the city.

"Well you better hurry up," Neroli said calmly. "Because here comes another contraction."

Arrived at hospital

The nurse quickly bundled Neroli and I into the delivery suite when they discovered she was dilated by 7cm. I seemed to be caught up with all the bustle and filling out the mountain of paperwork that was required.

I was still filling in her details on the medical form trying to remember Neroli's last name when she squeezed my hand so hard I thought she broke it.

Bitch.

3.05am

Healthy baby girl slithered out of Neroli. I bawled my eyes out for an hour.

She is so beautiful and I think I want a baby.

We named her Bailey and I phoned a bewildered Matt to tell him the news. We decided to wait and tell Tom together in the morning as we don't want to shock a four year old in the middle of the night. It was only then, for the first time, Neroli started to acknowledge her baby.

Arrived home

I'm exhausted but still buzzing. I so want a baby.

Millie turned up at the hospital after I had convinced her that what I had told her was actually true.

Sid brought along his camera claiming it was a miracle that Neroli never knew she was pregnant and wondered if it was the birth of Christ all over again. I didn't bother to tell him that it was unlikely Neroli was a virgin.

"Man what just happened?" Matt asked as soon as I opened the door. "I swear I dreamt that she was having a baby, I thought I was dreaming 'till I hit my head. No wonder I hit my head, the shock of that announcement in the middle of the night, freaky man."

"Did Tom wake up?" I asked Matt.

"Nah, wee dude is still sleeping." Matt sat down and shook his head in bewilderment.

"Man when I first saw her I thought she was hot, I didn't even realise she was fat ..." Matt trailed off, before continuing. "I think maybe the next time you invite your friends to stay you should ask them to take a pregnancy test first, and to think I was going to make a move on her and...."

"Matt!" I interrupted him. "If you'd let me get a word in, I didn't know she was pregnant and to be honest and I don't think she did either."

"How could she not know she was pregnant? I mean she wouldn't have had her period or anything."

"Well what I meant was she kept herself in denial all this time so I think the best we could do, sorry, I could do, is support her."

"Who's the father?"

"I don't know, someone who won't be seen again."

Matt sighed and stretched his hands and rubbed the lump at the back of his head. "So what are you going to tell the wee dude? He'll be awake soon."

"I don't know."

Matt thought about it and grinned, "I know, ask him if he has seen the movie 'Alien' and tell him that last night while his mum was sleeping alien's came down and did all sorts of experiments with her, and this morning an alien burst through his mum's tummy and gave him a baby sister."

"I don't think he would have seen the movie Alien Matt, he's four."

"Ah, right."

I picked up the phone and punched in the numbers that were on the piece of paper I retrieved from my pocket.

"Whatyadoing?" Matt stifled a yawn.

"Ringing Neroli's mother because from what I can gather she didn't know about the pregnancy either."

On phone to Neroli's mother

The conversation is a bit awkward and strange. But even stranger when she suggested that Neroli stay with me.

I finally managed to convince her that her daughter, and grandchildren, were better off with her and it might even be a good idea that Neroli fly up and not drive the journey.

I mean god, what am I, fixer of everything.

Breaking the news to Tom about his new baby sister was surprisingly easy.

"Cool." He said and turned his attention back to Thomas the Tank Engine.

Poor bugger, no doubt he's used to surprises.

On phone to Millie

Complained about Neroli hitting on male nurse when

supposed to be concerned about baby. Both agree she's not changed; thank goodness she was staying in hospital before going back to her parents.

Also told Millie that Mrs Crankshaw offered to mind Tom while I did Debbie's shift at the weekend. Millie relieved that she doesn't have to mind Tom over weekend 'cause cannot cope with demon child and both surprised that Matt had gone to visit Neroli and baby every chance he got.

On phone to Mrs Crankshaw

Set a date for the Kinky'n'Nice party which was to be held two weeks from now in the back room of the town hall. Thanked Mrs Crankshaw for support over Neroli and casually mention Jake's name to her as I have not seen him for sometime. She said hasn't seen much of Jake either but said he has been busy with the farm.

Have a feeling the old woman is covering for him.

In Ranor Hotel

Needed a drink (and small hope that may run into Jake), parked on bar stool next to Stubbs.

"So you and Matt are an item eh? I thought you were shagging Jake Crankshaw."

Stubbs, such a gentleman.

"Er... I'm not doing either," I don't think he believed me.

"Did you ever hear about Jake's brother?" Stubbs asked.

Small town pubs are great for gossip.

"Yes," I said, "Jake told me he ran away after his father died or something."

"Oh yeah, there's that." Stubbs said leaning towards me a little too close.

"But they had a huge falling out over a girl Jake was going out with and then of course there was the question of the farm."

This was getting intriguing. "What like?" I tried to sound as unsuspecting as possible.

"Oh there was some argument with the brothers over the division of the farm. Jake wanted to divide the land and sell small parcels and Rick wanted to keep it as one, this started after their old man got sick, don't know what the outcome was there. Then the girl that Jake was dating at the time was also dating Rick," Stubbs paused to take a swig of his beer before continuing, "so I think Rick just couldn't be bothered and left."

"Sounds like they are both as bad as one another," I said.

Stubbs nodded his head in agreement. "Yeah, but that happens between brothers sometimes. Rick will come back one day and they will probably kiss and make up."

Time to go, Stubbs's hand is now resting on my knee.

Next morning

Bloody hell, Neroli's starting a trend. I discovered six little yellow chicks running around the chook pen. They were so cute I couldn't resist a hold, even if that meant braving the rooster.

I opened the pen and the bastard thing flew at me again. "Right!" I shouted at it, "that's it, you're dead."

"Yeah, we're going cut you up," said Tom coming up behind me.

I bustled Tom into the car to drop him off at Mrs Crankshaw's before going to do the Saturday morning shift for Debbie. Tom had voiced his protest about going to Mrs Crankshaw's as he wanted to go with Matt.

After explaining that Matt has got to go to work, his protest went on 'till the discovery of the baby chicks and it was only the promise that he could name one if he went to Mrs Crankshaw's, that he went peacefully.

Four year olds are such hard work.

Mrs Crankshaw's yard

Jake is there, he's so sexy. He was chatting with Max and getting ready for a days work. He waved out to me as I delivered Tom to the door.

He's so hot and would father good-looking children.

After work

"I'll take the wee dude to see his mum." Matt announced as we sat down to eat the pizza Matt brought home for lunch after we both finished our weekend shifts. Millie and Sid still hadn't arrived to fix the roof, they were meant to be here by now so Millie and I can go to the hardware store and choose paint for living room.

Tom's eyes lit up like a power station with that announcement, I couldn't say no.

I'm also tiny bit relieved that Matt's willing to take him off my hands for the afternoon.

"Matt you're spending an awful lot of time at the hospital," I said. Matt played it down through a mouthful of pizza. "Yeah well I have to go into the city anyway, so might as well go in and say hi." I also thought it was a good time to ask him when he's moving out.

He shifted in his seat, "Ah, well, was gonna talk to you 'bout that."

"Oh god Matt," I cut in, "don't tell me you haven't sorted things with your mum."

"Nah, stuff mum, I got plans of my own now but I just need a few more days."

He looked at me with pathetic eyes, "I promise ya man, true to my word I've sorted something out, just give me a few more days."

I sighed and folded my arms. Uncomplicated rural life is bloody complicated.

"Alright," I agreed. "I'll give you three more days as long as you do me a favour."

"Yeah cool man, anything, just name it."

"I want you to help me kill the rooster, tonight!"

In garden

The afternoon sun was relentless, the sweat seemed to drip from me as I pulled the weeds from the vegetable patch that Sid and Mrs Crankshaw had planted. Millie and Sid phoned to say they were not coming because the car had broken down and will come later on in the week.

I must admit I'm a bit relived as I'm not in the mood for renovations.

I cranked up the old lawn mower that I found in the shed from the previous owners.

It was something that should have been in a museum.

With a puff of smoke it was away and I started going up and down the lawn, stripping the grass as I walked behind it.

I had just about completed my task when Jake turned up armed with an enormous bunch of flowers.

Stunned, I cut the motor on the rickety lawn mower.

"For you," he said, thrusting the flowers at me.

Speechless, I held them up to my nose to breath in the scent, they didn't have one.

"What's this for?" I asked him. "Ah well I have been busy lately it's kinda an apology for not seeing you."

Pft and to think I thought Jake didn't like me.

I launched into telling him about the eventful week I had, his eyes widen in such a cute way as I told him about Neroli's secret pregnancy followed by the not so secret birth and having to break the news to her mother. I stopped to take a breath when he interrupted me.

"Speaking of secrets you haven't told anyone about us, have you?"

I had to think about it, after all I did tell the midwife who delivered Neroli's baby and the nice young girl who served me my latté, and if I remember rightly, that lady on the phone who was seeking donations for some charity. But I'm sure Jake's not meaning those people.

"No I don't think so, besides Millie of course," I said. "Why?"

"I just think we should keep this between us, for now anyway."

Seems fair enough.

I realised I looked and smelled a fright and excused myself for a shower. Jake hinted that he had about an hour to spare and that we were coming into a drought (even though we just had four days of sodden rain but will play his little game, so sexy), so it might be a good idea that we share water. I couldn't agree more, I mean you have to conserve wherever you can, even if that means sharing the shower with another person.

And I'm really, *really* pleased that Millie and Sid are not here or Matt, Tom, Neroli and baby Bailey. Too crowded.

Also I'm starting to think that Neroli having a baby, Matt visiting her with Tom, and Sid's car breaking down is a sign from above that Jake and I are meant to be together because wouldn't be having sex in every room otherwise.

At pub

Jake's gone home and I'm so hungry. Matt and Tom were still at the hospital so I jumped on a bar stool and ordered a wine and a toasted sandwich.

I had made plans to go and see Neroli tomorrow with Millie and maybe do a bit of shopping while I was in the city.

"Hello Lisa." I turned to see Maggie climbing up on the bar stool beside me. A very large man with an untidy beard and long hair that was tied at the back stood beside her, she introduced me to her husband.

"What brings you here?" I asked her as her husband moved off towards a crowd of regulars mooching round the poker machines.

"Just a quick drink before picking the kids up from my brothers," she replied.

Maggie had six children so I can imagine her brother must be a saint if he has all of them there at the same time.

"I'm glad I've caught you," she continued as she took a sip of her drink. "I have wanted to catch up with you all week. I have something personal to ask." She looked embarrassed so I thought I'd spare her the question and just come out with it, obviously Stubbs had told her.

"Yes I did sleep with Matt Horton," I started. "But it was a mistake and I didn't know how old he was, and yes he is staying with me at the moment but there's nothing going on it's just..."

"Matt Horton?" Maggie looked puzzled. "Oh dear, I'm so sorry Lisa, I was going to ask you if you and Jake were an item, I didn't realise you were seeing Matt."

"No I'm not seeing Matt."

"Oh shame," Maggie took another sip of her drink. "I would have paid to see the look on Pamela face." I had to hand it to Maggie, as reserved and quiet as she was she wasn't backwards at coming forward.

"So are you seeing Jake?" she asked me again. "I know he took you to the dance."

Jake's words earlier that day about keeping it quiet ran through my head.

I took another mouthful of wine before pondering my answer. Maggie was the sort of person that could keep a secret but I wasn't about to risk finding out.

"Um no, I'm not," I said crossing my fingers behind my back, "we're just friends."

Maggie studied my face for a moment and I could feel myself go hot. I mean yes I have been known to tell the odd white lie but I wasn't very good at it.

Maggie smiled.

"That's good," she said, "I thought it was my duty, you know, from one woman to another, to warn you about Jake. He's a lovely guy and all but he can be a player."

My insides felt like they had stopped working.

"Player, you mean like a flirt?" I asked taking another gulp of my wine. Maggie shook her head

"No, not so much a flirt, it's just that..." Maggie shifted in her bar stool, she looked uncomfortable. "It's just that he has other interests."

"Like what?" I croaked. My mouth was so dry I faked a cough to try and cover my distress.

Maggie looked around before leaning towards me.

"Look, can you keep a secret?" she whispered.

The door to the bar swung open just as I was about to answer and Tom ran towards me.

"Aunty Lisa!" he called, "are you ready to kill the rooster yet?"

Matt was right behind him wearing camouflage army style cargo pants and a black T-shirt, all that was missing was the black face paint.

"Oi! No children allowed in the public bar." Rodney shouted to Matt from behind the bar.

"I'm not staying long," Matt shouted back, "I'm just here to see Lisa."

I was aware that all eyes were on me. "Not you," I hissed at Matt, "he's talking about Tom."

Maggie patted me on the hand.

"I'll talk to you later," she said as she moved off.

Oh god don't go.

Matt sat down in the vacant bar stool when Maggie moved off. "So when do you want to kill this rooster?"

Rodney came over with an orange juice for Tom who was now perched on Matt's knee. "Best time to kill a rooster is after dark," he gruffly told Matt, "element of surprise."

"What do you recommend?" Matt asked him. "An axe or the neck breaking?"

"Excuse me!" I interjected. "There is a child present, I don't want him to start having nightmares."

"I reckon we should chop his head off." Tom piped up, licking the orange juice from round his mouth.

"Kid's right," Rodney shrugged, "probably the best way to go.

Now get this kid out of here before I get complaints." Matt and Tom got down from their barstools.

"Are you coming home?" Matt asked as I desperately looked for Maggie. I saw her across the bar engaged in conversation, I missed my chance, bloody Matt. Now I'm dying to find out Maggie's secret about Jake.

2.00am - Operation Rooster

"Arrgh!"

"God Matt, don't sneak up on me."

"Sorry, my bad."

We tiptoed around the chicken coop.

Tom was tucked up in bed, despite his and Matt protests, I didn't want a four year old in my care witnessing the death of an animal.

"Right I have my plan." Matt whispered as he took out a piece of paper and unfolded it. It contained diagrams that looked like Tom had scribbled.

"We go in through the door," he proceeds, as he pointed to the scribble.

"You throw the sack over it and grab it and bring it out to the chopping block shown here in diagram b."

Impatiently I grabbed the paper off him. "We don't need this," I hissed, and screwed the paper into a ball. "Just have the bloody axe ready when I come out."

I made my way through the pen, the rooster was nesting in its box.

This was a test for me, if the rooster wasn't so bloody nasty I wouldn't have even considered killing it, my heart was thumping through my chest as I quickly threw the sack over its body and scooped it up.

Scwaakkk!!! It started flapping it's wings as I made a dive for the door and out to where Matt was waiting.

"Quick, hold it down," he said. The rooster was making a lot of noise and flapping it's wings, I held it on the chopping block and closed my eyes.

When Matt raised the axe behind his head I suddenly felt sick. I couldn't do it.

"Stop!"

I let go of the rooster. It ran off just as the axe landed on the chopping block.

"Awwhh man, what ya do that for?" Matt protested.

The sack that contained the rooster was running off into the darkness.

"I couldn't do it Matt, he knew what was about to happen, it's not right!"

Scwakkkkk! We turned our heads in the direction of the rooster. The sack had stopped moving.

Matt and I slowly made our way towards the sack whispering to each other not to scare it. Matt pulled the sack away and I stood with my whacking stick in hand.

The rooster lay there on it's side clearly not moving.

"What the..?"

"I think it's dead?" Matt said leaning over the rooster.

"Don't be so sure, it could be pretending." I said.

"Nah man, I think it's died of fright or something, we'll wait a few minutes and see if it goes cold."

Back inside 2.15am

My hands were still trembling.

I stood there in a daze as the kettle started to boil. I'm definitely not cut out for killing animals even though it was a good idea at the time. In hindsight have learned something about myself tonight but that's not good if I'm to become a farmer's wife. Imagining all the packaged meat in the supermarket isle and all those poor defenseless animals, sure the rooster was nasty but he didn't deserve to die. I could've built him his own pen, it could be like a solitary confinement for roosters who decided to play up.

I could rescue many animals and declare a no-killing zone, and I could become a vegetarian, for real this time.

I poured the steaming water over the teabags in the mugs.

Matt came into the kitchen and frightened the bejezzes out of as I turned to see him holding up the limp rooster.

"It's definitely dead, I think we frightened it to death."

Matt's lips started to curl at the sides.

I warned Matt that it wasn't funny that the rooster was dead and then we both rolled round kitchen in fits of laughter.

Okay, it's a tiny bit funny.

Maternity suite

I rang the buzzer to the maternity suite. Visiting hours were not officially open for another 5 minutes but because Millie and I had Tom with us we thought we are classed as family who could visit as often as we like.

I'm a bit worried about Tom; he had been quiet all morning after running outside to find the dead headless rooster hanging from the clothesline. Matt had hung it there the night before to let the blood drain from its body.

Tom despite all of his talk about killing the rooster screamed his little lungs out from the very sight of it.

Neroli was propped up on her pillows with little baby Bailey clamped to her breast. Tom jumped on the bed and delivered his mother a big hug.

"Where's Matt?" Neroli asked as Millie and I made a beeline for the only chair available.

"He will be here soon," I said as Millie beat me to the seat.

Neroli shared a room with four other nursing mothers who all hushed us as Millie scraped the chair along the floor.

We gazed at the little bundle for a while, so cute with her little pink squashed face. It was hard to imagine Neroli had hid her belly away from the world.

I so want a baby.

"So, looking forward to going back home to your parents?" I asked. Neroli handed baby over to Millie who looked so awkward with it.

"I'm not going home," Neroli said as she smoothed down her blankets.

"Pardon?" I seemed to be having trouble hearing her.

"I'm not going home, I'm staying."

"No!" I cried before I could stop myself. Millie's head shot up from goo-ing over the baby. Neroli gave me a surprised look.

"I mean, ha, ha, don't you think you would be better off going back to your mum?" Millie tried to hide her grin behind baby's head.

"No I don't want to go back to Mum's," said Neroli, picking an imaginary piece of fluff off her sleeve. "Mum didn't really want me back there, anyway Taromeo seems a nice place to settle down and raise children."

An involuntary squeak escaped from my throat.

"And I'm kinda in love." Neroli added.

"What? Since when?" Oh god, not another bloody secret.

"Neroli, have you got a place of your own lined up?" Millie asked her as she handed the now crying baby back to Neroli.

"No, no, Millie, don't change the subject. Neroli who are you in love with?"

"With me," came the voice from behind. Matt had arrived and Tom leapt off the bed into Matt's waiting arms. "Hey there wee dude," he said as he sat down at the end of the bed.

"Very funny Matt," I said before turning back to Neroli who was vigorously rubbing Baileys back in attempt to bring up her wind.

"So Neroli, let me get this straight, you have decided to stay because you have a crush on a guy. Great Neroli, sooo responsible."

"Pot calling kettle black," Millie mumbled.

Matt put his arm around Neroli. "I have an announcement to make. As of this morning Neroli and I have our own place. We can move in as soon as Neroli comes out of hospital."

Smutty moment between Neroli and Matt so I turned my head away.

I still do not believe that Neroli's in love with Matt. Matt's too young to be in love and Neroli has only just met him. Neroli went into a great story about having a crush on Matt when he first came to stay and then Matt started coming to see her after the baby was born and realised they were meant for each other.

Matt nodded. "That's right; her, me, little dude and the little dudess."

"Matt, does your mother know this?" I asked.

"Yeah, just been to see her. I thought she would go psycho but she said, whatever, as long as I don't move back home."

Cafe

"I could see that coming," Millie smirked.

"Oh did you, were you going to let me in on it?" I asked.

"Oh come on, you're not that blind and plus it makes sense, look at the way Matt is with Tom, they adore each other."

"But Matt's too young to take on a ready made family." I protested.

We ordered our caffeine fix and found a couple of seats overlooking the busy city streets.

"That's his decision, get over it Lisa. Why are you so down anyway, you have a face like a hostile lemon?"

I was so pleased Millie asked, it took her a while to notice.

"It's Jake," I sigh.

"Maggie asked me last night if I was seeing him and of course I lied and said I wasn't 'cause Jake and I decided to keep it quiet and she starts to tell me something about Jake, something not nice I'm guessing, and she never got round to telling me."

"And why do you want to know?" Millie asked.

"Because we are sleeping with each other," I spelt it out slowly for Millie.

"But not seeing him."

"What's the difference?" I asked.

"I thought you were happy with the way things are with you and Jake. Sex with no strings attached. Friends with benefits, wham bam now piss off."

"Well I changed my mind, I want a baby, with Jake."

Millie looked me in the eye. "The renovations are still on aren't they, or am I wasting my time?" Then she added silently with her intense stare, to think about my answer very carefully.

"I've course not," I scoffed, turning my red face away from her. Jake would want me to move in with him anyway after we married, family farm and all.

"This guy is obviously doing your head in." Millie said in a tone I don't like as she slammed her cup on the counter to intensify her point.

"My advice is to stop seeing him until you sort out what you want."

"You don't understand," I mumbled.

Millie rolled her eyes before checking her phone which I could tell was Sid from her ring tone, she has a special one for Sid.

"You still haven't told me why Sid and you broke up," I said.

"Because it's something that's going to take a lot of explaining," she said as she slung her bag around her shoulders, "and I've got to go to work. I will come and see you next weekend, in the meantime, sort yourself out." She leaned over to give me a kiss on the cheek.

"You're a dope, but I'm glad you're my friend."

Back home

Despite a successful shopping spree, I'm still a bit down and I had Jake on my mind all the way home. I pulled into my drive, turned the car off and gazed towards the clothesline. The headless rooster had gone; Matt must have taken it off when Tom saw it this morning.

I was barely out of the car when Matt arrived home with a ute load of empty boxes.

"Neroli is allowed to come home tomorrow," he announced as he came into the kitchen and grabbed a beer out the fridge. "So I'm going to start packing our things and move in the day after tomorrow."

"Great," I mumbled. I should be rejoicing but my thoughts are still with Jake.

"Um Lisa," he put down his beer and turned me around to face him.

"What!" I snapped.

"It could never have worked between us you know that aye?" His eyes were full of pity.

"What are you talking about?" I asked as I pushed past him.

"You and me," he continued, "I know it must have been a bit of a shock about me and Neroli, but you have to move on and I know you will get over us eventually."

Oh my god.

"Matt I'm not upset about Neroli and you as a couple, I'm happy for you. I just hope you know what you're doing that's all."

"So you're not in love with me?"

"What? No, god no Matt, I never was."

"Oh that's all right then, I mean like, that could have been awkward eh."

Matt's so bloody full of himself.

"So where did ya bury the rooster?" he asked as he took another swig of beer.

"I didn't, I thought you took care of it."

"Nah, didn't touch it."

I felt a chill through my body, if Matt didn't touch it and I didn't touch it, then where did the headless rooster that was hanging from the clothes line go?

"Maybe the cat took it," Matt said as he left the kitchen.

"So where are all the feathers then?" I said to the empty doorway.

I went outside to see if I could see any evidence of a headless rooster. Someone must have removed it, as the string that was holding it to the clothesline was also missing. If Randy Puss had removed it there would have been a frayed string, wouldn't there?

Oh god, I felt another wave of depression come over me again. A ramshackle house, I'm crazy with love for a guy who has a secret, my best friend has got two boyfriends, my house-guests are shacking up together and someone's stealing dead poultry from my clothesline.

I felt so sorry for myself the tears started falling down my cheeks. I sat on the grass with my head on my knees.

"What's wrong Aunt Lisa?" Tom came up beside me.

"Are you sad about the rooster dying too?"

I looked up and smiled at him as I wiped the tears from my cheeks.

"No buddy, I'm sad because everyone has found love and I'm going to be all alone."

I'm pouring my heart out to a four year old; Tom knelt down to my eye level.

"You shouldn't be sad Aunt Lisa, you've got the man who lives in the forest."

"You mean Jake who comes here sometimes; well he's not really my boyf..."

"No, the man who lives over there," Tom pointed to the forest. "The one who took the rooster."

Facebook Status Update.

Lisa Collins: Has anyone seen my dead rooster?

Lisa went from 'In a relationship' to 'It's complicated'.

Lisa likes: Stop the Slaughter of Animals.

11

At police station

"Well I cannot do much about your complaint until we catch someone in the act," the policeman said, as I sat opposite his desk.

It was the same policeman that visited me about the illegal hunting. It was a small station sprawled with a few posters about illegal substances. To the right of his desk is a small bench with tea and coffee making facilities, a filing cabinet and one small sofa and a few leaflets stacked on the table. A far cry from the busy police stations you see in the movies with bad guys been led in in handcuffs and typewriters clicking and the buzz of phones ringing constantly.

In fact this station looks like it used to be somebody's garage and they added a rug and a glass door.

I'm now wondering where they put any bad guys that they arrest.

"But however I'll make some inquires," he continued, snapping me out of my thoughts. After Tom's shock announcement, Matt and I searched the forest for any evidence of the hunter or the dead rooster but came up with nothing.

"The wee lad did give us a description," the policeman went on. "But I don't think Jake Crankshaw would be into stealing headless roosters off clotheslines."

"He didn't say it was Jake," I explained for the third time. "He said this man looked like Jake."

"Yes well, all the same," the policeman said, shuffling papers on his desk. "We will follow this up. We are taking this seriously, trespassing and stealing are serious, even if it is a dead rooster."

Outside station

I rummaged around in my bag for sunglasses. The heat hit me as I stepped outside from the cool air conditioned comfort of the station.

A familiar sexy voice appeared behind me.

"Did you make bail?" Jake stood there in his dusty jeans and his equally dusty white singlet top that showed of his tanned muscles. So sexy.

"Would you bail me out if I was in trouble?" I asked him in an equally good humoured tone.

Jake simply laughs. I'm slightly taken aback by this, wanted to shake him and yell 'well would ya?'

"Actually, the police might be around to ask you some

questions." I started to explain about the rooster. Jake's smile disappeared when I mention Tom's mistake of telling them the hunter looked like him. He didn't speak at first then he shook his head and muttered something like "pff kids eh," and then walked off. I mean, what is his problem? I didn't say Tom said it was him; I only said Tom reckons it looked like him.

Back home

Missed a call from my parents, must phone them.

Matt had finished packing and now was loading boxes into the back of his work vehicle that he had borrowed from his patient, understanding boss.

"What ya think?" he asked as he threw back the tarpaulin to reveal a beautiful crib all draped in white lace that had gone yellow at the sides. "It was mine when I was a nipper, Mum said that Neroli could borrow it." Matt puffed his chest out with pride.

"Matt, I think Neroli's a very lucky girl," I said as I took a closer look at the crib.

Matt looked at me sideways. "Um Lisa, I thought you got over us?" he said, slightly exasperated, "we had this conversation remember?"

"Oh god! Matt for the hundredth time, no I'm not in love with you! I think it's sweet that you look after her is what I meant."

"Oh, yeah, well I've also brought these," he said opening the car door to reveal baby's blankets and a mountain of toys. "I'll just take this stuff round to the house."

Tom jumped into the passenger seat beside him. So cute that Matt and Tom have finally found each other.

Arrival of Jake

I'm shocked at the arrival of Jake with a parcel of fish and chips. Jekyll and Hyde thing wearing a bit thin, we must have a talk.

After a meal of greasy fish and salty chips Jake leaned back on the sofa feet outstretched and patted his tummy and suggested sex.

I'm thinking about the conversation with Millie yesterday. Jake and I would most likely have sex, then tomorrow he wouldn't acknowledge that we are anything more than just friends, it wasn't good enough for me any more.

Time to put my big girl's pants on and deal with it, as Millie would say.

I took a deep breath.

"Look Jake, I think I like you, a lot, I cannot go on just being friends and having occasional sex. I want more and if you're not comfortable with that then..."

I trailed off leaving the answer hanging in the air.

God I think I'm going to throw up.

I glanced at him, he was staring at his boots looking like he was deep in thought; I sat there with my heart in my mouth waiting for him to say something, anything.

Oh god, I should have kept my mouth shut.

"I, ah, will just go and get another drink," I mumbled.

"Lisa wait," Jake grabbed my arm and pulled me down on the sofa. "Listen," he said putting his hand on mine. "I like you a lot as well and I am sorry, you see, the reason is I'm not afraid of commitment, I'm just afraid of getting hurt."

I remembered the conversation with Stubbs in the pub about Jakes girlfriend, I was about to mention it but Jake's not shutting up.

"I guess my brother disappearing as he did..." Jake trailed off again, I went to speak but Jake's stealing my thunder again. "Look if you want to make a go of it then we take it one step at a time." He was looking at me now his eyes were searching.

No need for talk, Jake said it all. I gave him a long and sexy kiss and Jake suggested we have sex.

On phone to Millie

"I'm in love Millie," I whispered down the phone. Jake was in the kitchen making coffee, I kept my voice low so he wouldn't hear me. "He stayed the whole night."

"Fantastic," Millie said with a dry tone. "But did you have to ring me so early on a Monday morning to tell me that!"

I felt like I was in a real grown up relationship. Maggie's yet to be revealed secret about Jake was still niggling away but Jake's a sensitive, lovely guy, the secret can't be *that* bad.

I hung up on Millie as Jake handed me my coffee and announced he has to go do farming things and asked if I wanted to come with him. I thought about chucking a sickie from work but knowing my luck, somebody will see me doing cattle rounds with Jake and go back to tell Debbie.

On porch

Feeling the morning sun on my face and feeling wonderful. Jake and I had talked for most of the night; he told me a bit more about his childhood and growing up with his twin brother and how his brother broke the families heart with his teenage rebel ways, putting his father into an early grave and how he didn't attend his father's funeral, just disappeared and no one had seen him since.

He also talked about the girl who broke his heart years ago and how he wanted so much to marry her, only for her to laugh in his face when he tried to propose on stage after winning first prize for the wood-chopping at the country fair five years earlier. After learning more about him I could understand why he kept his distance.

Who could blame him, all the people in his life that he loved, either died or left him.

Shit! Late for work.

At work 20 minutes late

Debbie was showing off her wedding photos in the staff room on the morning's break. The room was full of congratulations and curiosity, as a prison wedding wasn't really the norm. We had all chipped in and brought a beautiful silver candlestick from the staff at the rest home.

Debbie was touched as she turned the candlestick over in her hands and thanking everyone for the efforts, until the cranky grounds-keeper called Jim broke the magic when he commented that the candlestick would most likely be used on her new husbands next victim, before being sold at a pawn shop to help fund his next criminal activity.

Everyone departed to go back to work and I gave Debbie a hand with the usual routine of the Monday mornings linen change.

As we stripped beds and remade them, I told her about the weekends events of Neroli and the baby, Matt and Neroli and of course, Jake.

"Wow, all in one long weekend, I didn't know you were interested in Jake Crankshaw."

"Well we have been seeing each other for a few weeks now but we kept it quiet."

"Why?"

"Oh um, I don't know really."

"And Matt Horton's shacked up with your friend?"

"Yeah..."

"And she's just had a baby and you knew nothing of her pregnancy?"

Debbie shakes her head and smiles as she threw me another batch of dirty sheets. "Lisa, you do attract a lot of drama into your life."

Slightly uncalled for, it's not like I go looking for it.

My mobile started ringing, I checked the display screen, it was Mrs Crankshaw. Ever since she's been organising the Kinky'n'Nice party the woman has been calling me non stop. I ignored it and switched off my phone.

I stuffed the stiff heavy sheets into the industrial sized washing machine and punched in the appropriate wash cycle. The water started running into the machine and I turned to prepare the next load when Debbie came in with yet another load

"We must go out for a drink sometime," Debbie said as she turned to leave the laundry.

"Oh that reminds me," I said as I pulled the invitation out of my pocket.

Mrs Crankshaw had given me a bunch of invitations to give out for the Kinky'n'Nice party, that's perhaps why she was calling me, to check up on my progress. But in fact I almost forgotten they were there 'till this morning when Jake spied them sitting on my dresser. I handed one to Debbie.

"I don't know if it's your sort of thing but if you wanted to come along and have a good laugh."

"Are you kidding!" exclaimed Debbie as she skimmed through the invitation.

"Nah you're right, silly isn't it? But it wasn't my idea, it just... "

"Oh no Lisa, I'll be there, don't you worry, I have a husband in prison, remember he's still got eighteen months inside and no communal visits left."

"Oh great," I said as Debbie checked her pager.

"Gotta go, see you tomorrow."

I was shocked, I had only 15 minutes left on my shift. Being in love makes your boring day go faster. I haven't thought of anything else except Jake since I saw him this morning. I was going round to see Matt and Neroli after. Matt had texted me earlier to say they were on their way home and to call around after I had finished my shift.

Bakery

"Morning Lisa, or should I say afternoon," Tim said checking his watch.

"Hi Tim, how are you?"

My phone rang, Mrs Crankshaw again, I ignored it.

"Millie's fine." I said, beating him to the post.

"Yes, I know, I was at her place this morning."

"Oh?"

"Great about Jake."

At Neroli, Matt, Tom and Baby's house

I was greeted by Tom who insisted I come see his new bedroom. I toured the wee cottage, which was full of furniture. Matt had stuck Stars Wars posters all over the walls of Tom's bedroom along with a Stars Wars bedspread. Tom was in Star Wars heaven. Baby Bailey was fast asleep in her crib. I goo-ed and clucked over her for a while. I had to hand it to Matt, he has done so well, I just hope Neroli's grateful.

My mobile rung again, I looked at the call screen, it was Mrs Crankshaw, what the hell is so bloody important! I couldn't ignore it this time, otherwise the woman will be hunting me.

"Sorry," I said to Matt and Neroli as I flipped open my phone.

"Hello Mrs Crankshaw."

"Lisa dear I have been trying to phone you all morning, what's the point of having a phone if you're not going to answer it."

I was ignoring you, I thought to myself.

"It's Jake!" Mrs Crankshaw sounded panicked.

"Jake!" I sat bolt upright, "what's the matter with him?"

"His mother died this morning," Mrs Crankshaw voice cracked, "I thought you should know."

At Jake's place

I don't know what I'm going to say to him. I've never met the woman. But how bloody inconvenient though, just when Jake and I were going to be a proper couple, his mum up and dies.

No, stop it, I told myself, it's not her fault and it could bring Jake and me closer together.

I noticed Pamela's oversized SUV parked outside. Jake was sitting on his sofa when I walked into the living room. Pamela was sitting beside him, too close I may add, she jumped when I came into the room. "Oh Lisa didn't hear you knock." I looked at Jake and he looked pale, "Jake," I began, "I'm so sorry. Mrs Crankshaw just phoned."

"I'll go make some more tea shall I," Pamela said as she got off the sofa, Jake gave her a fond smile. I waited 'till she left the room and made my way over to Jake to hug him.

"Thanks for coming," he said, shifting in his seat to avoid my hug. Bit startled by his coldness but then everyone deals with things differently.

"Apparently she took a bad turn through the night and they tried to call me then, but of course I wasn't here and you know, I don't carry a mobile or anything so they got the doctor to her, but she died before Aunty could find out where I was."

I felt a pang of guilt, while Jake and I were busy shagging his mum was dying.

Pamela came back through carrying the tray of tea followed by Mrs Crankshaw. For the rest of the afternoon there was chatter about the funeral arrangements, I tried to busy myself with making tea and washing up. Pamela was now sitting beside Jake once again.

Honestly does that women have to be involved in everything!

Things got heated when Mrs Crankshaw suggested that Jake should really try and get hold of his brother.

"I don't know where he is," Jake snapped at her when Mrs Crankshaw suggested it.

"Okay then," she said calmly, trying not to upset him. "Then what we should do is put a notice in the national paper and hope that he will see it."

"Well you could," said Jake coldly, "but the funeral's the day after tomorrow, let's hope he has time to get here."

Mrs Crankshaw gasped. "The day after tomorrow! Jake that's too soon, what about the viewing and remember you've got cousins that need time to travel from their various destinations."

"I have already spoken to the funeral director, everything's taken care of, Mum had planned her funeral so it would be what she wanted."

"But Jake," Mrs Crankshaw pleaded with him, "it's still such a rush, why can't we hold it on the Friday."

"Well, I've made my decision," he said standing up. "Now if you'll excuse me I want time to myself."

Mrs Crankshaw had tears welling up in her eyes she looked across at Pamela for support but she just shrugged. "Well it's his mother," she said before exiting the room.

I went over to Mrs Crankshaw and put my arm around her beefy shoulder. "Don't worry about him," I said handing her a tissue, "he'll come around, he's just a bit upset and there is a lot to think about."

"You're right dear." Mrs Crankshaw sniffed and patted my arm. "You're such a lovely girl and I know you and Jake are good friends, his mother was a lovely women Lisa, you would have liked her a lot."

I'm so bored and have nothing to do so I tapped on the bedroom door.

"Jake I'm going, I'll come back later. Jake?" The door swung open and Pamela appeared.

She closed the door behind her before speaking. "He's sleeping now," she informed me.

"Oh well, could you tell him when he wakes up that I'll be back later."

"If I'm still here," she sighed and looked at her nails, "I've to fetch the kids from school."

"Okay well, I'll just leave him a note then." I scribbled 'Back soon, love Lisa.'

"I'll leave this beside his bed then," said Pamela as she took the note from me. God what is she, his bodyguard!

Back home

Missed another call from Mum and Dad.

A quick shower and change of clothes as I need to get back to Jake's before Pamela snotty Horton gets back and takes over Jake's life again.

Jake has also got to eat so I was planning on making something for dinner and taking it there. I'm not exactly Jamie Oliver so I'm thinking macaroni cheese would be fine. But what if Jake doesn't like pasta? Well, too bad, that's all I can manage in such a short time frame.

Phoned Millie to tell her the news

I told Millie about Jake's mum. She said she knew because Tim told her.

"Oh, okay, I also heard he stayed the night last night."

"Yes, he's stayed a couple of times now, why?" Millie sounded defensive.

"You live an hour away Millie, what does he do, drive with his erection?"

"Ha bloody ha ha."

"What about Sid?" I pressed on. "Is he there when Tim stays over, I mean come on Millie wouldn't that be a bit weird."

"Sid's not here at night, he works now remember."

"Oh that's right."

I yakked on to Millie while I set about making my tea dish, I was in the middle of telling her about Matt and Neroli's love nest when I stopped to listen, I could hear the banging coming from the ceiling again but this time it was a lot louder.

"Lisa are you there?" asked Millie down the phone.

"I'm here, the banging started in the ceiling again."

"I thought you were going to get the exterminator out?"

"It was on my 'to do' list."

"Oh Lisa, you would have to be the worlds greatest procrastinator."

The thumping and banging was getting louder, I walked around the house trying to locate it. I had a terrible freaky feeling it's coming from the secret room.

"Millie," I whispered down the phone, "it's coming from the secret room."

"Well there are rats in there remember when we first discovered that room, one shot out then."

"Yes I know but Millie this doesn't sound like rats."

"Then open the door and find out." Millie said nonchalantly, like risking my life is no big deal.

"Alright but stay on the line and if I scream, hang up and call the police okay."

"The police, don't you mean the exterminator?"

"Millie I'm serious, what if it's a burglar?"

"At four in the afternoon, doubt it, but okay then, go in."

"Ready?"

"Ready"

Secret room

The door creaked just like in a horror film. I stopped to listen but the banging noise had stopped.

I'm feeling very freaked out. It must have come from this room as the noise had just stopped dead. But very relieved it's not a robber.

But it must be very big rat. Either way the noise has stopped.

"All clear," I said to Millie down the phone, "banging stopped, Millie, are you there?"

I waited for a reply "Millie?"

"Sorry," she said as she came back to the phone, "I just had to go to the toilet."

Back at Jake's house

There were a lot of people coming and going. It was a very busy evening. My macaroni cheese was outdone by Pamela's cottage pie, which Jake was tucking into a second helping of when I arrived.

I hardly had Jake to myself since the passing and the brief time I did have alone he seemed to shut down like I wasn't there.

Mrs Crankshaw put the advertisement in the paper for the next day to try and get hold of Rick, Jake's younger brother. Mrs Crankshaw was still upset but she did manage to convince Jake to move the funeral one day, to the Thursday, which Jake agreed too. But any mention of his brother was normally met with a snappy response from Jake.

Max, who had arrived after me, had a talk with Jake, who in turn, apologised to his aunty for the harsh words, and he agreed that she should go to the local policeman and see if they could locate Rick through national information with the hope that they could reach him. "I was going to do that anyway," she whispered to me as she put her coat on to go down to the police station "I know he's my nephew and I love him, but he can be such a stubborn arse."

Night before funeral

I finally had Jake to myself. No sign of Jake's brother. Pamela left for home to be there when her husband arrived, he was returning from yet another business trip, to attend the funeral.

I stayed over and it was an awkward night of a silent dinner followed by more silence watching TV. Jake lay beside me in the darkness. He wasn't asleep.

"Jake," I whispered to him, no response.

It had been like this all night. "Jake listen," I tried again, "I'm here to talk to."

"I know," he said reaching out and patting my thigh. We lay there in silence. It was playing on my mind all night to get Jake to talk about his brother as there were still a few anger issues. Could they be so important that he should pretend his brother didn't exist. I knew I was treading on eggshells mentioning this but I had to try.

I cleared my throat.

"Jake."

"Hmm."

"Are you still angry with your brother?"

"Lisa, drop it," he responded coldly.

"But Jake," I pleaded, "whether or not there are issues between you two and from what I understand it's over a girl, you are still brothers and you're acting like you don't care whether or not he comes to your mothers funeral."

"I'm not acting, I don't care. I don't care much for him at all." Jake threw the sheets off the bed and sat on the edge, "look Lisa!" there was anger building in his tone, "you don't know enough about what went on okay, so just drop it."

Our first fight. It should be very momentous occasion with lots of tears and make up sex but I'm too bloody angry.

"Then tell me!!" I shouted back. "I'm trying to understand, I'm trying to be here for you and I thought if you talk about it then it might help."

"What? You think I need *you*," he turned to look at me, his eyes cold.

I sat frozen. I felt like a knife had cut through me. Not angry anymore, now I just want to cry. "I'll go," I whispered as I climbed out of bed, which I felt like was in slow motion.

I could feel the lump in the back of my throat, the tears were spilling onto my cheeks as I fumbled round in the dark for my clothes and stumbled to the door.

"Oh for god sake!" Jake spat. "Lisa wait," he reached out and grabbed my wrist. "Look I will tell you, but then promise you will drop the subject. I'm not in the mood for talking about it okay. I'm sorry, but I've been under a lot of pressure. It wasn't just one thing with Rick, it was a whole lot of things.

Rick didn't have the passion for this farm, all he was interested in is money and trying to compete with me." He stopped and sighed, his voice was gentle now.

"It all started over a girl I had been dating, Rick had stolen her from me, but that was just the beginning, you see before Dad got sick, he semi-retired, handing the running of the farm to Rick and I.

Dad still kept his hand in but basically he stood back while I made all the decisions over the day to day running of the farm and Rick helped and took over the bookwork. But by the time Dad got sick I had found out that Rick had been irresponsible and ran up a lot of debt so the farm was in the red.

He had been pushing for a long time through Dad's illness to cut the farm into smaller parcels and sell it."

I remembered what Stubbs had told me about the feud the brother's had over the farm, but Stubbs told me it was Jake who wanted to sell the land.

He must have got the story wrong.

Jake continued. "He was always greedy, Rick, nothing or no-one else mattered. When I told him about Mary, the girl I fell in love with, he did everything in his power to take her away from me, all the lies he told her," Jake broke off.

"Is this the girl you wanted to marry, does she still live here?"

"No, she moved away after that."

Phew, last thing I need is competition.

Jake continued. "Anyway we paid off some of the debt and kept the farm going but then Dad passed away and the next day Rick had disappeared, no note, nothing, and it wasn't 'till after Dad's funeral that it was obvious he had gone, and then I learned he had run up more debts."

"Mum was devastated, with Rick gone and losing her husband as well, her health started to suffer and of course I couldn't look after her, thank goodness for Uncle Max and Aunty Barb." He turned to look at me. "So no, I'm not quite ready to forgive him yet."

Jake fell silent; I put my arms around him and his head fell onto my chest.

What a bastard his brother was, nothing like Jake. Maybe it was a good thing that he's not around, and his poor mother, how could her son do that to her after losing his father?

"Jake I'm sorry," I whispered. "I don't blame you for being angry."

He sat back up and looked at me before his eyes fell to my chest. "Are you still going to stay?" he asked, tracing his finger round the shape of my breasts.

"Do you feel better?" I asked.

"Oh yes," he said, taking my hand and placing it on his groin, "much better."

Make-up sex, so much fun.

Facebook Status Update.

Lisa Collins: What to wear, what to wear.

Lisa changed her 'It's complicated' to 'In a relationship with Jake Crankshaw'.

12

Day of funeral

I sat in the back row as the congregation started moving in. I was lucky I managed to get a seat, the whole town seemed to be here, local shopkeepers shut down for the morning, there was only skeleton staff on at the nursing home, the only thing still running was the local school. Up front I could see the coffin and it sent shudders down my spine. It could very easily be one of my parents up there and the very thought got me all choked up.

Which reminds me, I must give them a call.

The sound of the music coming through the speakers pulled me from my thoughts as the minister asked the congregation to rise. I stood up, I could see Pamela through the crowd, near to the front with her Basil Fawlty husband. Maggie was on the opposite side, two rows up from me, she turned to smile at me and I waved back.

The doors opened and in entered Jake with Mrs Crankshaw beside him, followed by Max, a rather robust young woman and a gangly looking young man. I'm guessing they were the Crankshaw offspring.

"Hi Lisa," whispered Tim as he squeezed in beside me.

"Oh hi Tim," I whispered back.

"Did I miss anything?" he asked as if he just stepped into a movie theatre. The family sat down in the vacant pews in the front row. I saw Pamela reach forward and put her hand on Jake's shoulder.

"How come you're not up there with Jake?" whispered Tim.

Yes it should be me consoling him but you see this morning just as I was leaving to go home and get showered and changed, I asked Jake if he wanted me to be by his side, he shook his head and said he didn't want to be smothered.

I waved my hand at Tim as if it wasn't bothering me. "Ah, you know it's a family thing."

"Yeah, s'posse." Tim shrugged.

The minister asked the congregation to rise again to sing Amazing Grace. Have to admit, I'm a bit bored, not being insensitive but it's far more interesting if you know the person.

I engaged Tim in whispered conversation by asking him questions like, who is sitting over there and did he use caged eggs or free range in his pastries? Jake had now got up to speak. He talked about his mother's interests and what it was like growing up, no mention of his brother. Jake looked like he was holding it together, every now and then his voice broke and he paused to get himself together, my heart broke for him.

Next Mrs Crankshaw got up and spoke about her sister-in-law and the early days in the CWA. My gaze shifted to the stained glass windows. It was a beautiful sunny day and a gentle breeze was flowing through the open doors of the church.

I noticed a man standing outside the church doors just off to the left a bit where he could not be seen. Looks very familiar, I'm very sure I've seen him before. Strained eyes to get a better look at him.

Oh my god!

I recognised his clothes, it was the hunter!

Tried to locate the policeman through the faces of the congregation, to tell him of suspected rooster thief. No sign of policeman, which was typical. Whole town turns up and the one person you need is not here.

Casually glanced at hunter again, he caught my eye, I couldn't see his face underneath the wide brim hat and untidy beard, but I could feel his gaze cut straight through me, daring me to tell on him. I quickly tore my gaze away and nudged Tim. "Don't look now," I whispered, "but who's that guy outside standing just to the left of the doors?"

Tim turned and strained his neck to look. "I don't see anyone," he whispered back.

Tim's right, there's no one there. Strange, but obviously not a funeral goer.

Maybe he just stopped by to see why the whole town, besides

policeman, are packed inside a church on a sunny day and is now off to steal more roosters.

A few more people got up with memories to share and then Mrs Crankshaw's plump daughter got up and spoke about the early days growing up on the farm and she mentioned Rick on a number of occasions. I couldn't see Jake's face but I could see his shoulders tense up every time Rick's name was mentioned.

Finished (thank god)

I felt like a fish out of water amongst the congregation outside the church steps mumbling things like 'lovely service'. Tim looked like he felt the same way, I moved over to where he was as he puffed away on a cigarette. I must admit Tim looked good in his suit but I still find it difficult to see what Millie sees in him.

Jake and family members were now crowded round the hearse saying their final goodbyes.

Tried to engage Tim in conversation again, I asked if he was seeing Millie again tonight.

"She's coming down here." Tim said, "I thought she mentioned it to you."

Bit put out, Millie was my friend. "Oh well no, she didn't, but that's okay, she's always got a bed at my place anyway."

"Um actually Lisa, I think she's staying with me."

"Oh, of course," I stood there trying to find something else to say.

Why did Millie pick the quiet ones?

I looked around to see if I could make a hasty exit when I saw him again, the hunter, in the background leaning on a lamppost taking in the crowd. I tried to grab Jake's attention but he was being smothered with hugs from the townsfolk.

Anyway it's not a good time to be pointing out rooster thieves.

Tim was now engaged in conversation with some elderly gentleman. I looked towards the hunter again just in time to see him cross the street and disappear out of sight.

I moved towards Jake through the whispered conversations as to why Rick hadn't shown up and asked him if he wanted me to accompany him to the cemetery. Pamela overheard and told me that its family only going to the cemetery.

But Pamela went and she's not bloody family.

Arrived home

I feel drained. Funerals do that to you whether you were close to the person or not, all the emotions of those around you seemed to drain your emotions.

I don't remember pulling my car to a stop, I don't even remember getting out of the car, my eyes were fixed on the house because there in the side wall were two bi-fold doors.

Sid and another young guy, who I was introduced to as John,

were packing up their tools amidst the wood shavings.

"Sid," I gasped, "it's fantastic!"

"I tried to call to say we were coming, you didn't answer. But your back door was unlocked anyway."

I stared in awe at my new doors. I opened one and walked into my living room; there was so much light in here now, I couldn't believe the difference it made.

I thanked both men over and over until they handed me the bill.

Sid was sitting on the porch with a beer in his hand when I returned after seeing his builder friend off.

"Thanks Sid," I said once again.

"No problem," he replied draining his bottle and opening another. "Do you mind if I stay here the weekend?" he asked, "it's just so peaceful out here."

I couldn't say no, Sid just spent three hours putting doors in. I said he could and then realised that I may have invited Tim over for dinner in a desperate attempt to make conversation. "Um Sid, what's Millie up to this weekend?" I asked. He looked at me puzzled. "You mean you don't know? She's here already, she came down with me, she's at that guys place."

Awkward silence before asking if he's okay with that.

Sid shrugged and stood up. "Well nothing I can do about it, fate is fate and obviously the universe doesn't want us to be together. I'm going for a walk," he snapped.

On the way to Jake's house

I had left Sid meditating with Bonnie and Clyde. I told him last night that I had invited Tim to come round with Millie tonight and he said that it's okay he was going down to the pub anyway.

I drove down the road towards Jake's and I could see Pamela's SUV pulling out of Jake's drive again. God that women is unbelievable, what is she doing, delivering more casseroles? Jake must get really sick of her. She pulled to the side of the road as I drove closer and waved me down.

What does she want now, to tell me that I cannot see Jake again, what was she, his mother?

Oops, that was a bit insensitive, but she certainly acts like it. I wound down the car window.

Wanted to ask her if Jake can come out to play, but I decided against it.

"Hello Lisa," she trilled out her car window, "on your way to Jakes? I've just been there myself picking up my dishes from yesterday."

Is that what she wanted to tell me, that she picked her dishes up, well that is just thrilling!

"Anyhoo," she trilled over the top of the running motor, "I have your invoice here for the goats." She leaned over and handed me a white envelope through the window.

"If it could be paid by the end of the month that would be great."

Her SUV roared off, and I opened the envelope.

The invoice was for two x boars @ $50 each, plus GST, plus interest of 2% for late payment.

Interest?

That bloody sly, pruned face woman, interest! For late payment. I was fuming, wait 'till I tell Jake, then he will be able to see through that women once and for all. I slammed the car into gear and headed off towards Jake's.

At Jake's house

"Jake you'll never guess what Pamela's done."

Jake called out from the bathroom and said to give him a moment. The place looked like a bomb had hit it. I made myself useful and started clearing the table, there was a stack of clean casserole dishes piled on the table, I flipped them over to see if any of them had names.

Most of them belong to Mrs Crankshaw, one of Pamela's that she must've missed.

I felt like accidentally dropping Pamela's dish on floor, after all she charges interest so she can afford a new one, but decided against it. I started to stack the mountain of papers that were littered over the table.

Underneath the mess were some house plans and a map of the farm.

I'm not being nosey but the house plans looked great. I scanned over them and realised these plans are not for just one house but for multiple houses. There were also survey applications and some plans for the drainage.

And they were all addressed to Jake.

What the hell?

Judging by all the paperwork, it looked like Jake was planning to build a whole housing estate.

"What are you doing?" came Jake's voice behind me.

I jumped in fright. "Um, just tiding up," I said as I gathered up the papers and put them aside. Jake came over and took them from me and put them in a drawer.

"I don't need a housekeeper," he said coldly.

"I'm sorry," I mumbled, "just thought I would help."

He slammed the drawer shut to demonstrate his dislike.

Great, back to Jekyll and Hyde thing again.

"So what has Pamela done?" he asked, his eyes darting to the invoice I still had clutched in my hand.

"Oh! Well she's invoiced me for the goats but she's added 2% interest for late payment! Late payment, she's only just given me the invoice."

"So?" Jake's voice had a sarcastic edge to it.

"Its only 2%, it won't break the bank."

"It's not the money, it's the principle," I trailed off; clearly Jake's not interested in hearing about it. He shrugged and moved off towards the kettle and started to fill it. My face was hot with rage, I tried to calm down while I watched him get two mugs down from the cupboard. Why is he acting like this? All moody and sullen you would think ...... oh wait, I realised he's only just buried his mum yesterday and now I want to slap myself for being so insensitive and spouting off to him about a stupid thing like an invoice. Stuffing the invoice in my pocket I moved towards him and slipped my arms around his waist.

"I'm sorry," I murmured, "how are you today?" His shoulders seemed to tense.

"Fine!" he pulled out of my grasp and reached for the milk, "I'm just a bit tired that's all."

I nodded in understanding, sensitive way.

"I've got to go and sort Mum's stuff out at the home."

Jake lit a cigarette and handed me my cup and I followed him to the front porch, trying hard to avoid the goat droppings left by Jake's four-legged lawnmower.

"I thought you only smoked after sex?" I asked as I sat down on the broken, weather beaten sofa.

"Lisa, give me a break," he snapped, "it's been a very stressful couple of days."

"Sorry," I murmured, "just trying to make conversation."

"Well don't!" he snapped even louder. He might as well have slapped me in the face, it had the same effect.

Jake rubbed his forehead in frustration.

"Sorry," he said, "didn't mean to snap it's just that..."

"It's been a very stressful time," I finished.

We sat in silence for a while looking out over the green pastures sipping our tea.

The scenery was breathtaking, the countryside seemed to go on forever and the cattle in the far off paddocks look like little white specks. "This is so beautiful," I whispered to no one in particular. Jake looked at me puzzled for a while then his face broke into a smile, "I aim to please," he teased. "I've got to go and collect Mum's stuff, so you want to come for a ride?"

I couldn't think of anything worse than collecting a dead woman's stuff but I wanted to be with Jake so I said that I would and he said "then after that we'll get in the car and drive to the city."

Ha, ha, so funny.

I asked Jake to call into Pamela's house so I could pay her stupid invoice after we drove back from spending the afternoon packing boxes at the home.

Not much to pack, a few nightgowns, photos and personal belongings. Must admit I was really bored and the place smelt like old people, so I was pleased to be out of there.

Jake was really sweet, holding my hand like teenagers do as we drove into the Horton's place.

It was every bit of what I imagined it to be. The brick two story grand manor with it's lion statues at the entrance to the drive, carefully pruned hedges and a pond in the middle of the sweeping lawn. It was so Pamela and I kind of wondered how the Horton's made their money, but then again if they charge interest on every bloody invoice then I'm clearly not surprised. Jake turned off the engine, I made my way to the door and rang the bell.

An older woman answered the door, her greying hair tied neatly back into a bun. She rubbed her hands on her checked apron. "May I help you?" she asked.

"I'm Lisa, I'm here to pay an invoice."

"Its okay Ester," Pamela's voice came up behind her, "I've got it."

The old lady moved off. "I'm just here to pay your invoice," I said to Pamela, who strained her neck to look past me.

"Oh Jake's with you I see. Ester!" she called the old lady back, "see to this would you," she barked as she pushed past me and headed over to Jake.

I handed the invoice to the woman while she instructed me to follow her so she can write me a receipt.

I stood in the office while Ester tried to find the receipt book on the huge mahogany desk.

There were ribbons and trophies all over the room from the Goat Society, Diplomas for Business Studies hanging on the wall. "So are you a relative?" I asked the old women trying to make conversation.

"Housekeeper and nanny. Name?" Ester asked me as she located the receipt book and flipped it open. So that's why Pamela looked so good I thought to myself, with a housekeeper and a nanny she doesn't have to do a damn thing other than meddle in peoples lives. Ester scribbled my name down and handed me the receipt as I handed over my cheque.

Pamela was still talking to Jake through the car window when I returned, she moved off as I opened the car door to the passenger side. "Thank you for settling that Lisa," she said as she made her way back towards the house.

Jake seems moody again as he said nothing and slammed the car into reverse.

Back home

I asked Jake if he wanted to come round as Millie's coming for a bloody good night. But he declined saying he was tired and not really in the mood for company, I took that as my cue to bugger off.

Matt's car was there when I arrived home.

God please don't tell me Matt has broken it off with Neroli already.

"Hey," Matt nodded to me as I entered the house to find him and Sid lazing about on the sofa watching Matt's DVD of 'Jackass'.

"Is everything okay?" I asked, warily looking round for any sign that he may have brought a bag of clothes with him.

"Wait for it," Matt sat forward and pointed to the TV, ignoring my question, "you should see what this dude does," he said to Sid, who was also eagerly sitting on the edge of the sofa "wait... wait... awhhh!!" they said in unison, "wicked man."

"Matt!" I snapped.

"What, oh yeah," he said turning his attention back to me, "fine, just returning the lawnmower."

"Returning? I didn't know you borrowed it."

"Yeah the other night when you were at Jake's – watch what he does now, watching, watching, awwhh."

Sid fell into fits of laughter.

Stupid movie.

I studied the contents of the fridge, I'm really not in the mood for cooking and didn't see why I had to as it was Millie who suggested having a bloody good night, so she can arrange the food. I shut the fridge, reached for my phone and texted Millie to pick up some pizzas in the village on her way out.

Very rude text message received back but I took that as a yes.

"How's it going with Jake?" asked Matt coming into the kitchen for another beer. "I've heard you two been shagging like rabbits. I'll just let Neroli know I'm still here."

"So things are going well with Neroli and the kids?" I asked.

"Yeah sweet," he nodded putting the phone to his ear. After murmured conversation Matt snapped his phone shut and now looking happy 'cause Neroli said he can stay for a bloody good night because she is tired and is going to have an early night.

I had consumed three glasses of wine by the time Millie and Tim arrived with pizzas'.

Sid sulkily announced he was going to the pub and Tim looked uncomfortable and insisted that he should be the one to leave. My eyes silently pleaded with Millie to do something but she seemed oblivious to the tension she had created.

God Millie's so thoughtless.

Sid walked out the door and I ran after him, pleading that he should stay and have some pizza at least, which he agreed.

Tim offered his hand to Sid when he came back through the living room, which Sid ignored. But with pizzas' consumed and more beers' drunk, both Tim and Sid let their guard down with one another. Tim, like Sid, was quiet by nature so the fact that they managed to say anything at all to each other, even though nasty at times, was in fact in itself, a miracle.

I was now onto the second bottle of wine, which was justified because we did have my new bi-fold doors to christen, which Millie approved of.

I wished Jake had stayed on, we were having such a bloody

good night. My stomach was sore from laughing so much. Sid and Matt disappeared outside at intervals and every time they came back their eyes seemed to disappear into their sockets and their silly grins seemed to get bigger. We were up to our sixth game of charades when Matt excused himself to go to the toilet. I was trying to guess what Millie was doing as she lay on the floor kicking her legs, "you're a dead ant," I called out and we both fell about laughing again.

Bloody good night.

"Um Lisa," Matt came back through to the living room looking slightly pale.

"What?" I said, wiping a tear from my cheek from laughing so much.

"Well I went outside for a slash and then I needed a crap, so I went to the toilet but your light's blown so I was sitting in the dark and .... well there's a light coming through your ceiling."

13

In toilet

Yes, definitely a light coming through a tiny crack in the ceiling. Sid turned all the lights in the house off just to be sure it wasn't a reflection off something. But there it was; a light coming from the assumed attic.

"We should make the hole bigger," said Matt. I shook my head, I could just imagine Matt with a hammer in his hand pounding away at the ceiling with debris falling everywhere.

Matt suggested that it must be the light that was helping the plants in the ceiling along and that it must be on a timer. Well he didn't say that exactly, because I managed to shut him up before he said it. Millie, Sid and Tim were looking at us bizarrely.

Matt up the ladder

Matt is taking boards off the window to the dope room, but strangely enough no light.

Millie, Sid and Tim looking strangely at Matt up the ladder.

Back in living room

Light still coming through ceiling in toilet. Not coming from dope room so I'm a bit puzzled. Tim spoke up.

"I remember coming here as a kid. Mum was friends with Flora, the previous owner, and the house pretty much looked the way it does now, but I remember Mum asking Flora about the attic and she said," Tim paused for effect; we leaned in closer waiting for his reply, "she said the stairs were blocked off." Tim looking enthused and glanced at our faces for a reaction.

"And?" Millie probed him.

"Well that was it."

"What a dickhead," Sid mumbled.

"Look," I said patiently to Tim, "we know there must be stairs, but where in the house?"

"The secret room!" Millie and I said in unison as she leapt to her feet and I rushed off in the other direction to grab the torch.

In secret room

"I can't see anything," said Millie. There was no sign of any stairs, just the old wardrobe. "What about that door?" asked Matt, pointing to the door opposite the wardrobe.

"No that just goes to the spare room," I said. "Besides the door's locked and we can't open it."

Tim looked about the room taking in the old wardrobe.

"This must be worth a mint," he said, "what's it doing in here?"

"We couldn't shift it," Millie said.

"Well we could shift it now," I suggested.

"Yeah I'll give you a hand," said Tim.

Sid turned on his heal and headed out the room muttering something about rats so we all took a side each.

"Ready, one, two…"

"Lisa!" Tim gasps while Matt let out an involuntary squeal.

"Oh god! What now, more rats?"

"No, I think we might have found your staircase."

A door

I'm so excited, bloody good night turning into a bloody great night. We were all surprised the door opened with ease and behind it was a staircase with the light beaming down from the attic. Millie pushed me in front of her saying it's my creepy staircase so I should go first. Murmurs of agreement from Matt, Tim and Sid. But then Sid decided not to go up the stairs, saying he's too stoned and the staircase is too steep and he'll stay down here just in case someone needs to dial 000.

Finally up staircase

I couldn't believe my eyes. Millie gasped and Tim simply said, "What the..?"

We reached the top only to discover the source of the light came from a lamp powered by electrical cords running through the attic and down through a hole in the floor.

In the corner was an old mattress with blankets and a pillow. Empty food packets littered the floor and tins' of cat food were stacked in one corner.

Oh my god Randy Puss. No wonder he looked so fat!

Back in living room

I had gone from drunk to sober in three seconds flat. Millie handed me a gin to calm my nerves. I was visibly shaken. I gripped the glass with both hands to steady myself enough to take a sip.

There has been somebody living in the roof, *my roof,* the whole time.

When I showered, when I sang and danced like no one was watching. Oh god, even when Jake and I were having *sex*!

I whimpered to Millie.

"Don't worry the police are on their way," she gave me a re-assuring pat on the arm.

"Well I'm outta here," said Matt.

"Yeah me too," said Sid.

"What! Why?" Millie snapped.

"Well in case you haven't noticed," Matt said, "Sid and I are off our faces on pot. We're not hanging about for any cops man."

"But you have to stay," said Tim, "they're going to want all our stories."

"Not mine," Sid said as he turned to leave.

Then it dawns on me; pot. "Oh no, Matt," I stood up in a panic grabbing him by the arm. "What about the dope in the ceiling."

"You're growing dope!" exclaimed Tim, his eyes like saucers.

"Lisa," Matt took me by the shoulders and looked directly into my eyes as if he was going to break into some meaningful words of wisdom.

"Deny. Deny everything," he said before he and Sid made a hasty exit.

Arrival of police

The police took their time arriving, apologising for their delay as there had been a brawl at the pub. Millie had taken them up to show them the room. I couldn't bring myself to go back up there, not yet. I could hear their murmured voices coming from the ceiling.

God how could I have been so stupid, how could I have not noticed I had a squatter. Now it was all making sense, the banging at night, food disappearing from my cupboards, the fact that Randy Puss never ate any food I left for him but weighed 250 pounds.

The police came back into the room followed by Millie and started their questions.

When satisfied that they had enough, I turned to Millie.

"What if someone mentally disturbed was living up there," I sobbed, "just waiting for the right time to kill me." Millie put her arm around me.

"Well I doubt that miss," the short balding policeman said. "If he or she wanted to kill you then they would have done it by now."

"Well that's reassuring," said Millie rolling her eyes.

The younger looking policeman looked at his watch. "Look we will have a quick look around outside, is there somewhere else you can stay tonight?"

"She can come back to my place tonight," Tim piped up.

"Great and tomorrow we will start our investigation, but it looks like you have a squatter so my advice is lock the doors tonight, take all valuables with you and a team will come out tomorrow."

On Tim's sofa

It's morning already and I have a headache. Predicting it was early as the flat was quiet and I'm in desperate need of a coffee. I was quite anxious to get back to the house but terrified that a squatter is sitting waiting for me with an axe.

My phone beeped an hour later after two cups of coffee and a couple of aspirin and me crying to the universe that it was unfair and it needs to stop sending me pervert squatters.

It was a message from Sid to say he's just returned to the house after crashing at Matt's and the police are here.

I scribbled a note to Millie and fished in my bag for my car keys but I had a sudden realisation. Did I drive here last night, is my car actually here? I looked out the front window to see my car in the driveway, which was scary 'cause I don't remember driving last night and I would have been like *1,000* times over the limit.

Back at mine and pervert squatter's house

There were at least three policemen scouting the place. The young stocky policeman greeted me.

"From what we found so far," he said, sounding formal like, "is that he or she gained access by entering through the back door and entered the attic through the door in the smaller room."

"But that door doesn't open," I said, "I tried it."

"Yes it was locked by key," he regarded me for a second before asking.

"Have you given keys to anyone, friends?"

I thought about it "No, I have only got one set. I often found my back door unlocked even though I was sure I locked it."

He nodded as he flipped open his notebook and scribbled something down.

"Well apart from a few Hustler magazines and of course the mattress and blankets, we haven't found a lot to give us any clues to who he might be, so we are guessing that he moved out a long time ago and forgot about the light or..." he trailed off.

"Or what?"

He took a deep breath. "Or he's using this place as a hide-out and we are also guessing it's someone you might know. Have you had anyone that might be known to have a fixation on you?"

"Sarg, I think we might have found another room," said his colleague. I followed them round the side of the house, "up there," the young constable pointed to the boarded window. My heart stopped beating while I stood there frozen in terror. Blood started to rush heavily in my ears.

I snapped back to the present, the sergeant and constable were both looking at me

"I'm sorry, what?"

"Do you know what is up there?" he asked.

"Um...no."

"Okay grab a ladder," he instructed. There was nothing I could do but watch what was going on in front of my eyes. The young constable pulled the ladder in position and started to climb.

Sid appeared at my side.

"Where have you been?" I asked.

"Feeding the hens and goats."

'Oh, thanks."

"What's up there?" Sid asked.

"The dope room," I whispered.

"Oh, well see ya."

They started attacking the board that Matt had put over the window. I shut my eyes and tried not to think about what prison life must be like.

"Whoever nailed this shut did a shoddy job," the constable shouted to his colleague below. I opened one eye as the board hit the ground below.

Oh god!

The constable shined the torch through the hole in the wall. "I'm going in," he shouted as his legs disappeared. It might have been 30 seconds it might have been 30 years but how long I had been standing there in absolute terror I didn't know. I had the same feeling that I had back in high school when I had been caught smoking in the male toilets (I only did that 'cause I was sooo in love with Andrew McMillan at the time) and standing outside the principal's office while they telephoned my mother, the absolute terror of the unknown punishment to come.

But I will just have to cope with it the same way as I coped with it back then.

Deny everything.

"Nothing up here!" The constable shouted as he made his way carefully back through the hole and onto the ladder.

I snapped back from my comatose state of terror.

"Nothing?" I asked.

"No, just an empty room," said the constable jumping the last few throngs of the ladder.

"We'll go and collect a few things from the attic for evidence and Mick, if you could nail that board back on and..."

"Hang on a minute," I interrupted. "What do you mean there's nothing up there?"

"There's nothing up there unless you count the cobwebs," he chuckled.

"I don't think so," I said, grabbing the torch from his hands.

I climbed up the ladder to see for myself. I shined the light through the hole trying carefully not to snag my sleeve on the jagged glass. The room was empty, all the marijuana had gone. The only thing that remained was a piece of frayed bailing twine hanging from the rafters.

Bloody Matt, wait 'till I get my hands on the little shit.

After promising they will keep in touch and that I should get a dog, the policeman left. Sid had come back moments after their departure.

"So are you busted?" he asked grabbing a beer from the fridge.

"No and I thank you very much for leaving me."

"So what did they say?"

"Nothing, it wasn't there."

"What wasn't there?"

"The dope you idiot!" I snapped, "Matt must have taken the rest. I can't trust that little shit anymore."

"But you don't smoke the stuff."

"But it's still my house."

"Yeah, yours and the hobo living upstairs," I let that one slide, for Sid that was his best attempt in humour.

We both stood in silence. I started reflecting on what to do now. It was so unfair, this was supposed to be my home and as I looked around I felt like this wasn't my house.

Sid broke the silence.

"I could stay with you 'till this was sorted out," he said as if he just read my mind.

"Thanks Sid," I smiled at him. "But what about your job and the alien watching, you can't just leave that, this could go on for a while."

"Pff ... it's nothing. I could get some temporary work on the farms' and it's my uncle's business that I work for, I'll explain, he will understand."

So it's sorted, Sid will be staying with me.

And in an odd way I'm feeling pretty good about that.

Lying on my bed later on that day, I gazed up at the ceiling.

All this time someone was living just above me watching me when I showered, dressed, slept, had sex.

Randy Puss jumped up on the bed beside me. "And as for you, you traitor," I said stroking his ears, "go find your owner and tell him to piss off."

A week later

The next few days went on as normal, you know, work, chores, Sid, Jake. Stranger living in ceiling.

I sat on the porch sorting the merchandise so it would be ready for the 'ladies party', as Mrs Crankshaw puts it. Jake had offered Sid a few days work helping out with calving, which was sweet of him.

Jake's reaction was solemn when I told him of the discovery and when I showed him the attic he went slightly pale and seemed edgy after that, as if it was my fault and somehow I had invited the squatter. But he hasn't mentioned it again since. I also had to admit I was disappointed Jake didn't offer for me to stay with him although Sid was here, I felt edgy and have even taken to showering in my underwear.

Millie had gone back to the city but promised to be back for the Kinky'n'Nice party in the weekend.

The phone rang as I pulled the crotchless knickers from the box, it was Sergeant Donald, the young policeman who investigated.

"Just to let you know we ran the fingerprints through but we came up a blank. I'm afraid nothing else we could do but suggest you change your locks, maybe get a dog for protection, things like that. I have a pamphlet on the subject, I'll post it to you. There are some really helpful hints in there."

So basically they said that the creepy trespasser had moved on, good luck to you and that was that. Case closed, don't call us, we'll call you.

Just bloody fantastic.

Slammed the receiver down. Now what? Get on as normal, sell the house, move back to the city. I needed a sign from the universe. After all, the universe is responsible for sending me into the country with hillbillies and pervy squatters, it should get me out of this mess.

Oh, the phones ringing.

"Hello."

"Hey man, what's up?"

"Listen Matt you little shit." I hadn't seen Matt or spoken to him since that night of discovering squatter. "Taking my lawnmower without asking is one thing but stealing the dope from me and not telling me is another."

"Whoa man."

"No you listen to me," I snapped pointing my finger at the phone.

"The cops checked out the room in the ceiling.

I was shitting bricks with the thought I could be caught with an estimated 100 plants of over dried dope and it wasn't there. If I had known that you had taken it, I wouldn't have had my life cut short with the worry."

"But I didn't take it man, god, chill out."

"Chill out! How could I chill out, and stop lying to me."

"I'm not."

"You are."

"I didn't take it, I swear on my manhood, I didn't take it."

"Your manhood! Matt just remember I have seen your manhood and I wouldn't be making promises with it."

"Whoa man, now you've gone too far."

"Shut up Matt and put Neroli on the phone."

"Hello."

"Neroli hi, did you know your boyfriend is an immature lying twat."

"Oh! Is he? Um, I didn't know that, um, thanks for telling me."

She must have handed the phone back to Matt as his pleading, whining voice came back on the line.

"Look Lisa I didn't take it, okay. I don't know how to prove it to you but please believe me I didn't."

I ran my fingers through my hair in frustration and tried to calm myself down. I sat there thinking about it. Matt may be a lot of things but I knew deep down he wouldn't do anything like that really, also it's not like he's the only suspect now since the discovery of the squatter.

"Yeah I believe you," I sighed. "Sorry."

"It's okay. Did you mean it when you said I had a small manhood?"

"I didn't say it was small," my mouth started to twitch a little.

"Oh sweet, but it's okay? Isn't it?"

"Matt did you ring me about something?"

"Oh yeah, so what happened at the pub the other night between Jake and my stepfather?"

"What night, what happened?"

"Jake didn't tell you? Aw man I wish I was there. The night the coppers came to your place to check out the squatter, yeah well apparently they had just been to a brawl at the pub, it was between Jake and my stepfather."

Pamela's husband? I tried to imagine Basil Fawlty type husband in a punch up.

"It started in the car park and no one knew what it was about because no one saw what started it and I thought you would know since you're shagging him and all."

I was puzzled. Jake never mentioned a fight, anyway he said he was going straight home after he dropped me off because he was tired that night.

Seems odd that he didn't mention it to me.

Why didn't he mention it to me?

Right, that's it, I'm going round there.

At Jake's house

Jake's happy to see me as I pulled up to find him just getting in from the farm.

"This must be your lucky day," he said planting a kiss on my cheek. "I've just finished work so you can take me to the shower and wash me clean. What's wrong?"

"Did you get into a fight the other night?" I asked.

"Oh, ha, ha, did you hear about that?" he said.

"Yeah, so what happened, why were you fighting with Pamela's husband?"

"I wasn't fighting, it was a disagreement."

"So why didn't you tell me the other day?"

"It wasn't important."

"It doesn't have to be important Jake I'm your girlfriend, you don't get into a fight every day so I just don't understand why you didn't tell me?"

"Okay calm down, I didn't think okay, I'm sorry. Charles Horton is just a total dick who I've disliked for a long time, it was a disagreement over a business thing. I went to the pub to pick up some beer and he was in the car park when I came out, are you satisfied?"

Okay maybe I overreacted a tiny bit.

Later in Jake's bed

"You're selling?" Jake asked me.

"That was the original plan," I said rolling onto my back. "Part of me doesn't want to go, but every time I step into the place now I feel uneasy."

"Why, because of that squatter? Whoever he is."

I nodded.

Jake rolled onto his side and propped himself up onto his elbow. "You can't let some homeless tosser push you out of your own house."

"Yes I know but it doesn't feel like my home anymore."

"So if you sell up? What would you do, go back to the city?"

I didn't answer Jake. I thought about my original plan of moving back to city. But I like it here. I'm far more suited to this lifestyle. I don't think I could go back to the noise and I like my job here, as hideous as it is sometimes, I do like it.

We fell silent for a while, getting lost in our own thoughts. I closed my eyes and started to drift into a semi conscious state when I heard Jake speak

"Then move in here with me?" he said.

I sat bolt upright.

"What did you say?"

"Move in with me."

"Are you serious?"

"Yeah well why not? Sell that place, move in with me."

Jake adjusted himself up on the pillows. "I would have to charge you lodgings of course, but you will be helping me out cash wise, so it's a win win, what do you say?"

What do I say? I say universe didn't have it in for me. It stuck that pervy squatter in my attic to make me sell the house so Jake would have an opportunity to ask me to move in with him and then I can become country wife like Pamela.

Yes, yes, yes.

I turned to him smiling. "Would I have to wash your undies?"

Facebook status update.

Lisa Collins: I hate pervy stalkers. Hate, hate, hate.

Lisa changed her 'In a relationship with Jake Crankshaw' to 'In a de'facto relationship with Jake Crankshaw'.

14

Now to break the news to Millie.

"You want to sell now!" she exclaimed.

"Well why not?"

"Because it's not finished."

Anyway we had a big, huge argument. She said that I wouldn't get the return on it. I said that I didn't care and how would she like it if a pervert squatter guy was watching her have sex and sing while shaving her legs, and she said that she is the project manger and in her opinion no one wants to buy a half finished house, and I said...

Never mind.

But now she's barely talking to me and she is so mad that I haven't even had they balls to tell her that I'm moving in with Jake yet, and besides I have phoned some estate agents and they said that prices have gone up in the area and after I told them that the house renovations were not complete they said that most people add their own finishing touches to a place so it's a waste of time doing renovations.

So my house is officially on the market.

I told Sid and now I'm standing over him while he rings Millie to tell her.

I'm not scared of her just, well, better she hears it from someone else first, give her time to calm down.

The word had got around town that there was a bit of trouble at my place but no one knew exactly what. Debbie asked me what had been stolen as she heard I had been burgled. Stubbs had told me that he heard from a guy called Dave whose sister works in the pharmacy that I was hiding some illegal immigrants. Millie had asked Tim not to say anything so he just shrugged when anyone asked him. I didn't want to tell anyone the full story. Well apart from Jake of course. I felt stupid enough that I wasn't aware someone was in my roof. So I told people that I had a break-in but nothing was stolen and the towns folk held an emergency community watch meeting two nights ago. Apparently they hadn't had any sort of burglary or break-in since 1979 or something.

Night of Kinky'n'Nice party

Millie's here with me and she has a face like thunder. But I'm pleased to say she's talking to me again even though she said something like....

Better not repeat it.

The back room of the town hall looked fabulous. Mrs Crankshaw had hung up red sheer fabric on the walls and draped black lace trim around the chairs. There were candles burning around the tables, a make-shift curtain hung to one side with a sign saying 'dressing room' and a buffet of food and beverages on trestles tables in the corner.

"Ah Lisa," Mrs Crankshaw greeted as she negotiated her chubby legs off a foot stool, "what do you think?"

"It's amazing," I gasped looking around. "You've done a fantastic job."

She patted me on the arm. "Thank you dear, I think it's best to be in the mood. Now let me have a look at the merchandise."

Millie lugged the boxes from the car as Mrs Crankshaw and I unpacked it all and laid it out.

"We should just put one of each line on display," I suggested, "and order forms at the end so they can tick off what they want and come and pay and collect by the door when they leave."

"Brilliant dear," Mrs Crankshaw beamed. "Millie dear that can be your job."

"Oh, okay." Millie answered.

"No I can do that," I said.

"No Lisa dear I've got a much more exciting job in mind for you," she said as she pulled out a red and black teddy with black fishnet stockings and suspenders.

"Here," she said throwing the outfit at me, "you can greet our guests at the door and hand out the order forms."

"You want me to wear this?" I asked in horror.

Millie snorted with laughter.

"Yes, oh Lisa don't look at me like that! I would wear it but it would look far better on you than on me."

"Yes but ..."

"And it's not cold tonight, you have to get with the theme Lisa, so come on." She ushered me into the makeshift dressing room.

"And after you put that on I have your headpiece here."

I emerged from the curtain. Millie curled over in fits of laughter as Mrs Crankshaw fished in her bag and pulled out a set of devil horns and fastened them to my head. "Now it needs something," she said as she gave me the once over.

"Shoes," Millie piped up looking at my feet.

"Ah yes what shoes have you got Lisa?"

"Only my flats," I said, trying desperately to cover myself with my hands.

"No you need heels or something, and put your hands down."

"I have some knee high black boots at Tim's place," Millie said.

"I could go and get them." Millie was clearly enjoying this as punishment for selling the house.

"I'm not your size," I hissed.

"Yes you are, I'll just go and get them shall I. Could I borrow your car?"

"No."

"Thanks, won't be long," she grabbed my keys out of my bag.

"Oh and you could hold this," Mrs Crankshaw said, pulling out a bondage whip from the box.

Opening of Kinky'n'Nice party

I'm feeling humiliated as I stand outside the entrance to the hall handing out order forms, wearing black lace and a bondage whip hanging around my neck.

Good turn-out though, the room was crowded already and it wasn't due to start for another ten minutes.

"Nice outfit," Debbie said as she came through the door.

"Shut up," I muttered back to her.

"No really," she said, "nice outfit, it looks gothic, I've got to get one of those."

I wonder how Jake would react if he sees me in this outfit. I must take photo of myself to show him later.

I spotted Maggie coming towards the hall. "Lisa," she said as she lowered her voice, "I really need to speak with you."

"Oh, okay give me a second," I said as I handed out more flyers to the old biddies coming through the door.

"I need to speak with you now," she insisted.

She waited 'till the last group were through the door. Maggie looked behind her before speaking.

"Well I don't know how to say this so I'm just going to say it. You see I have been trying to get hold of you all week because I had heard that you ..."

"Oh Lisa," snorted the familiar voice behind us. "That outfit suits you."

"Hi Pamela," I said, handing her an order form. She ran her eyes over me from head to toe, "it's um, well a bit tarty isn't it?" she said as she cocked her head to one side.

"That's the idea," I mumbled.

She turned her attention to Maggie. "I know this isn't the time but I really need to go over the application form for the gaming funding, it has to have two signatures on it."

"Okay, but I need a word with Lisa first." Maggie turned her attention back to me.

Pamela interrupted again, "this application needs to be submitted by tomorrow and if you hadn't been so unavailable," Pamela rolled her eyes, "I would have had it done it weeks ago."

Maggie turned back to Pamela and crossed her arms. "I'm surprised Pamela that you had time at all with all your extra activities."

"Oh, what is that suppose to mean? Maggie, I need this done now!" she hissed waving the form in her face.

"When I'm finished having a word with Lisa."

The two women stood glaring at each other, clearly both of them were not prepared to back down.

"Lisa dear," Mrs Crankshaw's voice was urgent as she appeared at the door, "oh hello Maggie, hello Pamela, hurry up Lisa, we're starting."

After Mrs Crankshaw's introduction of why we were here and

where the funds from tonight's sales were going, she pinned the poster size photograph of Betty lying in the hospital bed with her naked chest revealing the scars of where one breast used to be. Everything was going well. The wine was flowing, there were giggles coming from the older women of the group as they picked up every dildo on the table.

The more wine I drunk the more comfortable I felt in my outfit. Millie was flat-out taking money and distributing orders and I was too busy answering questions about products and dishing out food and glasses of wine to catch up with Maggie.

We had glanced in each other's direction and it was clear from Maggie's gaze that she needed to talk with me urgently. Pamela was still trying to pin Maggie down to talk with her about the stupid application but Maggie was avoiding her.

Mrs Crankshaw, who was now wearing a feather boa around her neck after purchasing a dozen tubes of strawberry flavoured massage oil, clapped her hands to get the rooms' attention. "Just before supper is served," she announced. "I would like to take this opportunity to thank each and every one of you for coming tonight, I hope you are all having fun. Now ladies, we have taken the trouble to order some oysters in tonight, yes, yes, quite a treat. Thank you and dig in."

The ladies gathered around the supper table still hooting and laughing.

I followed Mrs Crankshaw into the kitchen where she went to the fridge and pulled out another cask of wine. "Phew, they are going through the wine tonight," she said. "I'm so excited Lisa, it's going so well, Betty would be proud and it's all thanks to you."

"Oh it had nothing to do with me." I think Mrs Crankshaw may be a big part of why the wine was disappearing so fast. "Oh it is dear," she said as her eyes swelled with tears. "You know I'm so pleased you and my nephew are going to move in together, he's clearly smitten by you."

"Really!" I said. My heart did a little leap of joy.

"Oh yes, he talks about you all the time you know." Mrs Crankshaw took my hands. "And I think it won't be long before I'm hearing wedding bells, I can feel it in my bones."

I left her to it and rushed over to Millie to tell her what Mrs Crankshaw had said about wedding bells and her bones, but remembered that Millie doesn't know that I'm moving in with Jake yet, so best leave that for now. I'll tell her tomorrow.

I felt like a princess as I walked around the room, Jake is smitten by me and so he should be, just look at me I thought as I stole a glance of myself in the makeshift mirror.

I'm so sexy.

I took my sexy self off to ladies room. Hadn't been gone that long but did hear the commotion going on. It sounds like Maggie's voice had turned up a few thousand notches.

I didn't see what started such disturbance but the room was silent and everyone was focused on Maggie and Pamela arguing in the corner next to the tea and coffee.

Pamela was red in the face and towering over Maggie.

Maggie with her hands on her hips, looked outraged.

"You deliberately did this!" shouted Pamela. "Anything to try and make me look bad, I've never met anyone so bitter and jealous as you."

Maggie inched towards Pamela and started jabbing her finger at her.

"Fight, fight, fight," Millie chanted to herself.

"Well, let's just tell everyone here why I don't what to sign this stupid gaming form shall we?" Maggie turned her attention to the room.

"Who here from the CWA knows anything about an application form for funding from the gaming licence. Anyone?" Everyone looked at each other. "No? No!" Maggie continued, "that's because the funding was never discussed with any member because Pamela here had no intention of a children's nursery, she wants the money for herself."

There were gasps from around the room.

"How dare you!" Pamela hissed. "You have sunk too low this time Maggie."

"And I will also have you know," Maggie continued to address the room like a courthouse,

I think Maggie may watch too many lawyer programs, "that she wasn't acting alone in this were you? Pamela and Jake Crankshaw have been taking the CWA funds for the last year to fund their romantic getaways!"

My limbs started to go numb.

"Oh now you're just being absurd!" Pamela snapped, turning her attention to the stunned faces around her. "This women is clearly deranged."

"Me? Deranged?" Maggie was even more fired up now. "Yes that's right ladies, Mrs Horton has been having it off with Jake Crankshaw for years and I have proof."

Maggie fished through her bag and pulled out a photograph.

Now my whole body had gone numb, I managed to turn my head to Millie. She looked just as pale as I did. Maggie handed the photograph to the group. "Pass it round ladies you can clearly see Jakes hand on Pamela's ...."

"Give me that!" Pamela flew at the group and snatched the photo. "It's not true!" she pleaded to the room.

Maggie seemed to ignore her, "and the final blow, and this concerns you Barb," Maggie said to Mrs Crankshaw, who had appeared in the room, or she might have been there the whole time, I was too numb with disbelief to notice.

"These are plans that were submitted to the council by a property developer for a residential estate, Jake's property.

It seems the sale of the land was subject to council approval. In the mean time Jake needed to get out of town to avoid questions from the village and of course his mother, who knew at that time. She didn't have much time left so it was so convenient she died sooner then expected. So, Mrs Horton here has been secretly taking funds from the CWA so her lover can move away 'till the settlement comes in."

Maggie turned her attention to Pamela. "You had forgotten my husband's a lawyer who was now working for the same law firm that was representing the property developer." Maggie now had a smug look on her face, "I knew I smelt a rat when funds started disappearing from the fund-raising we were doing and after I saw you and Jake together the night of the barn dance it was then I decided to do a little research." Maggie slammed the papers she was holding down on the table in triumph. Pamela fell into a chair as her legs gave way and the colour had drained from her face.

My whole body was shaking violently at this stage. I wanted to run but my legs couldn't move.

Maggie looked across at me. "Oh Lisa," she said coming towards me, "I'm so sorry."

I backed away from her and Millie came up behind me and gripped my arm to stop me from falling backwards.

"I don't believe you," I said as tears started to run down my cheeks. Maggie stopped in her tracks,

"Lisa," her voice was barely above a whisper, "I tried to warn you, I really did, I didn't want to hurt your feelings in all this, I..."

The room started in an uproar as Pamela flew towards Maggie. "You evil scheming bitch!" she screamed as she grabbed the back of Maggie's hair.

Blood was rushing through my ears so fast I couldn't hear the roar of the voices around me, the whole room seemed to be in a silent uproar.

"Stop it!" yelled Mrs Crankshaw at the top of her lungs; the room fell dead silent, Pamela let go of Maggie's hair.

"Let me see that!" she snapped at Pamela who sheepishly handed over the photograph, "and those papers over there," she demanded.

Everyone sat silent. In the background the clock ticked away as Mrs Crankshaw flicked through the legal documents carefully reading each page after which she shuffled the papers in her hand and placed them carefully on the table. The group in front of her hastily picked up the papers. "Leave them!" Mrs Crankshaw snapped at the group and made her way towards Pamela, raised her hand and delivered a slap across Pamela's smug face.

WHACK!

Somewhere between the butchers and the bakers

I didn't know how long I had been running for. I don't remember running from the room and I could hear Millie's voice behind me yelling for me to stop. I sat with my back to the wall and burst into tears.

It can't be true, it just can't. Pamela and Jake having an affair? What about the money? It just didn't seem like Jake would do such a thing. My thoughts started to go back through the times Pamela and Jake had been in the same room. The night of the barn dance when I saw him and Pamela in that embrace when she was upset about something. Catching her coming back from Jake's place. God I have been such a fool.

I heard footsteps as Millie appeared. "There you are," she said, her voice was gentle. "You okay?" I shook my head as Millie sat down beside me. "I'm so sorry chook," she said putting her arm around me, "but good thing you found out now before you moved in together."

"You know about that?"

"I wasn't born yesterday."

More tears are flowing down my cheeks and Millie is such good friend, all nice and understanding.

I'm such an idiot, and to think I was going to sell my house after Millie's hard work in helping me renovate, just so I could go and move in with Jake.

She held me while I cried some more, eventually I wiped my cheeks.

"So," I gulped, "is Pamela still there?"

"No she took off right after you, her tyres screeching. She's probably ran home to her husband before this gets out."

"I just can't believe it Millie," I whispered.

"Yeah I know, but you will get over this, I know you will. Now come on, it's eleven at night and you're sitting in an alley dressed like a dominatrix." I forced a smile and pulled myself up on my feet.

"Millie?"

"Hmm."

"I need to see Jake now, I need to hear it from him, will you come with me?"

At Jake's place

Millie retrieved my clothes from the hall and I changed in the car. I couldn't face going into the hall myself. I thought of Mrs Crankshaw who was in a state, back at the hall being comforted by her friends, she must have been feeling the betrayal as well. Her brother n' laws farm being in the family for generations only to be sold off by Jake to some mindless money hungry developer. That would explain the plans I saw at Jake's place and why he had been so guarded. "God I'm such an idiot," I said out loud.

"His ute's not there," said Millie.

"I'll just have a quick look," I said opening the car door.

"You could just write 'Bastard' all over his house," suggested Millie.

I walked round the house, it seems Jake left in a hurry judging by the state of his bedroom with clothes littering the floor. I opened and shut drawers at random, the anger filling up inside of me. Millie appeared at my side and handed me a spray can. "Found this in the shed if you're up for it." I took the can from her and threw it into a corner. "I doubt if he will be back to see it. Millie come on, let's go."

Back home

I felt sick when Millie pulled the car into my driveway and the big real estate 'for sale' sign was staring me in the face.

I refused Millie's offer to stay, I wanted to be on my own. "Unless you had intentions of staying here," I asked as Millie pulled the car to a stop.

"No, Tim's expecting me, I need to talk with him anyway. I need to cool things with him."

"Everything okay?"

"Yeah fine, it's just that well, I still love Sid even if I could never be with him again. Tim's a lovely guy, I don't think it would be very fair."

I stared out the car window for a moment before turning back to Millie. "You never did tell me why you and Sid split up?"

"Lisa, oh god this is so humiliating," Millie said covering her face in her hands.

"What, what is?" I asked pulling her hands away from her face.

"Sid and I, well it turned out he's my cousin."

"Your cousin?"

"Yep," Millie replied smacking her lips together.

"Well how's that?"

"You remember I wanted to arrange that family reunion for Mum's birthday, and remember I told you that my mother grew up in an orphanage and she was separated from her sisters and brothers. Yeah, well after I did some tracking through the family files at the orphanage. I discovered Mum's younger sister was adopted and of course changed her name. It wasn't 'till I located the birth certificates and started following the path to her whereabouts and just as I thought this was it, I ended up at Sid's mothers place. Now you could imagine the horror as I discovered that Mum's long lost sister was Sid's mother."

My mouth started to twitch, the laughter was bubbling up inside of me. I cleared my throat and tried to compose myself.

"But marrying first cousins isn't illegal, is it?"

"No it's not illegal but it is weird," said Millie.

"But Sid's weird anyway so what does it matter."

"It matters to me, I'm just not comfortable with it okay. Imagine our children, they might end up with sixteen fingers or something."

"Or twelve nipples."

"Exactly! Oh shut up, you think this is funny don't you?"

"Well Millie, it's not the end of the world, at least your Sid didn't shag an older women, betray his family and lie through his teeth about it."

Millie started to giggle. "God we're hopeless aren't we?"

"Speak for yourself."

"Yeah well, at least I didn't end up in a threesome with tight-arse Pamela Horton."

"Yeah well," I started to giggle some more, "at least Jake wasn't my cousin."

"Yeah well, at least I wouldn't have to put up with Pamela's make-up smeared all over my pillow."

We were rolling round in fits of laughter.

I took a deep breath and wiped my eyes until eventually we calmed down. I patted Millie on the leg.

"Well look on the bright side," I said to her. "When you and Sid do have children and one of them is a boy, he'll be so popular with the ladies, you know, having three penis's and all."

"Three small ones if it's genetic. So you feeling better?"

"Yip."

"Do you need me to stay over?"

"No."

"Good, then piss off out of the car, I'm in dire need of sleep."

2AM

I can't sleep. I felt like I'd been thrown out on a big rubbish heap and no one wants me. And the voices in my head are so annoying asking questions like;

What if I did sell this place?

Would Jake have taken my money?

If I did move in with him would he have called the whole thing off with Pamela?

Oh god, I wonder where he is now?

Visions of him and Pamela together were not helping.

Randy Puss was asleep at the end of my bed. It was like he sensed that no one loves me and felt it his duty to keep an unloved mature thirty-something woman company like a cat woman. I need fresh air so I sat on the porch cocooned in my blanket and watched the gusty north-west wind blow through the treetops.

I thought about Millie and Sid discovering they were cousins.

Hee, hee, hee, so funny.

Cheep, cheep

A fluffy yellow chick appeared in front of me.

"Oh darling," I said to it in my voice that was only used for fluffy yellow chickens.

"What are you doing out here, how did you get out darling? Let's go pop you back."

I grabbed the torch and headed towards the chicken coop continuing to lecture the chick on the dangers of being out here alone.

The latch on the coop wasn't on properly, the gusty north-west wind must have blown it. I placed the chick quietly next to his roosting mum and did a quick head count of all the chicks. My eyes rested on the nesting boxes Jake had built for me. Tears started to well up in my eyes.

Oh god. I slide down between the boxes and started to wail, this is what I have become! Crying my eyes out over a man in a hen house.

I'm bawling so hard that I barely heard the gruff voice in the darkness.

"Don't cry," it said.

I stopped crying and let out involuntarily squeals of terror. I jumped to my feet so hard that I forgot about the nesting boxes and knocked my head. The impact rattled my brain and a high pitched sound appeared in my ears.

"Who's there?"

"It's okay," he said, stepping from the darkness into the vague light coming from the moon. "I'm not going to hurt you."

My eyes were becoming fuzzy and black spots were appearing

in my vision. I recognised his clothes.

The hunter. Oh my god he's going to kill me for telling the police on him for taking my dead rooster. He steps further towards me and now he's so close I can see his facial features between the black spots appearing in my eyes.

"Oh my god, Jake!"

"No," he shook his head.

I jumped back "You're not...."

"I never did like the way my brother treated you," he said.

Then everything went black.

15

In bed I think, can't be sure

My head throbbed against the glare of the light as I tried to open one eye.

Yip, I'm definitely in bed. My head is so sore and my throat needs water, it feels like sandpaper. Tried to get up but I feel as rough as a vegetable fiber recycled bag.

I heard a soft-spoken voice beside me.

"Lie still, is the light hurting?" it asked.

I attempted a nod, the soft spoken voice sounds nice. "I'll pull the drapes," it sung again.

I felt the bed bounce slightly and the sound of the drapes being pulled. I tried to open my eyes again.

"Better?" he asked.

My eyes started to focus again, his face started appearing in my line of vision as he sat down beside me.

"Jake," I mumbled.

"No, I'm Rick, how are you feeling?"

"Rick?" It was all starting to come back to me now, I reached my hand onto my head and felt the nasty lump coming through the bandage that was holding my head together.

"You have a nasty bump," he said, "here take these."

He helped me onto my pillows and popped a couple of painkillers into my hand. I threw them into my month as he held a glass of water to my lips, I swallowed the water, it ran down my throat like a dried up riverbed that felt the first few drops of rain after a three year drought, I found my voice.

"So how long was I out for?"

"Couple of hours. You're okay, just a nasty bump but I think we do need to get you to the doctors surgery when it opens and get you checked out anyway."

His face came into clear focus as the painkillers started to kick in. I studied his face; the scraggly beard had gone, his slightly damp hair was darker then Jake's, as was his skin.

It had more of an olive texture. I stared into his deep piercing blue eyes, there was a gentle calmness behind those eyes and I felt a flutter from inside. A feeling I have never felt before.

"So you're not going to kill me?" I mumbled.

He laughed. "I see you've still got your sense of humour, no I definitely am not going to kill you."

"You, you had a beard."

"Yeah," he said rubbing his hand on his chin. "I hope you don't mind I used your shower and your razor. I'll buy you a new one I promise."

I waved my hand at him, I mean what's a razor between strangers.

My stomach began to churn as a wave of nausea hit me.

"I'll go and make you a cup of tea and some dry toast, you probably feel sick because you had those painkillers on an empty stomach. Will you be okay for just a minute?" he seemed reluctant to leave the room, I attempted a nod, trying to keep my nausea under control.

"Thre .. thre.."

"Three sugars?" he said as he reached the door.

I nodded.

"Yes I know and not too strong, don't worry I know how you like your tea."

Much later, who knows, still semi unconscious

"Your friend's back with the car," Rick said. "Come on let's get you to the doctor," he helped me out of bed.

"Did you tell Millie I'm s.." I was struggling make any sense of the words out of my mouth, but at least my nausea had died down after the tea and toast.

"No, you text her, well I text her on your behalf. I found your phone in your bag, I hope you don't mind."

"Pff," I said waving my hand.

Trying to focus on putting one foot in front of the other.

"Have you met...?"

"No not yet," he said as I gripped his arm for balance.

"Oh she's great you'll lov.."

"Lisa!" Millie exclaimed as she hurtled in and took one look at me. "Oh my god! What happened?"

She turned her attention to Rick.

"Oh, so you came back then!" she said crossing her arms, "and I see you have dyed your stupid hair."

"It's not J.. J.. Jake," I stuttered.

"I'm Rick, Jake's brother," Rick explained. Millie looked puzzled as she turned to me for an explanation.

"I'll explain later," Rick said. "Right now I really think she needs a doctor," his voice strained, as he heaved my limp arm around his neck. "I've phoned ahead, they're expecting us."

Millie didn't say anything so I'm presuming she is lost for words for once in her life. Can't see her expression but I'm betting it's a puzzled one. I felt her grip my other arm and now I don't have to focus on walking, which is great as I think I'm going to throw up again.

Back home

Torch light in my eyes, prodding, cold thermometer under arm-pit, x-rays, and lots of drugs later, I was back in my bed, diagnosed with mild concussion combined with mild shock.

Clinical name for feel as rough as a vegetable fiber recycled bag.

Later

The room was dark, I'm guessing it was evening.

The door opened and Millie appeared. "Oh hello you're awake, I was just about to take off," she said.

"Is it night time?" I asked.

"Yip, you have been out for most of the day. I left you some dinner by the microwave, it's Chinese," she said.

I sat up in bed feeling better, I had a weird dream though, I dreamt that Jake came back and took care of me. No wait, it wasn't Jake or was it? Maybe my concussion was getting worse. Millie sat down on the bed and smoothed the covers around me and here's the freaky thing, it was like she read my mind or something.

Or maybe I had said that out loud.

"You know, that's what I thought," she said. "I thought it was Jake when I first saw him pretending to be his long lost brother, so I rang Matt and Mrs Crankshaw while you were at the doctor and it turns out Rick is Jake's brother after all. He explained what happened and how you bumped your head on the nesting boxes in the chicken coop."

Oh well that's fine, as long as it explains what I was doing in my own chicken coop at three in the morning. Never mind what twin brother of bastard ex-boyfriend was doing in the chicken coop at three in the morning.

"Him and I have had a long talk," Millie continued.

"And?"

"And you know what, he's actually okay."

Still hasn't explained what he was doing in my chicken coop.

She gave my arm an affectionate squeeze and stood up

"Anyway," she said, "better go, Sid's waiting for me."

"Sid's here?"

"Yes, he drove down to take me home."

"So, you cooled it with Tim then?"

"Broke it off more like it," Millie shrugged.

"Ha! So you can get used to the cousin thing."

"Yeah, yeah, whatever," Millie bent down to give me a hug. "Better go," she whispered, "there's someone here that has been waiting to see you all day."

Still in bed, but with strange man claiming to be Jake's brother sitting beside me

I can't believe Millie's left me with strange man in my state. But he seems nice, sexy like.

He's since changed out of his dirty scraggly clothes he was accustomed to and was now looking more like a human again, in a clean pair of jeans and a clean crisp blue shirt that brought out his dark locks.

"I've got a question?" I said.

"What was I doing in your hen-house?" he grinned.

Great, he's a mind reader too.

"I was waiting for my breakfast," he said.

"So you were stealing my eggs as well?" I said, tucking into the fried rice that Millie brought for me.

"Yip."

We have been talking for a while. I learnt something interesting, that Randy Puss is actually called Bonzo. Oh and Rick has been living in an old forestry hut behind my property.

"I've been there for a few months," he said launching into the actual part of the story, like it's no hurry to explain what he was doing in my roof.

Very, very surreal.

"I had come down from the bush for more supplies," he continued, "I discovered Flora and Bill lying dead under the tree out the back," he paused looking at the concern on my face. "You did know about Flora and Bill, didn't you?"

"Oh yes, but how come no-one knew you were there? I mean Jake told me you had disappeared right before your dad's funeral."

Rick held up his hand "I'll get to that soon," he said uncrossing his sexy legs.

"Anyway I had to tell someone about Bill and Flora, they didn't get out much and rarely had visitors, even the rural postie never came up the drive. So luck would have it Jake had his ute parked down the road that day so I slipped a note telling him," Rick paused, making sure I had processed that information, like I'm some blond with a concussion.

Oh wait, I am.

"So," he continued, "with the house unoccupied and winter upon us, I moved into the house after the funeral, it wasn't 'till the estate agent started bringing people through that I thought it's best I return to the hut."

"Until I discovered a key hanging by the oven that unlocked the door to the attic and well, you know the rest."

Randy Puss or Bonzo, obviously got bored waiting for Rick to pay him attention and came to rest on my lap.

"And you have been there ever since?" I asked.

"On and off," he lifted his head and those eyes locked onto mine. He held my gaze for a long time.

Turn away, turn away, I thought to myself. I seemed to be under a spell, he had a mesmerising peace about him, not to mention he was absolutely gorgeous.

No stop it. He's a lunatic that's been living in your roof remember.

"You know I remember the first time you moved in," he said not taking his eyes off me. "You were wearing those tiny shorts."

My whole body turned to mush.

No, stop it.

"Rick you weren't spying on me, you know undressing and all?"

No!" His voice was firm as he held his hands up in defence. "I'm no pervert. I wasn't looking through the ceiling at you if that's what you mean. I couldn't see you anyway, I pretty much moved back into the hut when you moved in. I only stayed upstairs when you weren't here or on colder nights."

I sat there in silence taking it all in for a moment. Here I was face to face with some guy who had broken into my house time and time again and for some strange reason I wasn't feeling angry about it. Realising Rick's eyes were still on me I stifled a yawn. "Well I guess I should be grateful you weren't some psycho," I shrugged, stroking Randy Puss/Bonzo's ears. "But I should charge you for rent."

He grinned as he sat up, taking the carton from me and moving closer, he took my hand. My skin tingled, but in a good way.

"I'm really sorry for any distress I caused you, I didn't mean to. I just needed somewhere to lie low for a while."

He moved off the bed and I got a glimpse of his butt. So sexy.

"Do you need anything before I go?" he asked.

"Go where?" I asked slightly panicked. "Surely you're not going to your hut?"

He laughed. "No, there's no need too now. I was going to go to Aunties, she was going to collect me. I just have to use your phone."

"Oh," my voice couldn't hide the disappointment.

"You will be okay here?" he asked.

"Well, you could stay here?" The words were out before I realised I had spoken them.

"Only if you want me to," he said, sounding half amused.

"Well you know," I said trying to sound casual. "It's not like you're a total stranger and it's late, Mrs Crankshaw will probably be asleep anyway."

He looked at me again with those deep sexy eyes. "Okay," he said in his soft spoken voice, "sleep well."

3.00am

Not sleeping well.

I crept into the living room and now watching Rick sleeping on the sofa.

No need to justify my actions, I just wanted to know what it felt like to spy on him for a change.

He's so sexy.

It still didn't explain what happened that was so terrible to make Rick disappear and not want to be found and of course the farm, why did Rick want to sell it off in the first place?

Why did Jake change his mind? After all it was Jake who was against it in the first place.

Rick looked so peaceful sleeping, I longed for him to wake up so I can ask him more questions. I sat down beside him and watched him like creepy obsessed crazy person.

He's so different to Jake.

With Jake it was a lust thing, with Rick it seems more than that. I had only known him for twenty-four hours and twelve of those were with a concussion.

But this person who sleeps before me seemed to be pulling me deeper into his soul with every breath he took. I wasn't sure I wanted to hear the answers but I still had so many unanswered questions.

4.00am

Finally Rick stirred in his sleep. He opened one eye and a smile spread across his mouth when he saw me there.

"How long have you been there for?"

"Oh, ah, not long," I moved in closer .

"What happened between you and Jake?"

"It's a long story," he mumbled. "Is that coffee?"

I held up my coffee mug for him to take a sip, he smacked his lips together. "Ahh that's better. You're shivering."

I appeared to be shaking like a vibrator on high speed.

Rick opened his blanket and I climbed in beside him, he pulled the blanket in around me. My body moulded into his like a hand in a glove as I rested my head on the pillow next to his, but facing away.

Uh, I can't get that close, we've only just met.

He took a deep sigh.

"Do you want the long version or the short?"

"Either."

"Okay," he began. "It all started before Dad got sick. Jake was going out with a local girl, they had been engaged about a year or so when I found out that he was having an affair with Pamela Horton, I caught them at it."

I sat up and turned. "It'd been going on that long!" I exclaimed.

"Yes, and will you let me finish," Rick said, pushing my head back on the pillow.

"Anyway, that's when things started to get nasty because Jake's fiancé was pregnant. Mum and Dad didn't know, and neither did her parents at that stage. I confronted Jake about Pamela when I caught them, and asked him what he was going to do about Mary. I tried to persuade him to call off his fling with Pamela. He basically told me he didn't give a fuck about Mary and Pamela was none of my business."

"Mary was distraught of course, when Jake told her he didn't want anything to do with her, she didn't know about Pamela. I took it upon myself to comfort her, be a friend, that sort of thing. So when she told her parents, they had a family meeting with our family."

"Jake denied the baby was his of course and pointed the finger at me, saying it was mine. No I didn't sleep with her, before you ask. So as you could imagine it was fairly messy."

"Dad, not knowing what to do, wrote a cheque.

Mary and her family moved away being Catholics and all, and the baby was to be put up for adoption." Rick took a deep breath like he just finished a marathon.

"So Jake's got a child somewhere. Funny he didn't mention it," I commented.

Rick shifted his arm into a more comfortable position and rested his hand on my hip. I'm feeling a bit funny at his touch but in a good way.

Rick continued. "With that mess over, I went away to college to do a degree in accounting, don't laugh, but I wasn't gone for long when Dad fell sick so I returned home. Dad handed over the running of the farm to us, Jake was in charge of course, I took over the bookwork as instructed by Dad and that's when I discovered the farm had major debts and was in the red."

"I asked Jake where some of the funds had gone and he started getting a bit defensive, sure he brought some new farm equipment but I had my suspicions that it wasn't all spent on farm equipment, learning also that Jake and Pamela were still together, I wondered then why a rich woman twice Jake's age was risking it all for a farm boy, so I asked Matt about Pamela."

"Matt Horton?" I asked.

He gave me a playful nudge. "You know who I'm talking about."

Oh god.

"Turns out Pamela wasn't rich, according to Matt, she had to sign a pre-nup when she got married. It was the Horton's money and Pamela wasn't entitled to any of it and being the person she is, I wondered if she was trying to get her hands on our farm. So that's when I got Dad involved."

So Jake and Pamela the whole time I thought to myself. God I'm such an idiot.

Rick spoke again. "Of course Jake denied everything, he was good at that, Dad had warned him that if it was true about Pamela he was to end it now and gave the lecture about married women and that sort of thing. But he also told Jake if he didn't pull his head in then the greater percentage of the farm would go to me, as at the present, equal halves were to go to me and Jake in the event that Mum and Dad should go."

"Jake appeared to pull his head in and told the family he had ended it with Mrs Horton and won back his trust with Dad."

"Except he didn't end it?"

"No."

We lay there in silence for a while, Rick was drumming his fingers lightly on my hip sending shivers through my body.

Not wanting to move from his touch but knowing I should before I ended up throwing myself at him, I abruptly got up, muttered something about needing more coffee.

Got into kitchen safely, using a lot of self-control.

God whatever this man was doing to me it was unfair. I have to be absolutely convinced he's telling me the truth, what if he turns out to be the rat.

"You don't trust me do you?" Rick's soft voice said behind me, as if he was reading every thought I was having.

Has there been a trend in mind reading that I don't know about?

I'm trying to concentrate on the task of spooning coffee into mugs without shaking but I told him that it was hard to say who I trusted because it was Jake who had told me that Rick was the bastard who caused all the trouble and stole his girlfriend, and I'm very confused right now.

"I wasn't the one having the affair with the mighty Pamela Horton," he said.

"Yes, but..."

"And I'm not the one who sold the farm off to the developer."

"Well yes, but..."

Rick held up his hand to say, let me finish, "I'm not the one who took off in the middle of the night."

"Well you did really."

"I'm the one who came back," he said.

"If you were the innocent one, why run off and not tell your family where you were, you didn't even go to your parents' funeral."

"I did go," he said looking at his feet.

"You should know, you saw me at Mum's funeral. You're the only one who did see me there."

I thought back to the day of the funeral and of course, the hunter.

I finished making the coffee and handed Rick his mug.

He took a deep breath and tried to compose himself, he really looked like he was going to cry.

He's not only sexy, but sensitive.

"Jake and Pamela were planning to sell off our farm and run off together. Jake couldn't do this with me in the way, so the night after Dad died Jake had offered me a considerable sum to disappear."

"And you took it?"

Rick nodded still looking at his feet.

"But why?"

Rick raised his head to meet my gaze. A single tear was now running down his cheek.

"Because Jake knew I had done something far worse."

16

Back on sofa comforting distressed sexy man

"I'm sorry, I'm so sorry," he said to me over and over.

I was still too stunned to respond, it was as if time stood still and Rick's apologies were bouncing off my forehead.

"Please don't think I'm a bad person," he whispered to me as he continued to stare at the contents of his coffee mug.

Since Rick had told me, I had been to dumbstruck to say anything, it was like my tongue had gone numb with the shock. I took a sip of coffee and tried to say something.

"You killed your father?"

No wait, that didn't come out right.

"You aided in your father's death?"

"I didn't want to really," he pleaded. "It was my father's wishes, he pleaded with us. Jake and I couldn't stand to see him suffer any longer and neither did he, oh god," he cried and put his head in his hands.

My heart went out to Rick. I have heard of families who wish they could end the suffering of their loved ones through the final stage of their illness. There had been much public debate on the issue but unfortunately for Rick, however great his intentions were, it was illegal. I placed my hand on his shoulder he turned to look at me. "Do you hate me?" he whispered.

"No of course not," I said. "What you did was brave, how dare Jake hold that over you." He fell into my arms as I hugged him. This beautiful man with an equally beautiful soul to match and not to mention his sexy body.

Oh god stop thinking about it, this isn't the time to be thinking about sex. A sexy man's confessing to euthanasia.

Rick pulled away from me. "God it feels better to get that off my shoulders," he said taking a deep breath.

"Did your mother know?" I asked.

"Yeah she knew. Dad asked all of us. Mum also thought it was for the best, even Jake, he volunteered to do it but he didn't. I had made Dad a promise that was to keep the farm in the family. He told me the story of when his great grandfather first came to the land and the generations of blood, sweat and tears that went into the land and he knew what Jake was up too. So that was his final wish, he wanted to see the farm stay in the family for another three generations."

"Jake had also made the same promise to him but after Dad died Jake and I got into a huge fight. Jake threatened to go to the police over what I had done unless I disappeared so he paid me out, a bank account was set up and Jake's been feeding money into it."

"But you didn't go."

"No, I had made a promise to Dad and I was intending on keeping it. Jake couldn't do anything 'till Mum's death anyway, so I hid. Kept an eye on things until Mum had passed away. I went to see her two days before her death, after she died I thought it was about time I made an appearance again."

"But what about Jake's threat?"

Rick paused and started grinding his hands together, "I think I should go to the police and turn myself in."

"No!" I cried, very sexy man doesn't belong locked away.

"It's the right thing to do."

I jumped off the sofa and knelt in front of him, I pulled his chin up to meet my eye. "You listen to me," I pleaded. "What you did was a humane thing your father asked you to do, it wasn't murder, it wasn't even manslaughter, do you understand, don't go to the police."

He looked deep into my eyes and held my gaze, his expression softened.

"You wouldn't think I was a bad person if I didn't?"

"Are you kidding, I'm begging you not to."

"Phew, that's a relief. I thought for a moment you were going to march me down there."

"What, you mean you never had any intention of going?"

I belted him on the arm.

"Not really, as I said, I don't do communal showers very well, I'm a bit shy."

I rolled my eyes.

"But what about Jake?"

"I saw Jake a couple of nights ago, we came to an agreement, I would allow him to sell off the land if he kept family matters to himself."

"You saw Jake and he agreed?" I spluttered.

"Of course he did," Rick replied with humour to his voice. "It's all about money, it always has been with Jake, also I think he was shocked to see me, so I signed the sales contract and told him to go."

Well that would explain why he appeared to have left in such a hurry the other night I thought to myself.

"But what about the farm and your dad's promise?"

Rick beamed looking like he had just won the lottery.

"Ah I didn't say Jake sold all of it, he agreed to only sell his half."

"So you still own half a farm."

"Yip."

I smiled, oh how the tides have turned.

"Now it's my turn to ask you something," Rick said as I shifted my position to the sofa beside him, my feet were starting to go numb from kneeling.

"What?"

"You weren't really going to move in with Jake were you?"

Rick's face was serious this time.

I shrugged. "Well I thought we had something..." I trailed off.

"I couldn't believe it when I saw him here," Rick started, "I prayed every night you would see through him. Me seeing Jake with you was all the more reason to hang around as I knew he was still with Pamela Horton.."

"Well you could have warned me," I mumbled.

"Did you love him?" Rick shot a glance at me.

I didn't have to think about it, meeting Rick I realised that what I felt about Jake wasn't real.

"No, definitely not. Why?"

Rick was silent and started to shift uncomfortably in his seat, he took a deep breath.

"I'm, um, just getting up the courage to ask you out."

My answer is definitely yes, I mean it's like we are meant to be together, I'd had a very cleansing night and have suddenly realised it's okay to be impulsive. Just go with the flow, it's perfectly healthy. I can sell this house and Millie will get her commission for project managing so far and I'll move in with Rick and have lots of babies and I will be a woman of the land.

Arrival of rural mail-man

"Morning Rob."

"Morning Lisa, got a parcel for you today and these."

He thrust a bunch of letters, mainly bills, into my hands, before sliding open the door and starting to rummage through the boxes of parcels' in the back.

"Have you heard the latest?" he called out from the interior of the van.

"What's that Rob?" I asked, fumbling through my mail.

"About old Jake Crankshaw?"

This town certainly doesn't waste time I thought to myself, but I suppose after Maggie's outburst with Pamela at the Kinky'n'Nice party with a great percentage of the women population present, I was surprised it took this long.

Rob pulled a small box from his van.

"This one's yours," he thrusts a box towards me. It was my book on self sufficiency, a back order off the internet. It was meant to be a present for Joe.

"I'm not one to gossip," he continued, "but did you hear Jake's left the district?"

"Hmm," I replied with a cool head, as I scanned my bank statement.

"Yeah, sold the farm, apparently to a developer. Looks like we're going to have a hundred new two acre blocks, some smaller I hear."

"That will keep you busy Rob," I smiled.

"Oh indeed!" he said thrusting his hands in his pockets.

"Seems him and Pamela Horton were having relations."

Bless Rob, he can be as bold as brass, but he can also choose his words carefully.

"Yes," I mumbled, "I heard that too."

"Well," Rob leaned in closer, as if he didn't want the birds to hear what he was about to say. "I had to go to the Horton's place this morning, seems Pamela has had a nervous breakdown," he paused, waiting for my reaction before continuing.

"Yes, Jake's up and left her, apparently she doesn't know where he is. Charles wants a divorce and naturally it all got too much for her. Charles was packing her things to take her to the Marta Hospital where she's been admitted. So the housekeeper tells me."

Poor Pamela, I thought to myself. So Jake's abandoned her and she lost her marriage. Well, if you play with fire.

"It's a good thing you didn't get tied up with him lass."

I thought back to my time with Jake, suddenly what could have been didn't seem such a bad thing, maybe it was fate and fate sent me Rick.

I look up at Rob's reddened chubby face.

"Yes," I smiled, "very lucky indeed."

Facebook Profile.

100 friends.

Lisa Collins.

Birthday 8th December 1975.

In a relationship with Rick Crankshaw (not Jake).

Likes: Singing in the car, scrounging in op shops, farming, decorating old houses, raising goats.

Dislikes: Mindless developers who cut up precious farming land to sell off to urbanites (bastards).

Member of the Country Women's Association.

About me: I'm over 5 ft tall, blond, spent brief time in property investment, which didn't work out due to discovering a squatter in ceiling and having my heart ripped out by Jake, who ran off with woman old enough to be his mother.

I have fantastic friends - Millie. And I'm so in love with Rick (used to live in my ceiling but not pervert or anything, he's also Jake's twin brother, but nothing like Jake, is sweet and sensitive).

Started a campaign: Stop the Slaughter of Roosters (please check out my like page).

Member of the Impulse Behaviour Management Support Group (as an advisor not actual member).

17

6 weeks later

I couldn't hold it in much longer. The tears started trickling down my cheeks. I glanced at Rick who was looking so gorgeous in his black suit, which was a relief considering it wasn't the suit he was meant to be wearing today. He met my eyes and gave me a wink. It was such a perfect day.

"I now pronounce you man and wife," the celebrant announced forcing me to tear my gaze away from Rick.

Millie and Sid exchanged a brief kiss as applause and cheers rang out from the congregation. I wiped the tears from my cheeks and watched Millie and Sid link arms and make their way back down the aisle as man and wife.

"I hear it's traditional for the best man and the bridesmaid to get it on," whispered Rick as he took my arm and followed the happy couple.

Rick wasn't Sid's original pick for best man. Rick stepped into the role after Sid's original best man, Stubbs, had his teeth knocked out last night at a pub brawl. So Rick was a stand-in as Stubb's couldn't attend the ceremony, he was being held, awaiting a court appearance on Monday for assault.

It had been a hellish few weeks following Sid and Millie's announcement that they were getting married after finally coming to grips with their discovery of being cousins. It only seemed appropriate that the wedding be held at *Abby'toir*, which I've since learned is actually called abattoir because it used to be the old slaughter yards. I was horrified, but as Rick said, is just a name so we voted that we forget the horror of the slaughter yards and change name to Abby'toir.

Forcing myself to release my arm from Rick, I put on my headset. You see I am chief organiser for Millie's wedding, I have finally found my calling. I have decided to become a wedding planner and I have already got my business cards and plan to open little shop in the village soon.

"Lisa dear!" Mrs Crankshaw called as she made her way through the murmurs of conversation as the guests rose and headed towards the free glasses of champagne. "Where do you keep a mop and pine'o'clean?" she whispered, "it's just that Betty has lost control of her waterworks again after she dropped her tray of sausage rolls and got such a fright, the poor dear, and well to be frank with you dear, some of the sausage rolls are a bit soggy."

I groaned inwards. I had asked the CWA to do the catering for the reception as it was a low key affair with finger food, but it was a decision I was now regretting as half the members are over eighty and insisted they take regular breaks for cups of tea and to massage their corns.

"Okay," I sighed, "I'll grab another tray of rolls from the freezer while you clean up Betty's mess."

"And she may need a change of underwear," Mrs Crankshaw whispered. "Could she borrow a pair of yours?"

Not a good thought, and I'm slightly offended that Mrs Crankshaw would even think that my lacy g-stings would cover Betty's ass. But at this point the guests were expecting to eat soon, I had pee over my kitchen floor and no sausage rolls. "Fine, second drawer," I sighed.

I have also decided not to sell the house. I mean, what's the hurry, and the best bit is that Millie and Sid have moved in to take over the renovations so I can concentrate on my wedding planning business and I have some fabulous ideas for building a granny flat on the end of the house and maybe turn the old killing yards into an animal shelter and run a petting zoo, and maybe use the old house for wedding venues. I haven't exactly told Millie all my plans yet but I'm sure she would think that's a great idea.

Millie came up behind me and pulled me into an embrace, saying how beautiful the ceremony was and how I'm her bestest friend in whole world and blah, blah. As touching as this moment was, the truth is that Millie had quite a few glasses of champagne before the wedding and it took a lot of black coffee to get her sober enough so she could stand straight throughout the service and not slur her words. Sid appeared at her side and I have a sudden rush of joy for them both. They look so happy.

I so want to get married.

Rick came up beside me as I adjusted my headset, and handed me a glass of champagne. "Thought you could use this," he said and planted me a kiss on the cheek.

I'm so in love.

Ever since that night when Rick had asked me on a date, things have been great. He's so sexy and very sensitive.

Rick is now living back in the family home and the place looks great. He is in the process of renovations and the one hundred and fifty acres that Jake didn't manage to sell is thriving. He cooks dinner for me and occasionally he takes me up to his hunting hut at the back of the property and we just sit up there for hours drinking wine and eating cheese. He's so cool.

But I've decided to take things slow with Rick, yes I sooo want to have his babies but I am convinced that if Rick loves me and is serious about our relationship then we will take time to get to know one another.

And after Millie dragged me off to an emergency meeting, the members of the Impulse Behaviour Group said they couldn't agree more.

"Hey Lisa."

Matt approached with Tom at his heels.

Neroli and Matt are doing great, and we're all so surprised that it's lasted this long. Baby Bailey is now three months old and she is just the cutest little thing.

I so want a baby.

"Um, hate to tell you this but there's something wrong with the wedding cake."

Rick planted another kiss on my cheek before moving off to talk to Maggie who has stepped down from the CWA and I have a tiny suspicion she has nominated me for President, voting will be happening at the next meeting in a month's time.

"What now!" I hissed.

"Well um there are holes in it."

I couldn't believe it. I gave Matt and Tom one job and that's to keep the flies off the wedding cake while Mrs Crankshaw organised a fly cover to put over it. Adjusting my headset I stomped over to the marquee where the cake was sitting.

"Lisa dear!"

Mrs Crankshaw is now hollering at me. Honestly why doesn't that woman use the walkie-talkie I gave her?

"Lisa!"

She is hollering at me even louder now, but I'm just going to ignore her. I quicken my pace, with Tom and Matt on my heels.

"Lisa come quick, it's urgent."

Ignore her.

I made it to the safety of the marquee and the wedding cake looks like Swiss cheese.

"Oh god Matt, what the hell?"

"Hey it wasn't my fault," he said defensively. "I went to get a beer and asked Tom to stand guard and when I came back it was like this."

"The flies were getting on it Aunty Lisa so I had to stab them with my light saber."

I open my mouth to tell Matt what a dumb-ass he is and suddenly a high pitched buzz stung my ear. I whipped off my headset like a poisonous spider and discovered Mrs Crankshaw standing beside me talking into the walkie talkie.

"Lisa dear!" she starts to yell into the two-way.

I took a deep cleansing breath.

I explained to Mrs Crankshaw that she is standing too close and no need to use that because I'm right here.

"So what's the point of having it? Honestly Lisa, now what's the number for the fire brigade?"

Now I'm running towards the house in new stiletto sandals with my headset dragging behind me and Tom on my heels. Ran into the thick haze of smoke in the kitchen and there's much arguing going on between CWA women on whose job it was to man the ovens. I threw the burnt sausage rolls into sink and heard a shriek coming from marquee.

I arrived back at the tent where Bonnie and Clyde were on the tabletop eating their way through the starters. Rick came over and dragged the offending goats back to their pen (in his sexy manner).
Sid had let them out claiming that they too should join in on celebrations.

I spotted Tom heading towards the kitchen with garden hose in his hands. I screamed at Matt to stop him.
Too late, the sounds of shrieks coming from kitchen and the CWA woman running as Tom lets loose with the hose claiming he is a fireman.

I ran towards the demon child to stop him before the food is ruined, when my headset got caught on a chair leg and now I'm lying in the wedding cake.
I closed my eyes and wished it was a bad dream.

I can hear chaos and laughing all around me.

"Lisa?"

I snapped my eyes open at the sound of a familiar voice.

Oh no! I knew there was something I was meant to do.

Mum and Dad were towering over me with very alarmed looks on their faces.

"Lisa what is going on?"

The End

9 780987 375018